MY BURIED LIFE

PRAISE FOR DOREEN FINN

'Authentic and edgy, this is a sharply observed and extremely witty contemporary novel. Whether writing about lust, longing or loss, Finn's writing is sensuous and insightful. Her description of Eva's struggle with alcohol is especially visceral. A work full of beauty and truth.'

> – Niamh Boyce, author of *The Herbalist.*

'In language that is both lyrical and exquisite, Doreen Finn brings us on a journey of loss, love, hope and redemption. We are captivated by this superbly plotted and perfectly paced story.'

> – Mary Stanley, author of nine novels,
> including *Missing, The Umbrella Tree* and *Searching for Home.*

'Doreen Finn has created a loaded pistol in Eva Perry, an embittered poet whose creative voice has been silenced by a series of personal blows. When Eva returns from New York City to her native Ireland with the death of her estranged mother, a tangle of family secrets begins to unravel. Finn's language showers sparks as Eva confronts her own difficult nature and her family's clouded past.'

> – Janet Fitch, author of *White Oleander.*

'With insight and compassion, Doreen Finn takes us on a journey of understanding with Eva, an uneasy returned emigrant with alcohol issues. In lush, atmospheric prose, Finn charts Eva's griefs, old and new, and her path to forgiveness and light.'

> – Nuala Ní Chonchúir, author of *The Closet of Savage Mementos.*

MY BURIED LIFE

Doreen Finn

NEW ISLAND

MY BURIED LIFE

First published in 2015
by New Island Books,
16 Priory Hall Office Park,
Stillorgan,
County Dublin,
Republic of Ireland.

www.newisland.ie

PRINT ISBN: 978-1-84840-407-6
EPUB ISBN: 978-1-84840-409-0
MOBI ISBN: 978-1-84840-408-3

British Library Cataloguing Data.
A CIP catalogue record for this book is available from the British Library.

Typeset by JVR Creative India
Cover design by Mariel Deegan
Printed by ScandBook AB

New Island received financial assistance from The Arts Council (*An Chomhairle Ealaíon*), 70 Merrion Square, Dublin 2, Ireland.

10 9 8 7 6 5 4 3 2 1

To my parents, Ted and Yvonne Finn.
Thank you both for everything.

CHAPTER 1

My brother was my favourite person in the world, and he died when I was 16. He was a long time dying when it finally happened, yet I live with the aftershocks still. They tremble around the spaces I inhabit, quieter now, but still daring me to forget him, challenging every attempt I make at redemption.

It happened so long ago, but it's all I can think about today.

Maude suggested I might read aloud something about my mother, a eulogy of sorts. You must be joking, I'd retorted. She hadn't been. I did not speak at my brother's funeral; to do so at my mother's would be ridiculous. A list of her failings, scrawled on airline stationery aboard the red-eye from Kennedy the night before last, might make for interesting listening. Despite self-medicating on in-flight whiskey and a fistful of Ambien, high-altitude sleep had danced beyond my reach. Somewhere over the Atlantic's tumultuous darkness I gave up groping blindly in the half-light for rest that would not come, and instead began to compile grievances. The incomplete catalogue crackles in my pocket. Someday I will refine it, hold everything up to the light. For now my head is too crowded, the sting of

1

buried hurts rising like late-summer sap. Today, I bid my mother adieu. It will be short. I will not linger. I can't.

I could have sworn the sun was shining this morning when I woke up. It was definitely one of those multicoloured September days, a jumble of yellow light at summer's lapsing, green leaves that haven't yet begun to consider turning, the whirring of airborne insects cutting through the quiet, and all that clean, apple-scented air. Now I wonder if I was dreaming, or just hung-over. Now, vertical sheets of rain feel as though they'll pierce my skin. I'm not complaining though. I can hide behind the deluge, maybe even fool some of the people near me into thinking that I'm crying. I assume that my closed eyes are keeping condolences at bay; certainly it means that I can't witness any pity or sympathy that may be coming my way. I'm not sure how I feel. Actually, I don't really feel anything at all. Except cold. And more than a little wet. My New York trench coat is useless here beside the open grave. Maude's hand rests in the crook of my arm. I cover it with my free hand. She squeezes my fingers.

The priest's words blend into something I can make little sense of. I imagine the raindrops splattering his small black Bible, wrinkling the tissue-thin pages in darkening spots. He has nothing to offer me, no comfort or insight that I could take from the occasion and ponder later.

The topsoil threatens to slide into the cavernous grave. The dutifully gathered shift as one around me, their shoes sucking the muck, betraying a collective desire to be gone, back to warm offices, dry cars, solitary kitchens.

I don't blame them.

Wet hands press my cold flesh. Murmured words sweep over me, blending in a toneless wash of indecipherable sound. Earth hits the coffin lid. *Thwack.* I try to focus on the eyes that line up in front of me, jet lag and a headache distancing me further from the kindness and awkward, fumbled mumbles of sympathy and solidarity. Out of sight, another graveside party sings a hymn, a slow, ponderous swell of sound. I hope my mother wasn't expecting that. It was enough having to organise the funeral. Thank God for Maude. She leans in to me, tells me she'll see me back at the car. A man offers her his arm and she takes it, her steps careful across the slick ground.

One by one, people leave. Mud the colour of espresso clings to feet and legs. The deluge continues its monotonous tattoo against every solid surface, echoing around the silent graves. Trees drip silver rain. It runs like mercury off the late-summer leaves.

A discreet cough. The gravedigger stands respectfully to the side, his spade slung across his shoulder. The gravestone is every bit as shocking as I'd imagined and leaves me swimming in grief I thought I'd buried years before. *Andrew Perry. Son, brother. 1970–1988. Rest in peace.* A couple of decades earlier and he wouldn't have been allowed to lie in consecrated ground. At least that much has changed.

My abominable mother. Could she have found a better way to drag me back from New York? The last cosmic joke she could throw my way. I bet you're laughing sweetly now, Mother dear. Plummeting to your dark eternity. Dropping dead so I'd have to come back and pick up the pieces I'd scattered so gracelessly to the wind.

This isn't what I'd planned, not what I'd imagined. I didn't need to see Andrew's grave. No reminders. No gravestones. No sitting on cold marble, weeping my aching guts out over someone who was never coming back. I can see them from where I stand, other mourners at other graves, throwing flowers into the abyss. What a waste.

Again the cough. I ignore him, the man with the spade. I have two people in this grave. He can wait.

Cemeteries depress me. The futility of visiting graves is not lost on me. I prefer the physicality of concrete reminders. A letter, yellowed with age, thumbed to transparency. A comb with a strand of hair. Poems. A bar of music. Grave kissing is for those without the lives of the departed sewn into the fabric of their days. Unfortunately for me, my seams are stitched so tightly I can hardly breathe at times.

I kick at the soggy earth. I'm empty. I retreat, and the man with the spade slides silently towards the slippery mound.

The mourners' black car waits for me. The driver reads a newspaper, some tabloid with a red banner and a soccer player's wife on the cover. A takeaway cup of coffee rests on the dash. The smell of burnt espresso is sweeter than Armagnac and fills the car like hazy desire. One inhalation and I'm gone, to a village coffee house, all bistro tables under a striped awning on warm days, conversation competing with the cacophony of traffic, a table with a view and a book to read when it rains, the outside world blunted by fogged windows.

The driver turns to me, his heavy frame expanding the material of his navy jacket. Dark thread stretches at the shoulder seams. 'Your aunt went on ahead. She said she'll meet you at the hotel.'

'Thanks.' I rub a hole in the fogged window. I can barely make out anything beyond the blurred glass. 'Actually, just take me home.' The last thing I want is more condolences from people I don't want to see and others whom I've never met. It isn't a big funeral, not by Irish standards, but there are still people there who'd want recognition of their attendance, want to tell me how much my mother will be missed. The truth is that I don't miss her, and I don't want to hear how others do. Let Maude handle it.

The driver does not offer to help me change my mind. I suppose years of delivering the bereaved to their doorsteps has taught him not to interfere.

We wind our way through lunchtime traffic. I've stopped trying to recognise streets. Nothing is familiar to me on these widened roads, this motorway where there were only fields, the enlarged houses, the empty apartment blocks reaching out of what seems to be every corner, long, glassy arms stretching to the sky. If this is Dublin, I don't know it.

The rain continues its staccato on the car roof. The driver has the radio on low. Bank problems, job losses, foreclosures, political scandals. It seems as though time has bent in on itself and nothing has changed in the years I've been away. On the surface everything is different, shinier, newer, but the soul of the place is still the same. Greedy, self-absorbed, corrupt.

The driver and I don't speak. At my request he changes from the news to a music station. Miles Davis blasts his way into the car, and I lean back, close my eyes, surrender to the hangover that drills my temples, the base of my skull, every nerve ending in my head. The half bottle of Jameson had seemed like such a good idea at the time. It always does.

The lavender oil in the bath clears my head slightly. A single candle glows like a Chinese lantern in the gloom. I sip from the tumbler of whiskey that sits on the edge of the white tub. Waterford, cut-glass, polished to perfection. Barely used. I'll make up for all that neglect.

My apartment in New York isn't much bigger than this bathroom. My mother kept the original black-and-white tiles, the floor-to-ceiling shelves. The cast-iron bath sits on claws. The fireplace, never lit, lets in a stream of outside air. It cuts through the steam like a knife. I shiver, either from the sudden cold on my hot face or because it's been eleven years since I lay in this bath and nothing has changed. The mottled glass in the window still clouds with the heat of the water, the lavender soap still melts in the same dish. The place is spotless, scrubbed by my mother twice a week. It's cleaner than any kitchen, and she lingers in every corner, on each shining tile.

My mother. All her rage and disappointment finally caught up with her. So much of it aimed at me, her perceived notions about her only daughter. She hardly knew me. I left, and my mother forgot me, cut me out of her life as simply and easily as if I'd been made of paper and she the sharpest blade.

I'd had to go, had no choice but to leave, or I would have died here, choked slowly to death in the corners of a house full of shadows.

Trying to conjure her is always difficult. What I see is her anger, the fire that never cooled. Her death was something for which I'd been bracing myself for years. I can almost smile at the ordinariness of it. A heart attack while gardening, collapsing over spring bulbs, her straw hat hitting the ground first. I have yet to shed a tear over her passing. I gave up crying over my mother years ago. Too much of a waste, of tears, of time, of any emotion. My mother, a woman capable of shattering icebergs with her eyes, has yet to merit my sorrow.

CHAPTER 2

It's still bright when I awaken. I roll over and lie on my stomach. The whiskey is gone and only the melted ice remains in the bottom of my mother's cut-glass tumbler. I drain it anyway. I pass my hand over my hair, damp from the bath.

The walls are painted yellow. The wardrobe is new, something plain, Scandinavian, blending with the clean paintwork. The blind is Roman. It looks handmade. Probably Maude. The shutters are white, restored fully and folded neatly to the side. The sash window is open twelve inches. It was swollen from summer rain when I struggled to push it open earlier. I drag my aching body from the bed to the window. The sun has found a gap in the clouds, and the garden is washed in a torrent of sparkling light, the sodden vegetation a lush, verdant green. The flowers, my mother's prized blooms, are everywhere. They spill out of pots, scramble up walls, wind themselves around the trunk of the apple tree at the end of the garden. The effect is startling, and after the grey Irish morning the kaleidoscopic colour lifts my mood. A blackbird trills out of sight in the garden. Rain still weeps from the gutters. These are sounds I haven't heard in over a decade, not from this exact spot. Dripping gutters and birdsong. The soundtrack of this bedroom. Pushing away from the window frame, I look around. There's nothing of me in the room I'd slept in till I went to New York. The faintest indents on the walls, smoothed and painted over, whisper of the shelves that once housed all my books, inexpertly erected by my brother in a fit of DIY enthusiasm, one of his many short-lived spells. The wall is cold under my fingers, the paint as dry as a chalkboard.

My suitcases are half-exploded bombs along one wall. I pull on a long-sleeved T-shirt and an old pair of jeans, all frayed knees and bleach-splotched unevenness. They should have been thrown out years ago, but they were my brother's. The denim is worn almost paper-thin, and they're as soft as felt on my hurting skin. I stagger ever so slightly. Nausea swirls, and I lean against the bed for support. I reach for the empty glass then let my hand drop. I ache for a drink.

Only the rustle of newspaper is audible. I sigh. I'd hoped to have the house to myself. Maude sits, still in her funeral clothes, her back to the window, reading glasses slipping down her nose. A rug is tucked around her lap. Her tights pool at her ankles.

'There you are!' She is older, so much older than I remember. Funny how I only notice it now. 'I was wondering where you'd got to.'

I slip into the armchair by the fire. The blackened grate is cold, blank. Sticks are piled neatly to the side, a box of matches on top, waiting for the first fire of the autumn. My mother obviously hadn't planned on dying quite so suddenly. My hands shake. I sit on them so my great-aunt doesn't notice. The drinks tray sits in the same corner as always. It's a struggle to stay in my seat, even though I know it holds only an ancient sherry and something else congealed and sticky in a bottle with a withered label. I don't have high standards though. Anything will suffice.

My name is Eva and I'm an alcoholic.

'What happened, Eva? Where did you go? We waited and waited for you.' Maude puts the paper aside, ready to talk.

I pull at a hole in the knee of my jeans. 'I felt sick.'

If Maude thinks otherwise, at least she doesn't say so. 'Well, it was a lovely send-off. Esther would have been happy.' Maude's eyes fill and she dabs at them with the corner of a tissue. She looks worn out. A tremor in her hand is barely discernible. I wonder if she's noticed it herself. Probably. 'Poor Esther.'

Rain spatters the window behind Maude, a flat sound in the hush of late afternoon. I spot a photo of myself on the mantelpiece. I remember Maude taking that, and her quiet pride. In it, I am holding up a book, smiling. I hardly recognise myself. Maude sees me, and nods at the frame.

'You were so beautiful then. Look how young you were, 18, and all that success.'

It's like looking at another person. My hair falls almost to my waist, the weight of it diminishing the curl. My face holds its extra flesh, that padding of youth, without a hint of self-consciousness. The photograph is fading, the colours a shade paler than they were.

'You're still beautiful, Eva. You need to remind yourself of that every now and again.'

I stand. 'I'm going for a walk.' I know what's coming and I don't think I can bear to listen. The last thing I want to hear is how I could improve my appearance. I know what I need to do: stop drinking and get my hair cut. Not now though. Too much for now.

'Now?' She gestures at the window behind her. 'But it's starting to rain again.'

'I don't mind. I just need to get some air.'

There's no room for argument. I've been living alone for too long to debate the insanity of going out in the rain. I don't have a coat other than the one I wore earlier, now draped in damp folds over the end of the banisters. It doesn't matter. I don't have to justify my actions.

I stand on the top step outside the front door. A woman I don't know screeches her sports car to a halt in the driveway next door, popping gravel under the fat tyres. She takes the granite steps at a pace dictated by her black skirt and a pair of skyscraper shoes, a laptop bag slim and expensive in one hand, a folder in the other. The expression on her face is as tight as her skirt. Our eyes meet. Instantly she looks away and slides a key into the front door. A phone trills as she disappears. This must be the new neighbour Maude mentioned. Terribly successful. Loaded, no doubt. Something about the law, a huge salary, a partnership by the age of 30.

I remember Kathleen, our previous neighbour. Kathleen, kind and open, who allowed Andrew and me to pick her loganberries each summer and mind her cat when she visited her daughter in London. Early on the morning of Andrew's funeral I had sat, numb, on the couch in the front room. The cold grate held that faintly depressing look of burned ashes and stray matches, the charred remnants of newspaper twists. Something, a feint *tap tap tap* on the front door, seeped into the hush of the oyster dawn. Kathleen, tired of crying, had taken a duster and a bottle of Brasso and was polishing the brasses on our front door, readying them for the mourners who would later congregate to eat sandwiches and pass around cups of tea.

That old, familiar crush of oppression gathers like a storm cloud over me. If I had a car and an infinite stretch of open road I would jump behind the wheel and zoom away. But this is Dublin, and there are no open roads, just these tangled streets, snarled and knotted with traffic. I tighten my ponytail and button my cardigan. Already I need to get away. Old habits don't fade.

Rainwater is pooled everywhere. I step into a puddle and it runs into my canvas trainer, shocking my sockless foot with how cold it is. God, what a climate. Even New York, with its winters that shred you, can't compete with Ireland for grey skies and rain that spills like paint from upturned cans.

The street is choked with cars. An old man fails to move on time and the traffic lights turn orange. A cyclist sprays me with water. I jump out of the way, but not in time to avoid the dirty water that soaks my legs. A bus rattles by, its windows bleeding condensation, its occupants inert, expressionless.

What has happened to Dublin? I pass a row of shops that, when I was a child, housed the butcher, the newsagent and a dry cleaner. Now there is a coffee house, a shop selling nothing but stationery and a lingerie store. I pause at the window. The display of lace and frills amuses me. I shade my eyes and look in, but a movement behind the glass catches my eye. A girl I was in school with leans against the counter. The shop is empty of customers. I move quickly away. I'm not interested in bland conversation, the vacant chatter of inquisition.

Just like the journey from the cemetery, nothing is familiar to me any more. The vaguely shabby village of my childhood has mutated beyond recognition: with its wine shops, copious eating places and specialist food shops it's no longer a poor relative of the city centre. Despite some vacant shopfronts and three or four restaurants that have recently closed down, Ranelagh gives off an aura of new money, and like new money it glitters like a rhinestone in platinum.

The rain is sudden when it starts again. It tickles my skin, soaking my clothes; it blurs my vision. It's like looking at the world through plastic. After the impenetrable heat of a New York summer, the cool that comes off the downpour is more welcome than I would have thought. My wet trainers slap the pavement. I walk on.

In the park the ducks swim in circles, oblivious to the rainfall that silvers their feathers and pockmarks their pond. The sky is dark, too dark for so early in September. The old bakery beyond the walls is gone, replaced by more apartments. They hang their 'For Sale' signs out like flags, small flashes of colour in the grey.

My brother and I as children had fed the ducks every chance we got. We fought over the bread and over who would feed the last piece, childish arguments that never lasted.

Andrew. My beautiful, fractured brother. It's still almost too much to think of him.

That's where my grief lies, not among spring bulbs and straw hats, but where my brother is, and in that shadowed room there's no space for mourning my mother, no bed upon which I can drape my tears. Andrew would have grieved for her. He would have known how to arrange the furniture, how to give his sorrow space to breathe. Me? I just locked the door and threw the key in the nearest well, not waiting to hear the splash of black water before it was lost forever.

Drops spill noisily off the leaves, gunmetal in the grey September evening, slicing through my thoughts. I turn away from the ducks and their relentless circling.

I haven't been in this pub since university, and even then it was never a regular haunt – too close to home for me to reach brute oblivion in peace. I prefer the scruffier version of the Dublin pub, where decades of smoke and spilled porter stain the upholstery and darken the floorboards. No one bothers trying to pick you up or cares what clothes you wear. I cut through the huddle of smokers at the door, wreathed in the brittle cloud of their own addictions.

It's busy inside. Office workers celebrate the end of the working day, commuters from the dreary new suburbs seek refuge from the weather and the traffic and their negative equity. I slink to the bar, avoiding eye contact with strangers. I shed my drenched cardigan, drop it on a stool. My hair is stuck to my shoulders like tar, and my skin is visible through my saturated shirt. Not my finest moment.

A guy polishes glasses behind the beer taps. He raises his eyebrows.

I pull a high stool close to the bar. 'Jameson, no ice. A double.' I touch an old water stain on the polished wood.

'Would you like a towel with that?' A brief smile, as sudden as starlight.

'I might just say yes.'

He slides the glass to me.

The smoky warmth of the drink is like crushed velvet on my tongue. I want to spin it out, make it last, enjoy it, but it's impossible. I sip and sip until it is gone, some feeling finally edging back into my cold limbs. I signal for another. It disappears in the same way. A dish of olives sits on the polished bar in front of me, Greek, all wrinkles and shiny black skin. Another change I missed. I wonder what the seasoned drinkers, the hardened alcoholics, make of this, the provision of olives in their pubs? It must seem as foreign as shops dedicated to selling only lingerie. Dublin has been nudged further along the scale of capital cities. Despite the collapse, it plays its part well.

The barman picks up my glass. 'Another one?'

'No thanks.' I put my money on the bar. A shout goes up behind me. A group of males wearing football shirts with the logo of some multinational enlarged across the chest slop pints over each other in congratulations at points scored. A mute television beams a rugby match into this corner of Dublin. It flickers distractedly on the wall.

'It's on me.'

I pop an olive in my mouth. 'Why?'

He shrugs one shoulder. 'No why. Just thought you'd like one.' He winks, and somehow he manages to make it look cool. 'Given the state you're in, and all that.'

I laugh. 'All right. I'll have another.'

As he pours the drink the barman holds my attention for a second longer than is necessary. I blink and focus on my glass. A soapy bubble of excitement bursts somewhere in my stomach. I swallow more whiskey, glance at him, smile when I see he hasn't yet looked away. I catch myself, sort out some money and place it on the bar. The notes of this unfamiliar currency are wet and flattened from being in my pocket.

'Another?'

I cover the glass with my hand, hiding the remaining whiskey from view. 'Thanks, but no.' Not having eaten all day, I can feel the effect of the booze in the languid stillness that has crept into my head. 'Not unless you want to carry me home.'

He laughs. 'Mightn't be the worst thing I've done today.'

He has longish hair and it falls over one eye in a way that is absurdly appealing. I think his eyes are green, but I'm afraid to look too closely. He's out of place here. He should be waxing a surfboard on a beach in Malibu or leading hikes up high-altitude mountain trails. He's probably fifteen years younger than I am, but it's hard to ignore the smile and the way his hair falls. I place my palms flat on the bar. My wet jeans are cold and stiff against my skin, but the Jameson is working its magic and the world is starting to look less sharp around the edges. I loosen my hair, which is drying in a clump on my shoulders, and smoothe my T-shirt. That warm feeling, the high I get from alcohol right before I'm drunk, intoxicates me. I straighten up on the stool. My sodden jeans no longer bother me. I sip at what remains in the glass. The desperation has passed, that need I have to drink, drink, drink. It's like swimming against waves, pushing back a heavy wall, and then the relief of breaking through into clean air, bright light. It covers me, and I'm filled with benevolence towards the world.

The barman pushes a fresh dish of olives towards me. 'So, your first time in here?'

I shrug. First time in a long time. I don't bother mentioning the underage drinking I did here in my teens, or how easy it was to get served with a slick of red lipstick and a bit of hairspray. Age limits were optional back then, or so it seemed. 'More or less.'

'I'd have noticed you if you'd been here.'

'Your bar, is it?' I swirl the last of my drink in the glass.

He flicks a tea towel over his shoulder. 'Not a chance. Belongs to my parents, but I help out.'

I smile at him. I can't help it.

He raises his brows. 'What?'

I shake my head. 'Nothing. Can a girl not smile?'

He leans on his forearms. They are burnished from being outdoors and the good summer. His white shirt is rolled to the elbows. I think about touching him, accidently, with my hands, and how his skin would feel beneath my fingers, but the thought is too much. I tip over that ledge, the one that changes everything in an instant. It's always the same with alcohol: one minute I'm bright and shiny, the next the claw of dread reaches up and grabs me, dragging me down to the depths again. He says something, but I don't hear. I look at him, but I can't really see him any more. My damp jeans suck at my skin. My feet are freezing. I push away from the bar.

'What, off so soon?'

'Afraid so.' I slide the coloured money towards him. 'Maybe I'll see you around?' I hope my speech isn't slurred.

He goes back to polishing glasses. A smile is aimed at his towel. 'Maybe.'

Something is sticking into me. I blink. What happened? I'm face down on the living room floor. Chet Baker unspools on the stereo. I left him on replay, and his heartbroken voice swims in the empty night. The street lights glimmer through the unshuttered window, throwing bloated shadows across my thighs. Moving hurts me. Pain rolls through my head. I pull out what I'm lying on. The empty whiskey bottle. It's only a half bottle, but so what? I bought it as a present for Maude. I don't even like bourbon.

Waves of nausea crash at the back of my throat. I'm afraid to stir. In the end I have to, stumbling through the darkened downstairs, out the front door, down the granite steps until I'm kneeling over my mother's cosmos, retching. Eventually it subsides and I come to a trembling standstill.

The smell of drenched earth is somehow soothing. At least it's stopped raining. I rub my face against the spiky grass. The wet ground soaks through my clothes and I drag myself into a seated position.

I wipe my face with the edge of my sleeve. I'm still wearing the clothes from earlier. They've dried into me. I pull at the thin fabric, feeling it peel from my skin. The African drums in my head have retreated to a tedious pulse, and I rest my forehead on my forearms. It's quiet, the traffic all but gone save for the odd taxi swishing alone through the empty night. The house is dark and silent, still towering above me in its imposing Edwardian manner. The red bricks of the terrace are dulled in the non-light. The long sash windows are shuttered eyes, keeping secrets hidden. It's a beautiful sweep of architecture, the uniformity of the houses, the exact precision of red bricks, twin pillars flanking each door, the fanlight, curved like an orange slice, illuminating each hall. Dublin is full of beautiful houses, their periods of construction bookmarking the city's history. They crop up everywhere, surprising the onlooker, elevating the town.

Maude's room in the garden flat is without illumination. For that at least I'm grateful. I don't want her seeing me like this, thinking that in all these years nothing has changed. I suppose nothing has, but I like to think I'm different too, in some ways.

I almost envy her grief. I'm like a fraud in comparison. It's so easy for her to be sad. Thinking of my mother leaves me with the thin, bleak feeling of lingering regret. There had been so much to say, countless questions that I had sidestepped all my life instead of just asking her. I never even knew why she left my father, and by the time I'd got around to wondering he was long dead, buried in some traceless grave in the bleak midlands, another farmer succumbed to the land that bound him.

Grief is an abstract painting. Nothing is ever as it seems, and the shapes shift constantly. Mine is so old, so deeply buried, that I'm afraid to take it out. There are too many facets to it, too many ingredients that have gone into its making. I am afraid of it. It scares me to think too much because I don't know how to approach it, never having dealt properly with it from the start. Andrew's death I barricaded myself from, building walls from bottles of booze, submerging myself in writing, studying and drinking until I was finally able to leave. It was easy being in New York, refusing to come back to Dublin. But now I am here, and this infelicity, this wretched sadness, hangs itself over me once again, like cobwebs gathering around me. My brother's ghost dwells everywhere in this damned house, chased out of corners each time a light is switched on, persistent as a migraine. I've never knowingly wished for solitude, but it's all that seems to come to me, iron filings to my magnet, and now it is all I know.

Orphaned at 37.

And love, in all its manifestations, has galloped away.

CHAPTER 3

An Indian summer has suddenly replaced the rain. The blackberries at the end of the garden finally ripen with the combination of sun and showers. I lie in the old string hammock and watch the wasps gather and disperse among the berries. The garden appears stunned by the unexpected onslaught of heat. The birds, barely vocal, prefer to sit in the trees and preen in the shelter of the leaves. My mother's late-summer roses, heat-starved, climb the trellising on the crumbling cinder walls, competing for space and heat. The herb garden Maude planted two decades ago struggles to escape its boundary of uneven rocks. Lavender, rosemary and mint sting the still, hot air. I'd forgotten the smell of home until this moment, and I inhale, the fragrances peeling back time.

Using my foot as a lever I rock myself back and forth, hoping for sleep. I've barely slept since my arrival, and even then, only when it's been alcohol-induced. Exhaustion scratches my eyes and weighs down my limbs, lies like a wet rag over my brain. Leaving my bed in the mornings is an effort I do my best to avoid. Maude likes to talk, and with my head stuffed with a hangover and no safe topics of conversation it is easier just to drift around the house.

Maybe I shouldn't have left New York so quickly. I grabbed at the first decent excuse to run. I mean, who could argue with a mother's passing, or deny me the chance to bury my dead? Yet I miss it, that injured city, miss being surrounded by a thousand buildings that are surrounded by another thousand, and so on, almost into infinity. Lying on the grass in a park, I always felt my insignificance in comparison with all that architecture, instead of being bigger than everything else, which is how I normally feel. Too much inside my head, no getting away from the darkness that sleeps within me.

I plan to return to Manhattan. Dublin is only temporary, a holding place until I sort out my mother's things, deal with the house, put my ghosts to rest. I miss New York. Maybe what I really miss is how it used to be, how I used to be in the city. I can live without the pounding of salsa from my neighbours' apartment, the shouting in Spanish at three in the morning, the bantams crowing at dawn on the neighbouring roof. This year has been so difficult, and once again I've found myself wandering in my head, a fish out of water in the city I want to see as home. Everything changed. It started to become difficult to get out of bed in the mornings. The gloss turned dull; the excitement drained away. My usual bottle of California red and *tostones* at the Dominican bodega in the Bowery suddenly cost twice what I used to pay. Rising rents, Pepe the owner explained. Is all about the gentrification these days. They don't care about no neighbourhood no more. All about the money. Man, they forcing us out soon. Isaac had wanted me to move further uptown, closer to NYU, closer to him, but after so much time in the East Village I wanted to stay, put down roots, be at home. Have somewhere to call my own. Even amid the clamour, the noise, the vortex of

New York, I've sought out a sense of place, of belonging. It has never been quite within my grasp, but I've reached for it, and kept on reaching. Until everything fell apart, I was getting there. My sooty corner of the East Village, with its tricky layout of one-way streets and cul-de-sacs, where I no longer get lost. It may be still shabby, but it's mostly residential, and I have finally started to settle, for the first time in my life. Tony, the Chinese mailman, knows my name. I am on nodding terms with the woman who runs the bagel place across the street from my building. The Australian barista knows I like my espressos double, long and hot. It takes time, all of it. I've invested my time, and for what?

My mother's voice doesn't help. Even in death, I hear her. She barely needs to speak: just one lift of an eyebrow, one brief flare of her nostrils, and I am put in my place. I could cover my ears, tell her to leave me alone, but it wouldn't work. It never has.

A shadow blocks the light from my face. I shade my eyes and look up. Maude stands over me.

'I thought you might like a drink.'

I always like a drink. It's one of my less admirable traits. Thankfully, to my great-aunt's mind there are no alcoholics, only heavy drinkers – heavy drinkers who can control how much they consume and can stop at any point. She doesn't judge me for my excesses; I do enough of that myself. *My name is Eva and I'm an alcoholic.* Squinting up at my great-aunt I smile at her, take the cold glass and sip cautiously.

'Thanks.' It is disgusting. Maude likes to mix cocktails, but no one has ever shown her how to do it properly and everything ends up a sweet, sludgy mess. I'm not fussy, however, and she knows that.

'Do you know what this one's called?' Maude squeezes herself into a garden chair, a green-and-white striped seat that barely accommodates her. She flaps a handkerchief at her throat. 'My goodness me, it's hot!'

The drink is thick and excessively pink. A wasp buzzes nearby and I swat at it. 'I've no idea.'

'Poet's Dream!' Maude toasts me, sips at her drink.

'Is that a joke?'

'Not really. I made it especially for you.'

I shake my head. We smile at each other.

'The book?' I ask.

She sips again. 'The very book.'

Maude has a book of cocktails and has shaken her way through it diligently. The book is ancient, a sale find, its pages faded with age and wavy from spilled drinks. I raise my glass to her. 'Thank you.'

'You're welcome, Eva. And who knows, maybe it will start you writing again.'

I cut her off before she launches into a discussion of my writing. I talk about that with no one, least of all my 89-year-old great-aunt.

I used to write, you see. Back when I was a functioning person with time flung out before me, a great big carpet of it, all those shiny hours and days and years stretching out in front of me, and words, more words than I could possibly put down on paper, bouncing around inside my head.

Because there were so many words, too many of them, I kept it simple. I wrote poems. Books of them. Hundreds of poems, written in notebooks, on random sheets of paper, sometimes even on the backs of till receipts, any paper surface that accepted ink. I wrote all the time, mostly to escape my home life, although I can only appreciate that now that I'm able to look back on it all. Poems kept me steady, allowed me to speak without a shake in my voice, let me find my own corner of the unsteady world I inhabited, the girl with the pen in the house of shadows.

I've always been subliminally aware of the huge darkness from which I've sprung. My mother was the wellspring of it all as far as I could tell, but she never told me anything about it, never felt she owed me an explanation of any sort. My mother, all my life, remained several leagues apart from me. Occasionally, if I sat still enough and observed her, in quiet moments I could almost see waves of secrets rolling off her, but that was the closest I ever got to knowing her. She kept herself apart from me deliberately, and she scared me too much to allow me seek the answers. She would pause in her digging, or place the rake aside, and in the stillness that followed she would rub her upper arms or smoothe her hair off her face. And I believed that if I could ever catch those secrets before they hit the ground and disappeared forever, I could claim some part of her for myself. Like sand, her secrets always slipped through my fingers. I never had a chance.

'It's good to have you home, sweetheart,' Maude says, taking another sip of her drink. She touches my knee, her fingertips rough from decades of gardening. Her hand trembles, and I feel like crying.

'Thanks, Maudie.' I want to keep her hand there, hold on to the tremulous affection, press her to me, but the moment passes and Maude's hand returns to fanning the handkerchief. The wasps, driven insane by the dual seduction of sticky pink drinks and ripened berries, buzz around us. We retreat into the privacy of our heads, but I feel nicer around Maude than I have in a very long time.

CHAPTER 4

I begin to run again. It's been a long time since I threaded the laces of my running shoes and pounded city streets, but a mixture of boredom and frustration forces me into filling some of the empty hours. Now on this hot morning I wind my way through the village, dodging delivery vans and prams filled with babies, destinationless, past the unfamiliar cafés and patisseries, the sleek office fronts and estate agents. Early traffic strangles the hot air with oily fumes, acrid and burning in my nose and throat. I duck into a delicatessen to avoid another girl from school, this one pushing a double buggy, full of purpose and determination. I have no need of news about people I haven't seen for twenty years, or questions about what I am doing. Even more, I must circumvent sympathies proffered by those who mean well.

Outside one of the few establishments that I actually recognise, the small fruit and vegetable shop with its striped awning and boxes of fruit, I stop. I lean against the wall and catch my breath. Sweat wets my neck, pools between my breasts. Even the wall is hot beneath my hand. Traffic snarls on the road in front of me, and a flurry of horns vibrates on the muggy air. I peel my T-shirt from my back, and as my breathing slows I look around me. The fruit is exhibited as it was when I was a child, the apples wrapped in purple tissue paper, the prices on small white signs behind each tray. I grab an apple from the display. Holding it to my nose, I inhale its clean scent. Fruit that fresh is hard to come by in New York City. Even at the market in Chelsea, with its artisan stalls and buskers, the fruit always seems a day out of date, especially in summer, when flies cloud the sweet produce and the smell of vegetables can make your stomach heave. I bite. The apple is as I'd expected, strong and sweet. It cracks against my teeth and juice squirts onto my chin.

As I turn to go inside and pay, a man exits the shop. We smack into each other, my cheek colliding with his shoulder. The apple tumbles from my hands, rolls onto the road and is obliterated by a passing car. Juice sprays itself in a foot radius around the black wet patch on the melting tarmac.

I open my mouth to shout at the man who almost dropped his two large paper carrier bags on impact. New Yorkers always shout first, breathing in the maxim with the toxic city air – always blame the other person, never yourself, and never apologise. Before I have time to articulate a syllable, the bags are lowered and an apologetic smile is replaced with the surprise of recognition.

'Hello! Jameson no ice, right?'

The barman from the evening of the funeral. Sean, I'd heard someone call to him. Sean, without his beer-stained white shirt and bartender's black trousers, with the same longish hair and a smile that appears to be aimed right at me. He doesn't seem to mind that I see him looking me up and down, that lazy once-over that a man twice his age wouldn't possess the confidence to perform. I wonder what he sees. I touch my hair. Still tied back.

I lower my eyes. A car, its owner frustrated with the immobility of the traffic, honks its horn behind me, the sound cutting the air between us. Others follow suit, the cacophony rendering conversation impossible. Such impatient drivers, such intolerance. Everyone racing to go nowhere. It's as bad as New York. The distraction gives me a moment to gather myself.

He looks good. In another life I would have allowed him to take my hand over the bar, draw me into the vortex of chemistry. I fight the impulse of attraction. I have no space in my overcrowded head for dwelling on an attractive man. I have the house to sort out, my return to New York to organise, my life to get back on track.

And yet I'm lonely. It's been a while since Isaac. I've needed the space I've created around me, but I've been too good at shunning people, too exacting in my desire to be left alone. Once, hesitation would not have crossed my mind. Men have been the easiest way around the black spots in my head, and I've willingly given myself over to them. Glancing at Sean in the midst of the car-horn-induced fracas, I wonder how he would feel against me, how warm his skin might be. His lips are full, flaking slightly. I push his shirt up in my mind, place my mouth on him.

'So?' He regards me. His shirt is fraying faintly at the collar. It's old, denim, and open to the waist. He wears a white vest underneath, and his jeans are low on his hips. Definitely fifteen years younger. At least. He has the flat stomach of a boy and the undentable confidence to show it off in ribbed white cotton. His arms are strong around the paper bags of groceries, but it's his hands that grab most of my attention, large, capable hands, with clean nails and smooth skin.

I blink. 'What?'

'Are you on for getting some coffee? You look like you need one.'

'I've been running,' I begin, by way of explaining my appearance.

'Relax. It's cool. I like the dishevelled look. Not too many can get away with it.' He nods at the café. 'Coming?'

I have to say no. It's too soon. Sure, I want coffee, and maybe him, but I also need to be careful. 'Okay.'

The café is housed in what had always been O'Brien's butcher's shop. In the place of skinned carcasses, displays of chops and sawdust on the floor are clean, sleek lines and an industrial-sized espresso machine. The smell of coffee beans is powerful, but more than that, the pull of the man holding the door for me weakens my resolve to stay away. I fill a glass with water from the tray set beside the till for this purpose. Not quite cold enough, but I'm so thirsty it doesn't bother me.

Sean's eyes appraise me as I refill the glass. 'Sporty, eh?'

'Hardly.' Sport is one great arena in my life that slides by, unexamined. Running for sanity doesn't count as sport.

We sit at the window table. The wooden venetian blinds are closed against the luminosity of morning, which still manages to sneak in through the gaps, striping the table with thin bars of saffron light. The door is wedged open, and the heat from outside elevates the temperature. Awkwardness seizes my throat, and I rub my palms against my thighs. My running shorts, an old pair I salvaged last night from the attic, are too short, and I'm conscious of how dusty I must look, how hot and grimy I am from my five-mile run through the traffic-crammed streets. I feel old, too old to be sharing a table with this boy. I stir sugar into my espresso, a spoonful too much. It gives my hands something to do besides tap nervously on the table, or sweat invisibly. Music plays in the background, something loud and guitar-driven. Its interruption is welcome and it masks my self-consciousness. I fiddle with the empty sugar packet, folding it several times. The coffee disappears in a few swallows. What I'd really like is a whiskey, but it's too early to drink in front of others.

Sean talks, and I watch his hands. They're beautiful. I see Raphael painting his Madonnas and his angels with those hands, the power beneath the tanned skin, all those bones and muscles working overtime. Three leather bracelets loop his right wrist. A chunky silver ring circles his left thumb.

He's an animator. Of course he is. Somehow, in the wedge of time between my leaving and my return, job descriptions in Ireland morphed into something infinitely more appealing. Gone are the generations of Irish teachers and bank workers, civil servants and insurance company employees, with their pensions, their reliability, their permanent jobs. In their place are the computer crowd, the artists, the young entrepreneurs. Recessions find it hard to penetrate the membrane of confidence and fake tans, the easy money and easier successes. I am exhausted by the gap in our experiences, aged by bridges I'll never cross. But he's beautiful, and I'm finding it hard to resist.

'So, what brings you home?'

Is it? Home, I mean? Dublin hasn't felt like home in many years. 'Family things.' No mention of my mother. I don't want her here, spoiling the moment. 'You know.'

'Such as?'

I wave the question away. 'Just some legal stuff. Nothing interesting.'

He points to his cup as the waitress clears the table next to ours. 'Would you like another?'

I push my tiny cup towards the centre of the table. 'Why not?'

'So look, are you busy? I've a bit of free time on my hands, and I only live around the corner.' He rubs his shoulder. His ribbed vest moves. A tattoo snakes over his skin. It looks like writing. Curiosity urges me to look closer, but I sit back in my chair. I shrug. 'Not really.' A tiny skip of excitement quickens my nerves. 'I need to find a job of some sort though.'

'What do you do?'

Explaining academic work is rarely easy, which is why most of us simplify and say we teach. 'I work in a university. Research, some teaching, that sort of thing.' I miss it. The new semester started this week. The beginning of the year is my favourite part, the new courses, new books and students, the possibilities. So much to find out, untried lecture material to test out on unsuspecting undergrads. My plans for a book on women in literature, which I must now set aside for a while. Thank God I didn't mention the idea to Isaac.

'That's cool.' He sounds like one of my undergraduates. He could be one of my undergraduates. My God, what am I thinking, sitting in a shaded corner of a café with this boy?

'It's actually really interesting,' I offer by way of defence. Isaac once proposed that the reason so many academics marry each other is because they never have to explain what they do, the conferences, the urgency of new material, the pressure to publish. To outsiders it can seem pointless, a luxury in a world that can little afford it.

It is not without bitterness that I reflect that Isaac himself did not find it necessary to marry an academic. There was no difficulty in pledging himself to life with a corporate heiress. No brownstone in Brooklyn for them, no commute over the George Washington Bridge each morning from the suburbs.

A phone beeps from the depths of one of Sean's grocery bags. He pulls it out, slides a finger across the screen. 'Sorry,' he mouths at me, pointing to the phone. As I wonder if it's a girl he's speaking to, he rolls his eyes at me, whispers 'Work.'

I shouldn't be relieved, but I am. My hand sneaks to my hair. Thankfully it's still tied up. If Sean were to see it loose, see the mess it really is, he'd make his excuses and leave.

I wish I had a sweater, anything to cover up this ridiculous T-shirt and outdated shorts. My fingers drum quietly on the table. The espresso has made me jittery, the molecules of caffeine marching up and down my veins. A woman squeezes past me to get to a vacant seat.

'So, listen, I have to split.' Sean rummages in his pockets for change.

Disappointment prickles. I quell it. What was I expecting? He's a child for God's sake. 'Thanks for the coffee.'

He waves away my thanks. 'You're welcome.' He grins at me. 'It was good running into you. Unexpected.'

Sean produces a pen from one of the many pockets in his jeans. 'Give me your number. We could meet up some time, if you like.'

I recite the digits of the home phone, embedded as they are in my memory, and remind myself to get a cell phone. If I am to be here for a while, the Bakelite in the hall won't suffice. Sean transcribes them across one of his paper bags.

'I run the same route every day,' I venture.

But Sean is already gone, hoisting his bags in his arms, sliding his thumb over the phone again. Someone shouts out his name as he leaves. High fives and fist bumps are exchanged outside in the street. I turn from the window. The coffee machine shrieks. The waitress drops a cup. It shatters and she swears. I can't place her accent. Eastern European, maybe.

I wish I felt easier around strangers. I wish I could just let them look at me and allow me to unsee my mother's loathing. I should have written my own number on his paper bag without being asked. Maybe even added an exclamation mark or two, or a smiley face.

My espresso is cooling, but I sip it anyway. It palpitates in my blood cells, a caffeine high that can be stronger than drugs at times.

The café fills up, the late-morning crowd weaving in and out. A mother parks her pram in a space near me. The urge to touch the sleeping baby is so strong that I stand up and head for the door. I thank the waitress as I pass her. She is filling bowls with paper packets of sugar, cleaning tables, stacking cups. She looks tired.

The sun spreads warm fingers on my back as I walk home. My keys jangle on a cord around my neck. The day lolls in front of me, clean, bleached, an empty sheet on which I have no words to write.

CHAPTER 5

The solicitor's letter is a surprise. I've been expecting a phone call, a summons to a dry office in a Georgian house, where I'd sit on my hands watching cars on the street outside and the last of the Spanish students meandering along the paths. Not so. The embossed envelope sits imperiously on the hall mat, a relic of times past.

My mother's solicitor requests a meeting with Maude and me, at our convenience, to read her will and put her estate to rights. Her estate. I could almost laugh if I wasn't so wary.

I don't expect much. Given my mother's ardent lack of affection for me, I can't presume upon her changing her mind at the last minute and leaving me her worldly goods. I don't know if she had savings, or anything of worth beyond the house. A couple of years ago and it would have sold for a couple of million. Obscene, the amounts paid for houses. And now look at it all.

It's unfathomable how little I knew of her, how far she kept herself from me. I, in turn, learned to keep myself from her, to turn away from questions, avert my face when doors were opened. I liked windows, because my mother's face wasn't at them.

If I hadn't been so terrified of her, I could have learned to hate her.

Maude is nervous about the meeting. Her arthritis is acting up again so the solicitor has agreed to make a house call.

'This is highly irregular, you know,' his desiccated secretary advised coldly over the phone when I rang her. 'Mr Bergin is a very busy man, not a family doctor.' I imagine her, all rules and rigidity, upright and uptight at her keyboard.

My mother would not have allowed such an attitude. I, on the other hand, meekly accepted the dictum of the frosty female, unwilling to enter into an argument with a woman so much older and more experienced in life than me.

No wonder my mother walked all over me. I allowed myself to be the mat upon which she wiped the feet of her disdain. I was too afraid not to.

My brother never understood what it was like for me with her. He tried, but he couldn't have known how I shrank from our mother and her loathing. She loved him, Andrew, her beautiful son. Maybe *love* is too strong a word for what my mother was capable of feeling, but in her own isolated way she was obsessed with my brother. The crumbs of affection I sought never fell my way.

Mr Bergin is due to arrive this morning. Maude came upstairs an hour ago to 'tidy up'. I watch her push the sweeping brush over the wooden floorboards, run a duster over the visible surfaces.

Her arm is warm, soft under my hand. 'Maudie, sit down. I'll do this.'

She shakes her head. No.

'At least let me help.'

'I'm quicker on my own,' she insists, pausing to wipe her forehead with the back of her hand. Her fingertips tremble. It's another scorcher of a day, more like New York in September than dreary old Dublin. The hall door is wide open, but no air stirs and the heat hangs heavily around us. Outside, the day is yellow, stagnant with humidity. My linen shirt sticks to my back and I tug at it. I need more clothes. In my rush I only packed enough for a couple of weeks.

'Maybe we should hire someone,' I suggest.

Maude's face is a still life of disbelief. 'Do you mean pay someone to clean the house?'

'Why not?'

'Esther would never have allowed it.' Maude starts sweeping again, her vigour pointed, exaggerated. 'Never. We do our own housework.'

'But you're 89, Maude.' And Esther is no longer here to decide things.

'What's that supposed to mean?' She glares at me.

I shrug. 'Nothing. It doesn't mean a thing. But maybe you should think about paying someone to come in and do your housework. That's all.'

'I suppose that's the way they do it in New York.' She almost sniffs with disapproval.

It is, actually. My apartment is a shoebox, but I have Isabel, a Dominican girl who comes in once a week to clean. I felt slightly guilty the first time she arrived, five years ago, but I got over it quickly. Isabel earns her money, and I am happy to pay her. She used to clean for Isaac. He gave me her number.

It's funny, but I still pick up the phone when it rings, thinking it will be him. Which is crazy, of course, because Isaac has no idea where I live in Dublin, or even that I'm here. I was vague in my request for a sabbatical, and he was in no position to argue or to question what I would do with the time. Of course, he bent rules to allow my late application, probably had to justify it to someone above him, but it's not my worry. Our correspondence was conducted via email and by letters slipped under his office door as I exited the building. I denied him a meeting with me, a chance to explain. He was too happy to oblige me, too guilty to say no. Someone will replace me easily, probably a postdoctoral researcher eager for some experience.

'Maude, I'll pay. But I think you should consider it.'

She sweeps past me, all 89 years of her.

I know she's just trying to fill the time till Mr Bergin confirms what my mother's will contains. She's worried. Maude has no home of her own. Her husband gambled everything they owned, leaving her homeless, destitute, when he died at 58 of a heart attack. She has nothing to worry about. My mother will surely leave her the house. Eventually I'll go back to New York, to my job, my research. Easy though it is to breathe with my mother not around, this isn't home. Not this shiny city, this receptacle of half-finished buildings, the place from which I ran.

Maude has been up since dawn, pruning, weeding, picking herbs and now cleaning the house. It's only ten o'clock, and I would still be in bed if it weren't for this meeting. I am a spiderweb of pain, that vague all-body ache that results from drinking too much late into the night. I finished off the congealed contents of the drinks tray in the living room, smoked some of the weed I smuggled accidentally in the bottom of my suitcase, a tiny packet left over from God knows when. I don't even know how it got into my case. I passed out on the floor as dawn silvered the sky and slipped in through the window. Maude's key in the hall door roused me. I'd wanted to get up when I heard her, but I couldn't lift my cheek from the carpet. She didn't say a word about it, but I still felt grubby for being that way in front of her, as though I were a teenager and drinking against parental wishes. Maybe if she came out and confronted me, insisted that I have a problem, it might be easier. But I come from a house where nothing is confronted head-on, problems are discussed in hushed tones behind closed doors, and voices brighten when the subject of the conversation comes into the room. This house is well practised in discretion. It holds its secrets like port in a corked bottle.

It makes it easier for me to drink and get high.

Mr Bergin arrives in a flurry of tidiness. He is small, neat and compact. Utterly trustworthy, which I suppose is why my mother chose him. He busies himself with files and sheaves of paper, while Maude fusses with a heavy silver tray of tea and sliced cake. It won't make any difference whether we feed the solicitor or not, but Maude isn't like me. I remove the antique tray from her grip and place it onto the dining room table. My hands on her shoulders, I manoeuvre her into a chair before dropping onto one myself.

A headache sighs somewhere in the back of my skull. I pull at a thread on the tablecloth. I wish I could lay my head down and sleep until this whole gathering is over.

I'm exhausted. My hair is bundled into a knot at the back of my head, and I'm thinner than I've been in a long time. I'm running every day to keep myself from thinking too much, but I do know that what I long for is to escape into the cool, scented spaces in poetry. I don't want to be here, in this hot room, waiting to hear how my mother is laughing at me from another dimension.

Maude is bright, expectant, but it's just a disguise. I've watched her today, seen how she smoothes her hair, brushes invisible wrinkles from her clothes. The tremor in her hand raises its level of activity, and I see her calming it with the other hand, hiding it. Mr Bergin won't judge her on how she looks, but it's the small actions that keep her busy, stop her mind from wandering into substandard care homes for the elderly who cannot afford anything else. I understand her fear and the shapes it takes inside her head, but I also know she'll be provided for. My mother may not have cared what happened to me, but Maude was the most important person in her life.

I attempted to reassure her. 'I'm the one who'll be left out, Maude. You'll be fine. You've nothing to worry about.'

'But Esther died suddenly. I don't know if her will was up to date, if she even had a will.' Maude had retied her apron, thumbed a mark on the kitchen table.

Mr Bergin now shuffles the papers and makes a tidy stack on the table. His smile is expectant as he regards us. 'Well, ladies, I do wish we were meeting under happier circumstances, but Mrs Perry has been exceptionally clear in her wishes, so this won't take too long.' He pats the papers. 'Let us commence. Maude Mary Gilmartin?'

Maude nods and tucks an imaginary strand of hair behind her ear. Her bun is tightly wound at the back of her head. She keeps her eyes on Bergin.

'Eva Catherine Perry?'

This is ridiculous. He's not selecting a jury.

'Eva?' He raises his eyebrows.

I pull at the thread on the tablecloth. The pipes gurgle upstairs. One of the window shutters hasn't been secured and it creaks slightly. This house is full of noises. 'Here.'

'Good, good.'

I want to focus on what this man has to say, but it's so difficult. The room is too warm, despite the open windows. The hot air hangs heavy and thick around us. The flowers

Maude picked earlier are already wilting. Two petals lie on the sideboard like two yellow commas. Mr Bergin talks about the will and its codicils. I rub my temples and sip the tea Maude has placed in front of me. I pick at the fruit cake.

'... and most importantly, the house.'

Details of my mother's modest savings have slipped by me, but I am alert now.

The house is for me. The house is for me under the strictest condition that Maude will live here for as long as she likes or until her death. As though I would suggest anything else. Maude covers her face with her hands. 'Thank you, God, thank you, Esther,' she says, over and over. The room is flooded with her relief. It pools on the polished wood of the table, runs over the edges. I reach across and touch her arm. She grips my hand tightly and squeezes her eyes shut. *Thank you, God.*

I don't think God has much to do with it to be honest, but for once I choose to keep this particular view to myself. I don't think God has much to do with anything, really.

I should have reassured Maude earlier. The one person my mother had looked after was Maude. Maybe it was because they were both widows, or maybe it was something more, but my mother had loved Maude. It made her less of a monster I suppose, although it didn't deter her from fucking me up completely.

Isaac used to complain that I lived at an emotional remove from him. How I laughed at his Central Park West psychoanalytical pretensions. I was having an affair with a married man, wasn't I? Not *affair*, my love, was his reply. A *relationship*. We're having a *relationship*.

It turns out, after all that, that it was only an affair. For him, anyway. And how I'd loved him.

Yet now I have a house in Dublin, where I don't particularly want to be, and I can't sell it because of Maude. So I suppose my mother did get one last dig at me. This house is not the keeper of a happy childhood. It does not sing out its welcome. I don't rest easily here.

We say our goodbyes to Mr Bergin on the doorstep and watch as he climbs into his shiny black car and backs it carefully out onto the main road.

Maude still looks stressed. I take her arm gently.

'Come on, Maude. Make me a cocktail.'

I know it's far too early to start drinking, but maybe I'll just have one. I need one, if only to help me smoothe out the tangles in my head, all those shrieking dervishes that won't let me be.

CHAPTER 6

So. My choice is clear. New York, or something constructive in Dublin. A job, preferably. Something short-term. My mother's funeral was nearly three weeks ago, and now I'm in the lingering phase of my return. Time to get proactive, make decisions. My ticket is open-ended, so I have options, but inertia keeps its nails digging into me, dragging me down.

A girl I know, a research fellow, wants somewhere to stay for a few months, maybe longer. I can sublet my place to her and cover my rent. I reply to her email before I have time to ponder. My place is hers, all 500 square feet of it, caught between the warring Puerto Ricans on one side and the Dominicans on the other. From my fifth-floor window I can lean out and see the Latter Day Saints' meeting house on the corner of First Avenue and Second Street, the second-hand bookstore next door, the bodega run by a Cuban widow and her disabled son. Graffiti tags sprayed on the dingy redbrick by kids from the projects on Avenue D do nothing to lessen the appeal for me. A Latino man with a squeegee and a bucket balanced on a length of wood across his shoulders cleans the walls, the doors, day after day. I don't know who employs him. Hardly the city. But he is there, every day, dutifully erasing the giant penises and cartoon breasts left there most nights by the disaffected kids with time on their hands and no better way to expend their anger. There is nothing in Dublin that could even vaguely rival the multihued vibrancy of the East Village. I console myself with the reminder of how much quieter it is. I don't wake at night to metal bins being thrown around as homeless men fight over someone else's discarded food, don't worry about being caught on the subway in the wrong neighbourhood at the wrong time. The consolation is meagre, but in this moment it distracts me.

Early evening settles its folds lightly around me. Maude is at her bridge game, and I'm alone in the garden. September is almost gone, yet summer is taking its time in leaving, procrastinating in warm, still days and orange sunsets. The house glows red in the dissipating light. I neck a bottle of beer.

I'm drinking way too much. I know there's a meeting I could go to, but I lack the conviction. I've been through it all many times, the meetings, the sponsors, but I always return to the welcoming embrace of booze.

I was 16 when I first got drunk. I'd heard my mother go to bed, and the house was quiet except for the noises in my head. My brother had been dead two weeks and I hadn't slept properly since. I couldn't bring myself to speak his name to my mother. I couldn't stop his name being shouted out loud in my imagination, and I slid out of bed and crept down the stairs, thinking I might leave the house, wander away forever into the ebony night. Disappear, just like my brother had done.

I remember it was dark, and how strange it felt, being up while my mother slept. The front room had some light from outside, and the drinks tray with its modest contents sat on the small table in the corner, where it still sits. Same tray, almost the same selection of bottles.

The sherry looked cloudy and reminded me of my mother sipping tightly from a tiny glass on Sundays and at Christmas, one inch in the bottom of the glass lasting her the whole evening, afraid of being loosened by one drop more. I chose the brandy and drank it straight from the bottle. It burned the back of my throat, forced tears into my eyes, and I almost choked on its strength. I coughed into a cushion so my mother, upstairs in bed, wouldn't hear me, then drank again. Despite its fire the brandy tasted familiar, like something I'd been waiting my whole life to try. When it hit my bloodstream it slowed me, quieted my brother's name to a whisper, steadied me. I sipped till the fire in my throat was unbearable, forcing me to put the bottle down. Something drove me, something I couldn't comprehend, and still don't. My mother had a brother who drank himself to death before I was born. Maybe I'm like him. Maybe there is flux between generations, rogue genes hijacked on the DNA highway and carried on. Maybe.

Almost accidentally I'd found something that helped me. Something that worked. And it was so simple. For the first few months it was easy to restrain myself. Fear of being caught stifled even the strongest urges to drink. Just the thought of my mother's rage tipping over me was enough to keep me from emptying every bottle in the house. Eventually, of course, I stopped caring. I did it all: watered down the contents of the bottles at home, stole from the supermarket – the big one near my school, never the small local one where I was known by name – pilfered money from my mother's purse to pay for it when I was too scared to steal, scavenged Maude's pension pennies. I daydreamed about getting drunk, about the glorious buzz alcohol drove through my veins, blunting my edges, editing my memory. I drank alone, always, and hugged my grubby secret to me. It was easy to go into myself, pretend the rest of the world had faded. I could count on booze to get me out of anything at all. I simply stopped caring.

Now, though, I don't have that wonderful abandon of youth. I know what it does to me, know that something is embedded so deeply in me that I can't just have one drink and be done with it. I've read the health warnings, know the signs of physical ruin. I've been to AA, collected my chips, fallen off more wagons that I can count, but I know that when things go wrong for me my silent friend is always there, waiting. Its hushed expectation follows me, its eyes watching perpetually. My guardian angel, clothed in black.

This dark thing in me appals me. It sleeps so soundly that I can forget it's there. Then it rises and I hide behind a curtain of booze.

I need to work. Otherwise, I'll have to go back to New York, and I'm not sure I'm ready just yet. I can't face the prospect of trudging through the want ads, calling up old contacts, holding out my begging bowl. My sabbatical has kicked in, my replacement already attending meetings in my place, marking undergraduate essays, drinking coffee in the shabby faculty lounge. I want to be there in so many ways, but this break is needed. And I don't want to run into Isaac. That's the main thing. A little while longer won't harm me.

Today's paper has thrown out a possibility: a boys' school needs an English teacher. Full hours, within walking distance, until Christmas. In other words, perfect for me.

CHAPTER 7

The principal practically hires me over the phone. 'We're desperate,' he readily admits. 'I've parents ringing me up to complain and we're not back a month.'

I can do this. I've subbed before, and it's not like I can't handle senior English. The principal misreads my silence. 'Why don't you give it a try? Come over and meet me anyway.'

We agree to meet at eleven.

The job is mine if I want it. I'm not going to languish in indecision, as is my wont. I've put on a new blue shirt, a denim skirt that ends above my knees and some high sandals I bought for the occasion, reduced to virtually nothing on a sale rack with the last of the summer offerings. The summer was hot, and my skin has retained the remnants of a tan. Outwardly at least, I appear less of a mess than I feel. If I so desired I could even admit that I like how I look on this lemon-hued September morning. My hair is smoothed into a ponytail. I've been neglecting it since Isaac left, and if I'm not careful I'll end up with dreadlocks. He loved to appease the angry curls, pulling his fingers through the strands. Since the day he closed the door behind him, I haven't had the energy to bother caring

44

for my hair myself. It's simply too much of a drag. Maybe I should just cut it all off and send it to him in the post. I can hardly imagine the consternation it would cause in his Central Park West apartment, the betrayal that would ripple along the expensive Italian marble floors.

The morning is warm as I walk. I pick up the first chestnut of the new season. It is shiny and new and I stuff it into my bag. Leaves are gathering along the footpaths, waiting to be scattered by children and crunched underfoot. If I were still writing I would love this day. New York in autumn is the best place to be. Manhattan empties itself of summer tourists, the chill on the morning air is a sharp sting after the sullen heat of August, and every photographer, painter and writer in the city is out trying to capture the colours, the scents, the flavours of the new season. I have all the words in my head, it's getting them down on paper that is the problem. I can compose poetry in my mind, twisting cadences and blank verse into double helices, winding metaphors into knots, but once I try to pin the phrases down in ink, they vanish.

I'm afraid even to pick up my pen.

The school is quiet, a rushed sort of silence that descends after the maelstrom of morning break. The door swings shut behind me. I almost expect to see mice scuttling across the worn maple floor, tiny feet sounding cacophonous in the empty silence. Nothing. A statue of Mary takes centre stage in the entrance hall, her hand raised. All the fingers are missing. Beside her, Jesus has two fingers remaining on his hand, a peace sign for all who pass by. Charts for match fixtures, chess club results and league tables for every kind of sport are pinned to the walls. Science competition results, woodwork contest rules. And the names! All the names, all those Daniels and Stephens, the Pauls and the Peters, spilling off the lists on the walls, filling the corridors with testosterone and the barely contained noise that I know pulses behind the closed classroom doors. The maleness of the establishment threatens to explode the building at its seams.

Mr Collins is seated behind his desk. If the school is male, he is its alpha. His own trophies line row after row of shelving, framed newspaper clippings jostle each other for space on the crowded walls, and a heavily autographed rugby ball resides in a glass case behind his head. I squint to read it, but I have no sporting references whatsoever, so I give up before I've made out one name. I imagine the man in a tight scrum in a bar, downing post-match pints and ruminating on points missed, bad referees, someone's hamstring injury.

We talk inconsequentially about New York, the weather, Ireland's chances in the rugby this season. I lie sincerely and convincingly, keeping my appalling ignorance of sport hidden from view. When we eventually meander into talk of the job, Mr Collins pushes his sleeves back and leans towards me.

'It's only till Christmas, but at this stage I'd hire anyone. Those bloody parents are killing me.' The same parents he stands with on sidelines, no doubt.

I slide my CV across the desk towards him. He waves his hand in its general direction but does not open it. His glance falls briefly on the cover page but returns to me immediately. A mug at his elbow has 'The Boss' picked out in red letters. A plate bears traces of biscuits recently consumed.

'So?' Mr Collins' expectation is almost luminous. His sleeves are like skins, keeping his sausage arms restrained. His neck is squeezed by his shirt collar. Never trust a man whose neck is wider than his head, my brother used to say.

I rest my hands on my lap. 'Why not?' Why not indeed. I need money, I must be occupied to keep me away from drinking, I must move forward. It's only till Christmas. Possibility lifts its head, expands inside my chest.

'Excellent, Eva. Excellent. I'm delighted to have you on the team.' He winks. 'The lads'll be delighted too.' He half-rises from his desk and extends his sporty hand. We shake. I am compelled to smile at him. He is so very sincere in his need.

I will start on Monday. Three days to gather myself. Three days. It's nothing. I must not be nervous. It's nothing that I can't do, guide boys through Jane Austen and Shakespeare.

As I turn to close the office door behind me, Mr Collins calls my name. I turn.

'Do we address you as Doctor Perry?'

I laugh.

'I'm serious. This is important stuff.' He coughs. 'And the parents love it. Keeps them in their place, if you know what I mean. Less likely to complain.'

'There's no need.' It's one thing in the university, among the undergraduates, but here in Dublin it feels, I don't know, fake, forced. I can only imagine the eye-rolling among the other teachers, the knowing looks as the biscuits are handed around.

'Right so. See you on Monday.'

I make it out of the building just before the bell rings and the school heaves with noise and a further surge of testosterone. Outside, the sunlight on the rugby pitch softens and grows warmer. I wonder about my decision to take this job, to stay in the place I left. It doesn't have to be New York that claims me. Plenty of good universities in other cities would do. But something tugs at me, some desire to uncover stones left buried for too long. I walk away.

CHAPTER 8

So I am 'Doctor Perry' in school. I don't know, maybe it gives him something to boast about, a name to drop among the ranks of the ordinary teachers. That sort of thing divides people, but I don't care. I'm not out for friends or a place to fall into.

My mother knew what she was doing. I can't be in the house without an income, and she knew I'd have to work, which would keep me here. It's as though I've simply inherited her life, living in the house of shadows, the place I ran from. I feel small and mean when I think of leaving Maude on her own eventually, but I feel the creeping dread of old at the prospect of Dublin for the rest of my life. Whatever good may have happened here in my absence has evaporated. I'm tired of the bad news, all the closures, the depressing statistics, the IMF moving in, taking over. The ballooning politicians' pay. Cuts in all the important sectors. What a mess.

Damn Isaac. I miss New York. If I told anyone how much I longed for the place they'd say I was crazy. How can you miss such a city, they would ask. A labyrinth of lost souls, so much poison and fury, noise and sorrow twisted into a giant clanging mass of upheaval. Yet if I close my eyes for one second too long I can hear its sound, a frenzied mix of Spanish and hard-edged jazz, of steam hissing from a manhole and the subway juddering to a halt deep beneath the city streets. What I love about New York most of all is that it's mine. My mother has no association with it, or my brother. I walked its streets without ever seeing something that Andrew had touched, liked, commented upon. Dublin is full of him, even though he disappeared from life long before he died.

The first time he tried to leave us was the biggest shock. After that it seemed that we just waited, suspended in the brine of our own disbelief, for the time when it happened for real. That first attempt was when he was 16. Sleeping pills and a bottle of vodka that he took to bed. Very rock 'n' roll. He had already read of all the famous suicides, Jim Morrison, Janis Joplin, Ian Curtis, so many others, and he decided to join them, add his name to the infamy. He hadn't expected a stomach pump and two months in hospital during his dreams of obliteration. There is no mercy in the unsuccessful leap towards death, no fingers to stroke your skin and assure you that all will work out fine. What's left is a gaping chasm where oblivion should have been, the cold faces of judgement surrounding the bed, the next world missing a new soul.

The second time, I was away, on a school trip that I hadn't even wanted to go on. Maude had persuaded me to go, insisting it would be good for me. Halfway through the second day my mother rang the hostel, her panic electric down the phone line. I raced home, the provincial bus service taking ten times longer that it should have. Andrew was in hospital, his wrists bandaged, medication keeping him in some kind of otherworld. After that he started to back away from us. No joy at being Lazarus, back from the dead. Piece by tiny piece, I watched him slip away from me. I couldn't stop him. It was as though my hands had turned to netting and he simply slipped through the spaces. I touched his face, but he couldn't feel me. I called his name, but he rarely heard. He stayed in bed all day, or in the armchair in the front room, the one by the window, just looking out at the main road. He barely ate, unless it was placed in front of him. My mother hovered constantly, like a fly I wanted to swat away. Her nervousness drove me mad. We competed for Andrew's attention, but all his focus was on the road outside, on the rain that smacked off the windows, the cars that edged along the busy street, the glare blinding us on warm days.

I envied other people, the girls in my school, even the teachers. I coveted their ease, their normal families, the way they could go home in the evenings and slip into that other life. I dreaded going home, back to that house of shadows, my brother already a corpse, my mother a wittering wreck. I tried to stay on in school each day for as long as I could, participating in supervised study, the book club, the school magazine, anything that kept me out and absorbed, and prevented me from being drawn like a magnet to the chair by the living room window.

It dragged on for over a year. My brother lost himself in that chair at that window. He looked like something left out in the sun for too long, faded, all his colour evaporated. There was little to hint at his former self, that bright, beautiful boy, athlete, guitarist, artist. He took his pills dutifully, and was polite to the counsellor he visited once a week. As the year progressed, the visits fell away. He seemed to possess neither the energy nor the interest to keep going. I knew it. We all knew it. He had lost hope. He stopped his banter with me, began to look at me through eyes that were opaque with an exhaustion I could not name. Our old childish references slid by him. He no longer wanted to read my poems, let alone critique them. This pallid, limp creature had replaced my gorgeous brother, and he inhabited the land of thwarted death, all the while plotting his next attempt.

I, in turn, stopped trying with him. I left him in his chair, drowning in the black airlessness of his mind. I took up running after my school activities, one more thing to keep me away from that shuttered house. I spent most of my time at home in my room, honing my poems, typing them up on Maude's heavy old Olivetti, each line pushing me a step further from the madness among which I lived.

The school is fine. I think I'm actually enjoying it. The boys are so young, so bewildered almost, that I'm amused by them. The older ones think they're men, but despite their shaven cheeks and the swagger most of them carry around with them, their boyishness, their downright youth, shines through. I have to teach them literature, help them unravel the beauty of language. I may as well absent myself from the room for all the attention most of them pay me. They're too focused on their exams, on what might come up on the papers. I try to steer them from such a bleak endpoint, but it doesn't work. It's so different from my lectureship in the university. American students demand more from their education than Irish ones seem to do, or maybe it's just that they're older than these children I observe crashing through lines of poetry, flailing around novels that they should be able to dismantle in one reading. There's so little focus demanded of them, just rote regurgitation of pre-learned notes. They're just kids. I want more for them.

It was the same when I was at university. Anything was deemed acceptable once some effort was made. I'd never survive if I were to do this for a long time. I listen to them, to their manly voices, picking their way through Austen, through Montague, butchering beauty with their mid-Atlantic drawls and imported American grammar.

Andrew read poetry, deciphered its mysteries, wrote music. He demanded something out of life, was never a passive recipient, not until his illness leached away his spirit. He fades sometimes in my mind and I can't see him clearly. I see a curl of brown hair, a hint of a smile, the thumbprint bruises under his eyes when his insomnia kept him wandering at night. But it's become difficult to see him properly as he flits in and out of memory, his shadow falling across my eyes. I try to see past it, but it's almost as though he deliberately stays just out of reach, a silhouette on the grass. *Move on, Eva,* I know he'd say if he could. But I can't. I am at home in the darkness.

School at least keeps me focused, stops my hands from reaching for the sticky contents of the drinks tray in the front room. I would hate for anyone in the staff room to notice the smell of booze on me. Ireland, despite its legacy of alcoholism and its legendary relationship with drink, is still not a place where addictions are freely discussed. Americans announce their habits with shocking candour, dissect their recovery with an honesty that I cannot share, only envy. And so in spite of my students' lack of obvious enthusiasm for English literature they keep me busy, and the fear of being found out is enough to stop me from drinking too much, on weeknights at least.

On my third morning a boy staggers across my path as I navigate my way through the corridors. Break time is over and the hallways are jammed with boys jostling each other, tripping each other up, throwing things. I drop my bag of books onto a chair outside a classroom.

'Are you all right?' I recognise the boy, a third year. A messer. Zippy, one of the teachers calls him. Zip the lip, Zippy. Something like that. There's a Zippy in every class in every school.

I search for an adult among the moving ocean of grey uniforms. My hand rests on the boy's shoulder. Something, a sound from him, stops me. I peer at him. 'Are you sick?'

Someone nudges me in the back. 'Nah, miss, he's just looking for the doctor.'

The boy laughs and high-fives his friend, who disappears into the throng. I stand, shoulder my bag, straighten my skirt. 'Go to class, Zippy,' I say, wishing immediately that I had a long list of witty putdowns for moments such as this.

'Here, what did you call me?' Affronted now, his humour fades.

A yelp of laughter from behind me. 'Zippy, she got you.' A slap to his back. 'Scarlet!'

Mostly I avoid the staff room, with its green walls, designated work spaces and lack of welcome. Maybe the *Doctor* in my title has made the staff suspicious of me. Possibly they envisage my conquering the place, capturing their tenure, slaying them. I don't really care. Jim Collins invariably greets me with smiles and comments on the week's sports. I nod my agreement, thankful never to be asked for reciprocation.

'Great game last night, Eva! Were you watching?'

I murmur that I was, sadly, busy.

'You missed a good one. They were on top form. The pack really did us proud, but when the last try was converted, well, I nearly met my maker.' Jim rubs his hands together, thrilled at the prospect of his life ending on such a high note. 'My poor wife was convinced they'd be stretchering me out. Great game. Great game.'

I vow to find out what a try is.

As I leave school at the end of my second week, a car hoots then slows alongside me. One of the teachers calls out from the driver's seat.

'Hey, it's Eva, right?'

I adjust the bag on my shoulder. The car stops, forcing me to stop too.

'Adam.' He jerks a thumb at his chest. 'History and English. We share some classes.'

A road digger starts up at that moment and the rest of his words are drowned. He keeps talking, however. I observe his mouth. He's asking me to join some of them for a drink. I shake my head. I have things to do. The library, a bookshop farther up Rathmines, some groceries to buy. No drinking this early. At least, not in company.

'Come on, it's only for a quick one.'

Two boys on bikes shout at Adam as they pass. He honks the horn in reply.

'I'm sorry, not today.'

'Oh go on. we won't eat you!'

'Another day I will, I just can't today.'

Adam's car is ancient, a Merc, all dents and patches of rust. Adam is someone I could have found attractive in another lifetime. Reddish hair, quite long for such a conservative school, hazel eyes, black frames to his glasses. Face still tawny from the warm summer. His clothes are a study in academic chic.

He catches me looking the car over. 'Runs on vegetable oil.' He pats the steering wheel as though it were alive, an overachieving child making its father proud. 'You'll have to come out in it with me. Quietest engine ever.' He pauses to shout at another coterie of boys, then turns back to me. 'Well, if you change your mind you know where we'll be.'

If he had suggested coffee, I would have said yes, and would have quite enjoyed the company of my temporary colleagues, but I cannot sit in a pub with strangers surrounded by the fizz and clink of booze splashing over ice, unable to drink everything around me. My mouth burns for a drink, but it will be a solitary one, later. I dig my nails into my palms, a trick taught to me by my first sponsor to stifle the urge. For now, at least, it works. 'Another time, okay?' I smile at him. He is so very attractive.

Adam waves out the window at me and drives off. I duck down a back street so he can't pass me again. The digger resumes its destruction of the concrete, the dust it throws up making me cough. A siren out on the main road splits the afternoon in two. For a second I think I see my brother running, just another boy in grey school clothes, running and laughing. But it's a trick of the light, this autumnal sunshine that inexplicably has appeared almost every day. And Andrew hasn't been a boy in a uniform for many years.

There is solace in the hush of the bookshop, the sweep of pages, the wash of ink. The smell of paper hangs on the quiet air. Picking up two books I want to read, I meander to the poetry section. I still check to see if my own books are available. They rarely are; the print runs ended, and because I failed to produce anything else my publisher just let me go. On occasion I've been known to search online for copies, and usually someone is selling, but the price of one penny isn't good for my ego, and they hardly ever go for more than that.

My brother would have laughed at me, at my secret internet forays into the world of second-hand books, fortified by a few glasses of whiskey. I prefer Irish, but I'm not fussy. After the first few glasses I can hardly tell them apart. Malt, rye, bourbon ... they all blend into one pleasing analgesic blur.

I can't write any more. I can do academia, but I am afraid to try poetry. I love academic writing, and relish the challenges of finding new slants on someone else's material. The library is my friend, all those dusty corners filled with abandoned papers that other people wrote about other people's work on other people, all of it essential to keeping the blood flowing through the department, justifying our expenditure. Not all of it is pointless, though. During my time in NYU, I discovered that I have an ability to influence others to think a little bit differently, something that gives me more than a little satisfaction. Despite my inherent reservation, I can stand up at conferences and deliver papers without ever losing my nerve.

But poetry?

The thing that got me through the blackest period of my life?

The one constant I believed would be my mainstay?

That disappeared a long time ago, and it's not coming back. I've done my mourning, let its coat-tails trail out of sight. It threatened to be my undoing, but I won out in the end. I've necked bottles of booze, been so high I could have floated, but nothing nudged the block out of place. Writer's block. How well it was named. Mine sat on my shoulders, cold, hard, immoveable. A block of Michelangelo's finest marble, all white and implacable, crushing me. I don't dwell on it any more. I used to, used to let days roll by without leaving the first shoebox I rented. I witnessed drug deals on the street, saw two shootings, countless carjacks, all from my desk by the window where I sat, willing the words to come.

And when they didn't, I forced myself to leave it behind. I had to, or I would have turned to salt at that desk. After that, academic writing was easy. While pursuing my PhD here in Dublin my undergraduate students had irritated me, partly because of their simplicity, but also because I saw them as little more than a barrier to my poetry. Teaching was part of my doctoral studies, but I did it with little grace. I was impatient then, too eager to get to whatever place I'd planned out for myself, too busy writing poetry to be worried about explaining Chaucer or Dickinson to kids who doodled hearts and names on their folders and kept checking their watches to see when they'd finally be free. I watched my students live their lives around me, applying lip gloss, fretting over match results, worrying over essays and deadlines. From a great distance I observed them, endured the tutorials and the banality, their lack of ability to see beyond the words on any page. I let them slip away, ran red markers over their essays and then gave them grades they didn't deserve because I simply didn't want to fight. I know it's not the ideal way to liberate minds at third level, but I was young, messed up, moving on. Shelving booze for most of my doctorate didn't add to my good humour, but it got me through. I'd never have made it while drinking.

I buy three novels and two essay collections. A book for Maude is a last-minute addition, something colourful and breezy. She's nearly 90. She's earned the right to easy reading. I haven't yet.

Outside, the afternoon is still bright and warm. The teachers are somewhere nearby, tucked away in a dark pub, dissecting their students, their classes. Adam is among them. Adam. The last thing I need. The absolute last thing I need is another affair – sorry, Isaac, *relationship* – with a colleague.

Isaac is a professor of English at New York University, where I work. We'd first met when I arrived in New York to interview for a junior teaching assistant position in a community college, where he was the external interviewer for the day. It was a favour from my thesis supervisor in Dublin, pity-edged, and in my desperation to go somewhere, anywhere, I took it. Junior teaching assistant on the Introduction to Poetry course. It saved my life. Flailing around in my mid-twenties I was a wreck, still wounded by my brother's suicide, ignored by my mother, heading in the same direction as my uncle. I'd started drinking again once my thesis was handed in, and had thrown myself into alcohol with a fervour previously unknown even to me. Two months into it, dwelling under that dome of booze, enveloped, womb-like, in its tentacled clutches, a phone call came through. Junior teaching assistant. Community college. My university sensitivities bristled, as my thesis supervisor had known they would. Take it, Eva, she urged. At least go and see them.

I saw the possibilities this position held for me, the tunnel I could escape through. It was a clean break with home. No association with Andrew, no way my mother could trail her loathing in front of me.

'You're Irish, correct?' His diction clipped, almost English. His eyes, coloured like moths, met mine, then resumed their perusal of my résumé.

'Yes.'

He didn't offer his family line. No Murphys or O'Briens there to be held up to the light, examined, no common thread of ancestry to be uncovered. 'I'm not sure this is the post for you.'

'It is.'

A pause, during which he tapped his pen against his tooth. Then a look, just the barest hint of raised eyebrow.

'It's only part-time.' The pen tapped on my application. 'You strike me as someone who wants something more.' He spread his hands on the desk. 'It's community college ...'.

'I'm aware of that. It's fine.' I'd just had years of study, of undergraduates' essays, of battling for funding. I'd have taken anything. I simply wanted to stay in New York.

Isaac was older. Mid forties. I was raw, clutching my PhD to me, half afraid it would be taken away. I was a fraud, a stealer of degrees. It had been too easy. I'd heeded the warnings about the years that would accumulate as I struggled with my dissertation, but I finished in less time than anticipated. My supervisor advised me to keep the thesis from taking over my life, but that was what I wanted, craved. A permanent distraction. Something that would loom larger than my dead brother, that would fill the spaces inside me that I poured drinks into whenever I could. I lived for those all-nighters, the weekends locked in the library, the deadlines, the chapters. I researched enough for two courses, yet still I finished a year earlier than planned. I barely breathed during term time, and it suited me perfectly. I bypassed drinking in favour of my research, let the poets I wrote about take Andrew's place in my priorities.

'Well, we need someone, and you're ready to start, so let's give it a shot.' His first smile threw me. My nerves steadied.

His real job, I was to learn, was chair of English at NYU. When I worked with him there, everything changed.

Affairs with work colleagues are too damn tricky, and someone always loses.

My new books in a paper bag, I take the long way home, avoiding the pub. I think of the bottle of wine in the kitchen, the red lozenge it will create in the bottom of my glass. It waits for me.

CHAPTER 9

The house draws me in. I am a fly, caught in its sticky threads. Being there without my mother is still strange. September has dissolved into October, and autumn is mellow now, resisting the pull of colder weather. The trees have turned, and conker shells scatter themselves along the footpaths. Now when I run I crunch leaves underfoot, let them disperse in the slipstream of my pounding feet. Still the hot spell throbs, funnelling colour into the city, lighting it.

My mother's things need to be sorted, and I can't bear the thought of it. Maude offers every day, and I should just let her. My idea of sorting involves inviting someone from the nearest charity shop over, presenting them with black bags and letting them take the lot. Her personal effects, correspondence and whatever else she squirreled away I will just burn. Her letters are in folders, marked with dates. I thumb them. Her organisation floors me. They're filed in order of date with the envelope stapled to the top. I push through them. Who has time for this sort of thing? Why wasn't she mothering me instead of stapling envelopes to letters? Where was the care of her daughter, the attention to detail there? It was always the same, the cold eye cast in the other direction of anything I might have been doing. Even my drinking. Especially my drinking. Secretive as I was, she had to have suspected something. Easier to ignore it. Something I have asked myself frequently in my life, the question that will never be answered: what did she blame me for? What, if anything, did I do? It seems self-pitying now, but I ask without seeking answers. My mother had her reasons, whatever they were, stretching years back into my childhood. She never liked me. Drinking eased the gap she left in my life, but it never really filled it. My mother's meanness to me as a child petered out eventually, ran its course like a river through desert lands, grew tired and faded away. Being ignored is merely a substitute, a fatigued person's bullying.

The old cardboard files give way to newer ring-bound ones for her more recent missives. One folder is marked 'Lexington Ave.', the letters printed in her neat hand. Inside is a thick sheaf of pages dating back thirty years, more, all in order, each one dated by my mother. The first half of them are typed, the deliberate lettering of an old office typewriter, like the one Maude gifted me when I was still a kid. There is nothing on these pages beyond my mother's name, our address, the date, an office reference code. A staple in the top left corner of each sheet is empty, but a tiny shred of paper caught on the metal in several of them hints at something about which I know nothing. My mother was never in New York. She knew no one in the States. Did an emigrant relative send her letters? Money? After leafing through the pages I am as in the dark as I was when I opened the cardboard folder. I put it to one side. My head is too stuffed today to take on anything new that needs working out. My mother's mysteries are just as unsolvable now as they were when she was alive.

It is surprising to uncover my own correspondence to her, neatly stowed. My hand stills, hovers over my writing, spiky anger bursting through the hurried scrawl. I don't read what is there. I know the details. Weather, food, work. The parks I walked in, museums I visited. Nothing personal, no plea for an answer. But she must have known, must have felt my need for a reply.

Her address book is pristine. Old addresses are neatly crossed out, new ones carefully added in. I flick to E, but there is nothing where my name should be. Same with P.

She didn't keep my address in her book.

This is not a new address book. There are names in it of people who died a long time ago. I remember this book from before I went away. I had three addresses in New York, but my mother seems not to have recorded any of them.

A bang against the windowpane shakes the hush of the bedroom. A bird lies on the grass below. I can't tell if it's still alive from up here. This is the best bedroom in the house, two windows overlooking the main road, and all the light a room could need. I lean my shoulder against the wall. The paintwork is cool against the thin cotton of my shirt. I look down. My bare feet are pale against the dark wood. My mother's effects lie scattered across the polished floor. The room was immaculate until I began the sorting. Even in death, not a thing out of place. Rigid control of environment was my mother's calling card.

When Andrew was in hospital she wrote to him every day. I was never privy to the content of those epistles, but my mother spent time each morning composing letters to her son. She wrote on pads of Basildon Bond, always blue or white, watermarked. These she covered in her neat, slanted script. I knew that no error lay in those ordered lines, not a missing apostrophe or misspelled word. In my eleven years in New York I received one letter a year from her, all of them the same: a short appraisal of the weather, two or three sentences about the garden, a reference to bridge games and a line about Maude. The format never changed. My birthday slipped by each year, unacknowledged; one more day in a year of days for her.

Isaac asked me about my mother at the beginning. A tiny village jazz club, a candle in a red jar between us, cigarette burns on the tabletop. I waved away the question, let it run off me like oil. Jazz tore up the air around us, gobbled up the spaces between our sentences, didn't allow for proper conversation. It suited me, kept things at bay. Mineral water fizzed in a glass on the damaged tabletop. I'd stopped drinking again. My meetings kept me sane, even if they didn't completely stop the craving. It was something I learned to live with, that persistent nagging behind everything I did, the unquenchable thirst. Work helped in the way distractions do, keeping it all at bay.

I dismissed the question. *What about your mother?* I dismissed it, yet still I craved Isaac's curiosity, needed him to draw me out, to let me speak about it all. Sure, by that stage he was my superior at work. Sure, I knew he was married, but none of that mattered to me. Not then, not at the beginning. I just wanted him to talk to me, to ask me questions no one had asked before, things I wouldn't have tolerated from anyone else. In the darkness of that underground club, with music zinging in our ears and the smell of weed thick on the dark air, I wanted him to stroke my bare arms, to pull me in, to talk to me. His eyes were green-grey, like moths, and they travelled over me.

My mother never loved me. That's what I wanted to say. I know that now, sitting here with her folders of letters on my lap, her stupid, pointless collection of correspondence. She loved my brother and she never loved me. I always thought there was something wrong with me, some part of me that was missing, because if everything worked properly my mother wouldn't have looked at me the way she did, telling me without ever having to say it that I was a nuisance, a waste of her time and money, one more piece of clutter in her house. And I suppose I wanted Isaac to know that about me, wanted him to look at me and see something different, not to notice my mother's loathing.

But I said nothing, because how do you put into words something that is held so deeply, a nugget of belief that hardens into a diamond with time and pressure from holding it so tightly? *What about your mother?* And I said nothing because I didn't want to be tainted by it, by her indifference to me. Not on that night, in that club, with those eyes like moths on mine.

I told him I loved him right from the beginning. It felt that way. After three years in the community college, I took over from a junior lecturer in poetry in the graduate school at NYU, who took a sabbatical followed by a nervous breakdown. Isaac, NYU's star professor of English, was on a career break when I was appointed. It was another three years before he reappeared, fresh from a stint in Paris, another in Sydney, and a third in London. Amazingly, I remembered him, remembered his name and his face, six years older now, but as arresting as it had been that cold spring day he interviewed me. He cornered me at a faculty reception to mark a new publication a week after his return. It was a big deal. A donor was in attendance, a New York millionaire with his sights set on seeing his name over a door somewhere in the building. Promises of money gather huge excitement in the world of the university, where funding always runs short of the mark. We are like survivors of war, scrambling over each other to get the spoils.

There was little in the way of introduction. 'So, Doctor Perry, I hear great things.' He held his wine glass as though it were a pint of beer, his elbow sticking out at an angle. A plate of sausages cooled on the table beside him. He pronged three with a toothpick. On the wall over his shoulder hung framed photographs of events like this one, stretching back decades. The room remained the same, the passage of time marked only by changing hairstyles. Across the room a glass was dropped. Someone laughed nervously. The donor's voice, loud, self-assured, rose above the clamour. I mentioned the abstract I'd finished the previous day, the paper on Eliot I was preparing. Isaac listened, really listened. The noise of the room swelled around us, but I had his attention. He refilled his glass from a bottle someone had abandoned. As he poured, I checked my watch.

'Leaving us already?'

'Soon.' I'd started going to meetings, and being around alcohol made me nervous. Each time a bottle popped, or ice clinked in a glass, the dark thing in me roused itself and stretched inside me. He was attractive, Professor Kraal. And married. I'd been privy to far too much departmental chatter, the rolling commentary on others' lives. Chinese whispers informed me of his wife, an heiress, and the Central Park West apartment they shared. The same whispers spoke of his solo sojourn abroad, of another woman, terribly distinguished in her field, who left her post in Barcelona for him, and of how it ended badly somewhere between Sydney and King's College.

'I'm impressed with what I hear. Eliot, Yeats, Cummings. This is exciting stuff.'

Like most academics, I am guarded about work in progress. So much possibility of it going wrong. But this man, the star professor, a brilliant light in the world of early twentieth-century literature knew my realm of interest. His passion for it surpasses mine. Isaac simply lives it, and there we differ. For me, it's still a job that I can leave behind. He can't.

He leaned closer to me, Chardonnay on his breath. He paused, his mouth almost touching my ear. 'Do you like jazz?' His hair, cropped against the possibility of receding, shadowed his skull. His skin, that skin, smooth, honey-coloured, unwrinkled. There was no paunch, no sagging jowls. He hadn't lapsed into that state of bewilderment that claims so many men in their fifth decade. He had more of the successful novelist about him than the chair of English at a good university. His beige linen suit sat lightly on his frame.

'I do, Professor.'

He downed the rest of his wine in one go. 'Then come on. We'll be late.'

'And my paper?'

'You'll get it done. I trust you, Doctor.'

And so it was. Our shared love of jazz was the excuse I used for seeing him, for spending evenings in his company in dark clubs all over Manhattan. It was easy to catch the subway to meet him and convince myself that it was just for fun. It was fun, in that giddy, uncontainable way that love always is in the beginning. Isaac didn't know about my drinking, not yet. There was no need.

Now I'm here and he is in New York. Someone else is doing my job, teaching twentieth-century poetry to undergraduates, guiding my doctoral students through their theses, publishing papers and going to meetings in my place. My apartment has been sublet, and I can't go back, not yet.

I shove my mother's letters in a recycling bag. I care not who wrote to her, what they told her. It won't help me unpick her, uncover her depths. She learned too well to hide herself, to pack herself into the tightest suitcases, bury her truths.

I didn't choose this house, but it shelters me for now. I'll work my way through each room, lighting sage in corners, chasing away the ghosts that linger.

But my personal ghosts still waltz to silent music, dusty candelabra lighting their spooky way.

Later, I stand at the kitchen window, John Coltrane's tenor sax fattening the silence of the early evening. The topaz light slips slowly away, and I finish the bottle of wine I started in order to shake the dust of my mother's papers off me. Irish days take forever to end, twilight at this time of year stretching on past its bedtime. I've stood in this same spot on countless evenings, watching the same scene smoothe itself out before me. There's comfort in that for me; no matter what happens during the day, it will end.

That's the thing about home. It tricks you into thinking that nothing has changed. But in the universe of our lives, nothing could be further from the truth.

CHAPTER 10

The window has darkened without my noticing it. The overhead light flickers insistently. A faint buzzing like a trapped bee is the only sound in the empty classroom. I've just finished marking the last of the essays, all thirty of them. Two exam questions on solitude in Emily Dickinson's poetry, with reference to five poems. The church on Rathmines Road bells the hour. Six. My hand cramps from holding my pen.

This is the first time I've stayed late since I started, but I don't want to go home. The emptiness of the house has grown around me, pulled me close. My East Village apartment, where I've lived alone for six years, has never seemed as vacant as the three storeys of red-bricked Victorian terrace that my mother threw my way. Staying on in school stretches the day out, lessens the time that I must spend alone at home.

I crave New York. Flashes of what I'm missing out on catch me at moments when I least expect it. Flowers in barrels at the Korean market on the Lower East Side. A ticket to an exhibition at MoMA. Reading a book in the park on a cold spring day. Ramen or sushi in the tiny Japanese place on Seventh, where you have to point at pictures of what you want because no one speaks English. Chinese New Year in Chinatown Park. It's better for me, right now, to be away from everything there, but it is difficult being here. Dublin is full of Andrew. He lingers like perfume in the house no matter how I arrange or rearrange the furniture. His room is bare, yet my hand is stilled each time I place it on the handle.

'Are you still here?' Adam leans against the door. His hands are stuffed in his trouser pockets. The sole of his shoe taps on the wood behind him. His reddish hair is burnt sienna in the faded light.

'Just finishing now.' I push papers into the desk, closing the drawer on the red marks I've scored across most of them.

'What're you working on?' He gestures towards the desk.

'Sixth years. Dickinson.'

He groans. 'Jesus.'

'The kids or the poet?'

Adam rubs his glasses on his shirt tail. 'The shit they've probably written. I can only imagine, if it's anything like the shit I'm handed on a daily basis.' He holds the glasses up to the light then rubs them again. 'Unless you have a few geniuses in here.' A phone beeps in his pocket. He takes it out, slides his thumb over the screen, smiles and puts it away.

I stand and reach for my coat. Adam is at my desk in a flash, helping me on with it. It's unnecessary, but nice. Isaac was that kind of man too, opening doors, helping with coats, carrying bags. A gentleman.

'Thanks.' I tug my hair free, shake it. It needs a cut.

'No problem.'

We walk along the quiet corridor. The dry smell of chalk and dust is gentled by the lingering silence of the post-class school. Our footsteps are hollow in the hush. A large portrait of a founding father catches my attention. Something is off. Adam sees me looking.

'Have you not noticed it till now?'

I haven't noticed anything.

'Look closely.'

The priest's face is vaguely familiar.

'It's Jim Collins. Some smartass Photoshopped his face and stuck it up. It's been there about three years now, and Jim still hasn't copped on.' Adam laughs. 'I see it every day and it always cracks me up.' He nods to a plaster bust of a former pope, his skullcap obscured by a Dodgers baseball cap. 'Same thing, there since last year, not a glance from Jim.' We laugh at the silly, boyish humour. This kind of fun is absent in university, where it would be regarded as childish from the lofty heights of academia.

Adam holds the main door open for me. 'Drink? Or something to eat?'

The burger place is one of those upscale joints so popular now in Dublin. The hipster waiter seats us at a long refectory table filled with other early diners. I am reminded of lunchtimes at school when I was a child. We touch elbows with the people on either side of us, but no one seems to mind. The music is loud, something jazzy and mellow. Adam removes his glasses. He fiddles with them while contemplating the menu, which is huge and laminated. Despite the quirky names carefully printed in rows and the exorbitant prices, the dishes are ordinary diner fare.

We order. Adam requests a turkey burger.

'I don't eat red meat,' he says before I ask. Not that I care. New York academia is every bit as neurotic about its eating habits as the celebrified West Coast. I am accustomed to meat-free, wheat-free, lactose-intolerant diets. I order a gourmet burger, whatever that is, and a mineral water. Adam takes a long swallow from an impossibly tall glass of wheat beer.

'Sure you won't have something else?' He nods at my water.

'Positive.'

He doesn't push me or berate me for being boring as so many Irish people would, as though drinking were a badge of honour, an activity only for the worthy. Waiters weave their way through the rows of tables, the music changes and becomes more insistent, queues form at the door. A girl with a snake tattooed on her forearm stands at a podium and takes names, writes down mobile numbers, turns large groups away. Traffic builds on the main road. We talk about school, about books we've read.

'So, this PhD, what's it in?' Adam raises a hand to the waiter, points at his glass.

I shrug one shoulder. 'Early modernism.' It seems so long ago now, all those years of study. Poetry and early modernism. My crutch in times of need.

'I'm impressed.'

I tip the last of my water into my mouth. 'Don't be. It was years ago.' I signal for a refill.

'Have you done much university teaching?'

'That's all I've done.' I allow the waiter to place a new glass of water in front of me. I could pretend it's gin and tonic. I could languidly sip it, hold onto it while I converse, not let it out of my sight. But it's only mineral water, and I can have gin when I get home. If I can find any. If my resolve fails. 'NYU', I say, by way of explanation. Pride nudges me, but I bite it back. My mother hated pride. She made sure I felt little of it, and guilty if some should mistakenly fall my way.

I miss my job. I miss it all, my office, the undergrads, even my doctoral students, with their thesis problems and tedious draft rewrites. I miss my colleagues and the papers I should be writing. What am I doing? Really, where did my courage slip away to? Why didn't I just stay, face things, let time work its magic?

'I started one.' Adam's phone lights up on the table between us. I expect him to break our conversation and smile at the screen again, but he ignores it. 'A doctorate, I mean. I did two years and gave it up.' He sits back. 'Realised I didn't give a damn about what I was researching.'

'Which was?' I can't help it. He has caught my curiosity.

'British maritime history leading up to and during the Great War.' He announces it, then laughs. 'It sounds a lot more interesting than it was.'

I grin. He leans back, smiles at me. 'Oh, you may laugh, but I bet you're dying to know the intimate details of Mahan's thesis.'

'Who?'

'Don't be coy.' Adam shakes his head. 'You know who Mahan was. You probably keep a photo of him by your bed.'

I sip my water. 'Tell me more.'

'I don't know if I should. You might expire with excitement.'

'Try me.'

'Well, there's the dreadnought model, template for all battleships.' He raises an eyebrow. 'Should I go on?'

'Please do.'

'Let us not forget the fact that British battlecruisers and torpedo boats led the Germans to develop their own lighter versions.'

Our laughter is loud, and irritates the couple next to us, but I don't care. This is the most I've enjoyed myself in ages, and as I watch Adam spill ever more obscure naval facts, and find myself convulsed, I can see why the boys love him. He doesn't try to be cool or funny. He just is.

He's how old, late thirties? More? I admire how easy he is in himself, how effortless his confidence is. His mother loved him. I see how that one simple fact can alter the whole person. I am in awe of people like Adam, who wear their self-assurance like a loose layer, who treat such bounty almost with neglect. The old darkness slides through my brain, and the desire for a drink catches me, as it invariably does, unawares. I don't know why it surprises me; the need is always there. I just have to keep it tightly sealed in its jar. I've been good for a couple of weeks now.

This has been a bad year for my drinking. All that time on the dry, and I slid right down the ladder, all the way to the last rung and beyond. It's been a bad year all on its own though. The booze just cushioned it.

Adam pays the bill. The queue for seats does not allow us time to linger. 'Shall we?' Adam puts his phone in his pocket and shakes his car keys.

I follow him to the door. Our seats are swallowed before we've exited. Outside, the line snakes to the corner and beyond. An autumn wind gusts along the main road, sending bits of discarded paper wheeling in the air. It starts to rain with a suddenness that surprises me. The wind catches my hair, whips it around my face. I try to hold it down. Can't have it getting even more tangled than it is. The air smells of metal. A Hallowe'en firecracker explodes somewhere off the main road.

Adam opens the passenger door of his vegetable-oil car. 'Hop in,' he says. I dither. 'Come on, you'll get soaked otherwise.' He pulls the collar of his jacket up. 'And so will I if you don't get in.'

I obey him. The rain has soaked us, even after the few minutes it has taken to walk to the car.

Adam puts the radio on. Donald Byrd fills the silence around us. It doesn't matter that we don't talk. There is humour in the quiet, an almost intimate quality. Beyond the confines of the car the rain washes down the gutters, gathers in puddles. The car smells of doughnuts, and Adam delivers me to my door.

CHAPTER 11

Sean is buying vegetables the next time I bump into him. Same place. I see him first, turning carrots over, checking tomatoes for marks. His hair looks longer, or maybe it's just flattened beneath his grey beanie hat. A heavy checked shirt is knotted around his waist, his jeans are skinny and a faded black, and his canvas shoes scream hipster. The look is less contrived on him than it is on the legions of boys slouching around Dublin dressed as he is, as though it's simply the clothes he put on this morning as opposed to an image he wants to project. Gorgeous. He's gorgeous. He doesn't notice me, and I busy myself with a box of limes. The limes are organic, unwaxed, and their scent squanders itself on my hands, a citrus sharpness that brings to mind margaritas, a crust of salt on a glass, a hot New York sun, happy hour in a village bar. There are only three other customers in the shop, and I try to slip out before Sean spots me.

'Hey! How are you?' Suddenly, he is beside me. What has happened to the dour repression of Irish males, all that kicking at the ground with scuffed shoes, hands jammed in pockets and no eye contact, the familiar traits that afflicted the bulk of the boys of my youth? All those emotions, boarded up like a derelict house. Sean brims with smiles, pleased to see me in a way that I don't understand. He didn't ring me. Funny how that should matter. The paper bag with my number scrawled across it shames me slightly.

The bag of limes crinkles as I shift it to the other hand. 'Fine, thanks. You?'

He pays for his purchases and drops his wallet in on top of his vegetables. 'Grand, I'm grand. Busy, but that's a good thing.'

I duck under his arm as he holds the door open for me. A dog, tied to a post, barks furiously at us. Sean laughs and rubs its head. He jerks his thumb at the café. 'I'm going in. I'm freezing. You coming?'

A double espresso lasts only a few minutes. I order a second. Sean stirs his mocha. He's working on an animated short, something he's hoping will lead to a commission. 'If it doesn't happen, I'm off. Australia, probably,' he adds, though I haven't asked where. Everyone is off to Australia this time around. There or Canada. When I left, the States was still the place to go, but not any more. There are other destinations, other magnets that pull. It seems that economic prowess opened Irish eyes up to the world, battered down borders and any kind of barricade to personal happiness.

'Sure,' I nod. 'Australia.'

'Not much time to work in the bar any more. Have you been in?'

I shake my head. I'm trying to keep away from booze. If I'm not around it I'm less likely to drink. It's so difficult, the huge draw towards substance. The consistency of addiction is its most exhausting feature. Nowhere to hide in its darkened rooms.

I got high last night, smoked the last of the weed I brought back. Miles Davis unthreaded on the stereo behind me and I did something I haven't attempted in a long, long time: I tried to write. Oh, it was pointless, I knew it at the time, but I was stoned, stoned and lonely, and it's been such a bad year, and I need to put some perspective on it, need to examine it all, and poetry used to help me do that.

It didn't work, and after a couple of hours of looking at the sheet of paper, covered in my initials and not much else, I gave up, finished the badly rolled joint and surrendered to the empty embrace of cheap upstate weed. It's easy to trawl the darkness around with me. Letting it go is one of the biggest challenges. Despair is indeed a glacial god.

Sean tells me about the animation he is working on. It sounds good, some ordinary children, each with a once-off superpower that can only be used for the improvement of the world. His hands move as he speaks, shaping his characters, and again I'm struck by their beauty.

In the middle of it, his phone rings. Without apologising, he grabs it, nods, nods again, and hangs up.

'Listen, I've got to split.' Sean stands, gathers his bags and pulls his hat on. His blond hair touches his shoulders. 'We should hang sometime. Give me your number again.' He smirks. 'I know I had it before, but don't ask me where it ended up.'

'The language of seduction was never better spoken.'

'Sorry.' In black marker he scrawls on one of his paper bags.

'Is this your routine?'

He stops writing. 'What?'

'Nothing.' I recite the home phone number for him. 'Déjà vu.'

'Yeah, sorry. I'm hopeless.'

'It's Eva.' I point to where he's written 'Aoife' before the number.

'Shit, sorry. Jesus. Eva. Yeah.' He grins again. 'Sorry about that.' He doesn't bother changing it, but I don't really care.

The dog is still tied up outside. Its barking is frenzied as Sean bestows one final pat to its head. The sound grates. I've always tried to live in dog-free buildings, a near impossibility in Manhattan. One dog, an Alsatian, was poisoned on my block last year. Someone, driven demented by the incessant barking and the owner's dismissive contempt for the many complainers, got to it, fed it poison, and the dog was silenced. The owner was a Dominican drug dealer, flashy in stolen sunglasses and expensive clothing. The animal had worn a diamond collar. I admired the bravery of the poisoner, who risked a bullet for peace and quiet. Everyone said it was a rival dealer who had done it, but I suspected an elderly neighbour, fed up with years of barking and fear.

Sean sees me watching him. He straightens, raises his hand in farewell and walks away. He shifts his groceries to the other arm, adjusts his hat and disappears from view.

I linger, scan the paper and drink a glass of water. The same waitress is there, her English thickly accented, her face full of absent smiles. I have no plans for the evening and no weed left to blunt the edges of empty time. There are things I should do, boxes I need to fill with Andrew's things, emails from the university I must respond to.

What I'd really like, though, is a drink. A mojito, with the limes I've bought, all crushed mint leaves and Caribbean rum, or a margarita, salt and lime juice colliding on my tongue. Summer in a glass.

At the next table, a girl fills out a form. A supermarket's name proclaims itself in loud red letters across the top of the page. She marks the boxes in black ink. What position does she seek? What qualifications will she downplay so she can stack shelves at unsociable hours? This is where Ireland is heading. I'm lucky to have my subbing job. While I'm here, I must be busy. I don't want to do what the girl is doing, seeking work for which I'm overqualified and spending my free time in a maze of wondering how I got into such a position. The girl sips at her coffee. A drop splashes on her form and she swears, swiping at it with her cuff.

A vaguely familiar face gives me a tight smile from across the café. I nod in response and return to the newspaper and its untrammelled reportage on the financial implosion. It's depressing. Pensioners losing their life's savings. Half-finished housing estates abandoned all over the country. Stocks and bonds worthless. I fold the paper and place it on the table. The woman who smiled at me stops by my table on her way out.

'It's Eva, isn't it?' She is older up close, her face already beginning to lose its definition, that softening of contours that cosmetics giants have built empires on. Her hair, secured in a shiny bun, is expertly coloured.

I attempt the vague smile of confusion. I have no idea who she is.

'I'm Suzanne. Susie. Susie McEvoy.' She laughs, and touches her hand to her breastbone. 'Actually, it's Susie Clarke now.'

God. Do I look that old? I do remember Suzanne. She joined my class in second year. I doubt I've given her a single thought since finishing school.

'I heard about your mother. I'm so sorry, Eva.' She places a consoling hand on my arm. Her rings flash.

This is why I avoided the lunch Maude had organised after my mother's funeral. This, the touch of strangers, brimming with imagined solace.

I nod at her offer of sympathy. 'Thanks.'

'It must be so hard for you.'

My smile feels as forced as it is.

'Have you anyone with you? Anyone, well, you know, to help you.'

'My aunt lives with me. My mother's aunt. She's wonderful.'

Suzanne's hand flutters again at her breast. 'Oh that's great. Family is so important at times like this.'

I cough and touch my fingers to my hair, which is twisted into a knot at the back of my head. A gap yawns between me and this woman. A baby starts to wail at a neighbouring table. The espresso machine roars.

'You know, we should go for a drink some time. I could ask Sinead too. She still lives in the area.' Suzanne starts to button her coat. It is black and expensive. I may be an academic, but I can spot Prada from a great distance. Worn to impress. 'We could have a good catch up with you.'

I remember her friend, Sinead. She had a thing for Andrew once, thought she could draw him out of himself. It was kindness, I know, that led her to call to the house at weekends, bearing offerings of mix tapes and books he might like, but after his initial enthusiasm petered out I was left to entertain her. Those awkward encounters were intolerable.

Before I can squirm my way out of the suggestion of a social gathering, Suzanne's phone rings and she answers it. She points towards it and covers the mouthpiece. She whispers in an exaggerated fashion, 'Work. Great seeing you, Eva!' She waves her fingers at me.

The door swings shut behind her.

Rain is crashing down when I leave the café. The shapes of the street are bloated, distorted by the deluge. The afternoon is as grey as sorrow.

If Sean calls me, I'll meet him. Why not? It's not as though I have something to lose. Anything is better than a dismal school reunion with endless chatter about who's doing what and with whom. No thank you.

CHAPTER 12

I meet up with Adam again. He'd cornered me after school, driving alongside me in his vegetable-oil car. A late autumn mist had settled upon the afternoon, blunting the last threads of daylight, quashing the crunch of leaves underfoot.

'So, will I see you again some evening?'

I shifted my bag higher on my shoulder. A car blared its horn, angry at the battered Merc for crawling so slowly along the main road.

'Your call, okay? Dinner, the cinema, I don't mind.'

I wanted to tell him not to bother wasting his time, to find someone more worthy of his attention. Instead, I heard myself say that Saturday was good, and now I'm sitting here, waiting for him. This is my first Saturday night in town since I was in my twenties. I feel like someone's maiden aunt among the in-crowd, the teetotaller at the party. The bar Adam picked is nothing like the smoky corners of Manhattan I frequent. This is a cavern of noise, this place in the centre of Dublin. I stay near the door, my coat in my hands, my bag clutched tightly. Around me, everyone is young. Too young. They should be at home, doing homework and going to bed early. It's November, and cold, but the girls are mostly wearing tiny skirts, with bare, tanned legs and teetering heels. Hair is almost uniformly streaked blonde, and straight. Make-up is anything but subtle.

I touch my own hair, always just a step away from disaster. My top is Erdem, a present from Isaac, and it feels wrong. My jeans are too tight. My new boots should be inches higher than they are. Sweat coats my palms. I can pretend it's the tension of meeting an attractive man on a Saturday night in town, but really it's being in the presence of so much alcohol that is making me nervous.

This is a mistake. What was I thinking of, agreeing to a night out with Adam? I'm too old for dating. It is ridiculous, going out on a Saturday night. I would have been better off slipping down to Maude and watching something on television with her.

I feel guilty for not spending much time with Maude. I know she's on her own and she misses my mother, and I try to see her a few times a week, but she always steers our conversations around to my mother, and I prefer to avoid talking about her. There is nothing to say, and I'm not a good enough actress to pretend that everything was fine.

Adam billows into the bar on a gust of glacial air. He spots me immediately.

'Eva! You're here. Sorry I'm late.' He leans towards me as though to kiss me. He is jostled by a crowd of women in feathers and L-plates and he falls into me. 'Sorry!' He says something else, but the words are swallowed in a sudden wash of thumping, frenzied music. He brings his mouth to my ear, but the effort of conversing that way for more than two words is futile.

I point to the door. 'Let's find somewhere quieter.'

The air outside freezes my face, but brings the relief of being able to move my limbs and hear my own voice.

Adam steers me along the footpath, his hand cradling my elbow. His apologies for the bar are profuse and sincere. 'It wasn't my choice. A friend said it was a good place.' He pushes his glasses up his nose. 'You can see I'm not the man about town that I once was. I'm surprised we didn't run into half of sixth year!'

I nudge him. 'Doesn't matter.' The footpaths are an ocean of people, a bizarre fusion of tourists, more girls in feathers and fake bridal wear, drunken teenagers and hordes of others out seeking love and oblivion. I tighten the belt on my coat and wrap my scarf twice around my neck. The wind funnels down the wide city street. Taxis idle at ranks. A siren splits the night.

Down a narrow cobbled side street the noise suddenly halves, then halves again. Adam keeps his hand on my arm.

The pub is small and narrow. The smell of beer and spilled liquor makes me want to weep. My sponsor always said I should avoid bars. Too much temptation, too high a risk of offending. I've been good these past couple of weeks. There's no booze left in the house, and I have not replenished what I've consumed. No emergency bottles, nothing to lean on. If there's something to fall back on, I'll fall. Every time.

I order mineral water. Adam has one of his wheat beers, all cloudy foam in a spindly glass. He glances at my bottle.

'On the dry?'

The bottle fizzes as I crack it open. 'More or less.' Water bubbles onto my fingers.

'For now?'

I wipe my hand on my thigh. 'For good, if I can ever get there.' Three men squeeze by. The barman takes their order with a nod. Three pints of Guinness stand idly, the foam rising slowly to the top. Fantasies about grabbing those darkening glasses and downing them in one go distract me from the man beside me. This isn't good. Pubs are not places I should ever be. The music of booze plays its overture around me, all those ice cubes clinking, the bottles popping, the glug of glasses filling. Even the dull thud of an empty glass on the wooden bar has its own particular sound, discordant, and in a lower key.

'How long have you been off it?'

'Nearly ten years.' Give or take, with many incidences of falling along the way.

'Right.' He pauses. 'Sorry.'

'What for?'

'Because this is the second time I've drunk in front of you.' He regards the glass in his hand.

'It's fine.' I suck on an ice cube. It numbs my tongue. I can see Adam wants to take the discussion further. 'Really, it's fine.' The last thing I want is some earnest conversation about addiction. *My name is Eva and I'm an alcoholic.* Adam is an intelligent man. No crash course in substance abuse needed there. I'm curious about him, and maybe I'd like to take it further. Let the darkness stay out of the equation for now. Plenty of time for revelation at some distant point further down the road.

We push away from the bar and squash ourselves into a corner. Adam's jaunty confidence seems quiet all of a sudden. I rip a beer mat, piling the pieces in an untidy heap beside my glass.

I hate when the hint of dependence causes a rift in any exchange. It embarrasses me, talk of my addiction, as though it were something I should control but can't. Isaac never let it bother him. I'd been in and out of drinking for a couple of years when we began seeing each other, but my job was too important to lose it over a bottle of booze, so I stopped.

It was every bit as hard as it should have been, with no poetry to write that would keep my brain from meandering into all those pockets of darkness, but I was able to do it. I've always been able to; wanting to is another story.

Where is Isaac tonight? It's late afternoon in New York now, daylight already extinguished, a cold mist rising off the Hudson. The street lamps are probably switched on, the dark mass of Central Park swelling in the half light. The park is visible from Isaac's apartment, that gargantuan dwelling on Central Park West, between 81st and 82nd that he shares with his heiress wife. The importance of those street numbers was unknown to me before I fell in love with him. A professor's salary, even at our highly regarded university, would not cover anything in that zip code. From my tiny corner of the Lower East Side, the Upper West was a place I barely thought of. The ballroom-sized dining room, five bedrooms for a childless couple, an incredible kitchen that was never cooked in.

Damn him. Isaac. Do I enter his thoughts? My nameplate is off my office door now, another's title stuck in its place. Does he consider me, ponder our final moments together, regret what could so easily have been? I regret it, can't stop myself thinking that it was all a terrible mistake. What I wouldn't give to be back there, back to last spring, heavy of limb under the weight of an unexpected heatwave, slippery with anticipation, and not stuck here, empty and alone. I miss him.

'So? What do you think?'

Shit. Adam. 'Sorry.'

'You're miles away.' He digs his wallet out of his inside pocket. 'Another water?'

My glass of water effervesces quietly, barely touched. Suddenly I'm exhausted by it all, the being here, the smells, the presence of so much booze. I can't do this. I like to think it's possible, sitting here in a bar, drowning in an atmosphere of alcohol, but it isn't, not really. Overwhelmed. I am overwhelmed. I want to go home, find a bottle of something strong and negate all the thoughts that keep tumbling into my head. The tiredness weighs me down and makes me feel slow. Pretence exhausts me, and it's too hard to keep up with it. My coat is wedged between Adam and me. I retrieve it.

'Listen, I should go.'

The disappointment on his face is almost flattering. 'Really?'

'Sorry, I'm just wrecked. I think I'm getting a cold or something.'

Adam stands too quickly, and the table wobbles, slopping his wheat beer. 'Look, it's my fault. We should've gone to the cinema.'

I shake my head. How kind he is. A good man. 'It's not your fault. I just need to go home.'

He pulls his jacket on. An older couple ask us if our seats are free. They put their drinks down on the table, a pint of Guinness and something mixed with orange. My water remains there, barely touched, the green label curling where I pulled at it.

We share a taxi. It's early still, and the queues for cabs have yet to begin. Town is packed. Lines have formed outside clubs, and hordes of drunken people lurch along the streets, shouting across the road at each other, stepping out in front of cars. The taxi driver swears, blares the horn and complains about girls puking in the back of his car. It's no life, he says, driving a cab on a Saturday night in Dublin. You'd want to be mad to do it. We murmur assent. The driver shakes his head. Mad, he repeats. I must be mad to do this.

Adam lives in Sandymount, but we're going by my place first. He leans back, pushes his glasses up on his head. What would it be to kiss him, to smoothe the planes of his face with the palms of my hands? His hair curls slightly, dark auburn and thick. A day's growth stipples his jaw.

The traffic is heavy leaving town. By the time we reach the Triangle, we are stuck again.

Away from the city centre, and the flow of alcohol, it's easier to be calm. I don't want Adam to see me withdrawn, sullen. There's still time to salvage the evening. I lean forward, tap the driver on the shoulder.

'Let us out here, will you?'

Adam pays; he will not accept my share of the fare.

'Which one's yours?' he asks, looking around at the terrace of houses where we stand.

'I'm farther up the road. I just thought it'd be nice to walk for a bit.'

'It's very nice to walk for a bit,' Adam says. His breath swirls on the cold air. 'So I'm not in the bad books then?'

'Don't be silly.'

Opposite, diners sit on patios under gas heaters. The doors of a pub swing open, allowing a roar of sound to gush out before being sealed off again. This is better; this is easier. No drunken hordes of tourists and hen parties, no one vomiting on the streets. It's a neighbourhood, in the way the East Village is.

'I'm getting old,' I remark.

Adam reaches out, twists a lock of my hair around his index finger. 'You're looking good on it.'

'I mean it. This is much more my style.' I gesture at the scene across the road. 'I don't like town when it's packed. Not sure I ever have.'

'I'm with you. The only time I go in is if I'm going to a play, or to meet someone.'

'Is this what they call middle age then?'

He drapes his arm on my shoulders. 'I'm afraid it is. Next up, pipe and slippers.'

'And bridge.'

'Oh, that's very adventurous.'

'And Velcro. On everything. Oh, and leaving notes to remind yourself to do things and then forgetting where you put them.'

His laugh is loud, and I feel suddenly proud of myself. It's been an age since I made anyone laugh.

'You're a funny chick, Doctor Perry.'

The weight of his arm is not a burden. His hand grazes my upper arm. Should I take it? I feel as though I should, but what does it say if I do? In the end I leave it, but I walk leaning in to him, his navy wool coat soft against me.

The sky is clear and shaken out with stars. A curve of moon hangs idly over the houses. It's grown colder. A glitter of frost sugars the cars parked on the street.

As we walk I point out pieces of the old Ranelagh, places that were around long before new money moved in and took over.

'A friend of mine used to live above the shop here.' We are outside a gallery, its window lit by a single spotlight. Inside, the walls are hung with paintings of varying sizes. An event had been taking place earlier, when I walked past on my way into town, a launch of some kind. Suited men checked invitations, consulted a list. Caterers unloaded trays from a van. 'Her family ran the shop, and they all lived upstairs. Seven kids. I don't know how they all fitted.'

'Did you like growing up here? Here as in Ranelagh, I mean?' Adam's face is in profile. We walk on.

'It was fine, I suppose.' But it wasn't fine, not really. Place is important only up to a certain point, and beyond that what matters is how you are at home, your family life. As a child, I was on the edge of things. I'd learned to be watchful from an early age, mindful of angering my mother over the slightest thing. Spilled milk, extra laundry, books scattered around. It was invariably the small things, because I was too fearful to do anything really bad.

'Are your family still living here?'

We've reached my house. Maude's bedroom lamp is lit. Light seeps around the edges of the window frame.

'No, there's just my great-aunt left.' I gesture at the garden flat. 'She lives downstairs.'

Adam faces me. 'My family are all over the place. My parents are still at home, but my two sisters are away, both married, neither of them coming back any time soon. My daughter lives in Sweden, with her mother.'

'You have a daughter?' Surprise shades my voice a tone or two higher than normal. This shouldn't be shocking, but it is. Adam has a child.

He smiles, a proud, proprietorial grin that can't help itself. 'I have the greatest child ever born. Annalie. She's 10, and amazing.'

'You lucky man.' The words are out, hanging between us. I want to take them back, but I can't.

'I am. I'm very lucky.' Adam blows on his hands. 'Christ, it's freezing. So anyway, what about your folks?'

'They're both dead.' I tug the belt on my coat. It feels strange to talk about them. It's not something I do easily. A boarded-up house, that's my family. Doors, locks, entry difficult at best. 'That's actually why I came back here. My mother died a few months ago.'

Adam offers sympathy, which I sidestep. Another day, possibly, but not now.

A taxi swishes past. I'd like to ask Adam in, but I'm not sure what that will mean, or where I even want to take things. Next time. Next time I'll offer coffee.

He makes it easier for me. 'Look, I'm going to turn to ice here, and so will you. You don't have enough extra flesh on you to keep you warm.'

'Thanks.'

'Seriously though. We can do this again, another night. Somewhere different.'

'I'd like that.'

His forefinger is icy as he trails it down my cheek. 'I like you, Doctor Perry. There's something about you that I don't find in most women I meet.'

Of course I should respond, but what can I say that won't sound contrived? Words, once my greatest strength, consistently fail me in moments like this when I need them most.

'And next time, I'll invite myself in.'

'Deal.'

He leans towards me, kisses my forehead. 'See you soon. Sleep well.'

It's only eleven, but tiredness lies heavy on my eyelids. Adam hails a taxi and waves as it pulls away.

The knocker bangs against the front door as it closes. The sound is hollow, and it echoes through the empty house.

CHAPTER 13

The photograph of Andrew was taken when he was 16, and good-looking in a way that no one ever really is at that age. There is a row of photos of him, five pictures taken at varying stages of his life. A toddler holding a kitten aloft. A small boy in rubber boots, standing in a field. One photograph of him astride the carrier of an adult's bike, and two others showing him with his guitar. I touch my thumb to his freeze-framed images. I don't know who took the photos; Maude probably. Maybe my father took the early ones. My mother had never owned a camera, hadn't thought to document her children's lives. The first picture of me had been taken on my Communion day. I was 7, at odds with the white dress and the ridiculous veil that had been forced onto my head. There are no baby pictures of me, no mother-and-child smiles on the wall. The only image I have of my father is a small black-and-white snapshot from my parents' wedding day. I'd stolen it from a drawer years before, a still of him in a sober dark suit, his hair neatly combed to the side. He had his arm stiffly on my mother's shoulder, public affection making him uncomfortable. My mother, in a pale suit, looked equally ill at ease, her new wedding ring prominent on her left hand. What made you get married? I've always wondered. Where are the obvious signs of love, or even connection?

I'd loved Isaac obsessively. It's the only reason I can see for being with someone, for putting up with all the shit and the marriage to someone else and the non-availability at the only times that actually matter when you're in love with someone. So Christmas I spent alone, Labour weekend, Memorial Day, all the big holidays when everyone has somewhere to go to with someone they care about. Everyone except me. I languished in bookshops, worked on my publications, attended readings, the cinema, walked the grubby streets of the Lower East Side, careful of stepping on manholes that blow steam in the air without warning, past the laundromats and the Puerto Rican market. If an invitation to a party, a barbeque, a Thanksgiving dinner came my way, I accepted. Americans are the truly hospitable people, their inclination to include everyone a genuine part of who they are. Irish people are effusive, especially with strangers. Suggestions to meet up are easily thrown around, yet rarely followed up with an invitation.

Partly to ward off the disappointment that wound itself in coils around my heart, but mostly to keep myself from reaching for the nearest bottle, I reminded myself how good it was to be free to do my own thing, while my lover put on a show with his heiress wife and their circle of successful friends. But ultimately I was on my own, and I hated him for it, then hated myself more for tolerating it. He should have left her. If he had loved me as he'd claimed to, he would have left her.

I loved him. I touched him constantly, watched him as he slept, burrowed into him, seeking out the temporary solace he afforded me. Always seeking.

I don't need a therapist to tell me that what I seek is my father. You'd think that by now I would have moved on from all that.

I want to avoid becoming my mother. She had never seemed like a real mother to me, not in the way that other girls' mothers were. She didn't wait for me to come home from school, cared little for my stories or my friends. She had never sought out my company, like I observed other mothers doing with their daughters. Even as a child I was more like a lodger, always feeling I was in the way, ever wary of disturbing the fragile balance of her moods, impotent as distant storms in the cold face of her fury. When I was pregnant, the prospect of imitating my mother had horrified me. Her sharp edges were flint on the tenderest parts of my skin, her coldness freezing me with a mere glance. In Isaac, I was able to leave my mother behind. He enabled me to be someone other than the nuisance I was to her, the rock that kept her grounded to a life she clearly didn't wish to lead. I never knew what caused my mother's darkness, her cruelty. Certainly, I brought out the worst in her. She was able to be around Maude and my brother, other people, play bridge, talk to neighbours, but for some reason I unlocked whatever tiny door sealed up her blackest night, and out it came, gushing towards me in torrents, sweeping me away in its slipstream. The mask was for others; I got the uncut reality.

I carry the pictures of Andrew downstairs and hang them on the living room wall. They deserve to be there instead of on my mother's bedside locker. She's not going to monopolise him any more. Pictures of the dead should grace the walls of every house. Andrew and I became so adept at not saying the names of dead people that we effectively erased them from our memories. Our father, Tom. Maude's husband, Pat, dead since I was 7, driven to a stroke by bad debts and creditors, and now Andrew.

Many cultures celebrate their dead, give them their own days of remembrance. Their names are spoken freely and without worry. Candles are lit, parties held in their honour. Mexicans have *Dia de los Muertos*, and the dead come out to play, dance, live again, shaking their skeletons till their clothes fall away. Candles burn in front of photos of the *muertos*, food is cooked and eaten, stories told. It's sad, in the way that death is always sad, but it points too towards a greater understanding of life. We're always moving towards death, and its inevitability should be a reassurance, but we shy away from it, wear clothes that are too young for us, fix our faces so we can fool others. And all we do is fool ourselves.

In this house, too, we moved away from acceptance. Photos were not displayed, their names and stories wiped away like chalk from a board.

That was my mother's way, and Andrew and I simply followed her lead, knowing no better. Mindful of upsetting her, we stayed away from the topic of our father until we became so used to not talking about him that we never did. Saying *father,* saying his name, saying *Dad*, felt awkward on my tongue, the unfamiliar enunciation wrong somehow.

In the secret conversations inside my head, he existed as I sifted through my memories of him, any recollections that I could paste in my mental scrapbook.

In the fading light, the front room is cosy. I lit a fire when I came home from work and it hisses in the grate, spitting occasional embers onto the wooden floor. If I stay here, I'll have to put in central heating. For now, the fires will suffice. A log collapses ashily and subsides. The photo of my father

I place on the mantelpiece. He is a snuffed candle. Gone. How different would my life be had he lived?

My father, still in his labouring clothes, the rough wool trousers and heavy cotton shirts of the small farmer, used to sit me on his knee each evening before dinner and read with me. My finger traced the shapes of the letters as he showed me how to make sense of them. He smelled of animals and earth, a scent that could never be fully removed, regardless of how hard he scrubbed with the transparent bar of Pears soap that my mother kept in the bathroom. How my mother hated the farmhouse bathroom, with its leaking taps and noisy rusting pipes, the omnipresent cold air that rippled through the ill-fitting window. She'd tried, with nice soap and clean towels, to bring some semblance of city living to the flat, bleak countryside, but it was a lost battle. There was always too much opposition, too many filthy hands and boots for her ever to have had a chance.

Invariably in his stockinged feet, to avoid having my mother complain bitterly about tracking dirt across the floor she'd swept several times that day, my father sat with me and my books. His big work boots he left outside the kitchen door, scraped clean and ready for the early morning call to milking, that rural alarm clock that never needed to be set. He kissed me profusely every time I read a sentence without a mistake. Even at the age of 4, I'd wished that it were my mother who spent her days milking cows and tilling fields, leaving my father to me. One evening I touched his face, his end-of-day skin farm-dusty, jaws roughening under their daily growth. My father caught my hand and kissed it, his lips flat on my palm, my entire hand fitting over his mouth. I squealed as he blew against my skin, tickling me. I squirmed, the coarse fabric of his trousers rough on my bare legs, but I didn't say anything for fear of hurting his feelings.

My mother turned from where she spooned potatoes onto plates, disapproval unfolding in the steaming air. 'Tom, if you've nothing better to do than excite the child, go and get me some more coal. And Eva, get up off your father. Go and wash your hands.'

That's what I recall, my mother's unending dissatisfaction, curdling in the fridge of her bad humour. Andrew was lucky he was at school, away from the strangeness of home. I was the one who played far away from my mother. I found kittens, and birds with broken wings, named all the cows in the small herd, chased hens and fell in love with words.

My child, my father had liked to call me. *Come here, my child. Sit beside me, my child. My child, my child.* My mother had never once referred to me thus.

Maude is watching television downstairs. Canned laughter and applause reach me through the floor. Imported American sitcoms. Maude loves them.

I can sit here alone, or I can go and buy something to drink, or I can go downstairs to Maude.

I go and visit Maude.

CHAPTER 14

Her name is Aelita, and she arrives ten minutes early. She shakes my hand as she introduces herself. A child holds on to the tail of her jacket. He is beautiful, with huge grey eyes and those high cheekbones so familiar among the Eastern Europeans I see around. I never know what to say to children, so I just smile at him.

In the kitchen, I show Aelita the cleaning supplies. I've placed them in a basket on the table.

'I'll need you to clean downstairs too.' I point at the floor.

'Clean, yes.' She mimes sweeping.

'No, the flat downstairs.' I show her the door beside the kitchen that leads down to Maude's flat. It is unlocked. It always is, in case an emergency should arise.

Aelita will come once a week, for three hours. I don't know if it's sufficient time, or too much, but she'll clean for Maude as well, so she should have enough to do. She hangs her coat on the hook outside the kitchen, above the shoe rack. She wears a grey sweatshirt with Cape Cod lettered in navy across the front, and sagging leggings. Her blonde hair is dark at the roots and she has pinned it in a haphazard bun. A diamante butterfly winks in the folds of her hair.

'I start today, yes?' she asks, reaching already for the basket.

'If you like.'

'Good.'

When I check on Aelita an hour later, she is mopping the hall floor. She has tied a green scarf around her head, and her face is red from the exertion of pushing the heavy mop over the floorboards. She stops when she sees me.

'I dry floor too.' She rests her hands on the top of the mop. The child sits at the foot of the stairs, pushing a small yellow car over and under his legs. I hesitate. Should I offer him the television? A biscuit? He keeps watch on his mother. I feel a pinch of guilt at keeping his mother from being with him. He is too small to be at school.

Maude has remained opposed to the idea of getting someone in to clean. 'I don't like it. I don't like the idea of paying someone to do what I should be doing myself.'

'It's only a bit of help, Maude.' The argument circled us, going nowhere.

'We do our own cleaning in this house.'

'I know, and we can still do it. This is just a bit of extra help, that's all.'

We sat in Maude's living room. The public health nurse had just left. Maude hadn't wanted her to visit.

'I'm fine, nurse' was all she had said when the nurse arrived.

'I know you are. This is just routine.' She examined Maude's leg, about which she'd been complaining. 'You need to stay off that leg for a week or two.' She wrapped a bandage around the offending calf. 'I'm sure your granddaughter is a great help to you.'

'Grand-niece. She's not bad.' Maude smiled at me over the nurse's shoulder. 'She's threatening to get a cleaner.'

The nurse sat back on her heels, examined the leg, then stood up. 'Good idea. Anything that'll keep you off your feet for a while.'

'I can't be here sitting around while some poor girl dusts the room. It wouldn't be fair.'

So I have arranged for Aelita to come on Wednesday afternoons while Maude plays bridge. She gets a lift from her partner, and I finish school early so I'm there to let Aelita in.

There are toy cars somewhere in the attic, old Matchbox miniatures that Andrew collected in a trunk that had belonged to my mother's parents. I wonder about offering them to the child. He sees me observing him, and he stills the circling of the yellow car.

Aelita finishes the floor. 'Down now, yes?' The child follows her closely, his hand reaching for the hem of her sweatshirt. The door to downstairs closes with a decisive click.

I offer Aelita coffee when she finishes. Darkness has slipped like ink over the afternoon. The old clock on the kitchen wall ticks insistently. Five o'clock. Maude will be home at any minute. I wonder if she'll notice the scrubbed tiles, the clean floors, then dismiss the thought instantly. Of course she'll notice. Maude is house-proud.

I hand over the money we agreed on the phone. Guilt edges its way into my head as I pay this woman who has cleaned my house. I don't know why. I pay Isabel to clean my tiny apartment every week and it doesn't cost me a thought. It's different here, somehow. Middle-class guilt still makes it hard to employ people domestically. Maybe it's easier if your money is newly won.

She refuses coffee. The boy keeps a proprietorial hand on his mother. I'll find Andrew's Matchbox cars in time for next Wednesday.

I point out the bus stop. Aelita shrugs, amused. 'Yes. We come to here on bus.'

Of course they did. I am about to extend my hand, but Aelita steps out the door. Halfway down the granite steps, she pauses. A hat is produced from her large bag. She pulls it down over the child's hair. It is shaped like a bear, with rounded ears, white knitted eyes and a black nose. She ties it under the boy's chin. He tugs at a piece of her hair. He sees me watching, and, feeling foolish, I wave, then close the door quickly.

CHAPTER 15

Adam's house in Sandymount sits among a row of similar dwellings on a quiet street just off the main drag. The vegetable-oil car sits, abandoned for the weekend. Salt has dried on its paintwork. Feathery grasses drift over the neighbour's low wall, dry now in this wintry air. The garden is quieted by the season, dry and wreathed in shades of brown. Two enormous terracotta tubs overflow with potting compost and chickweed. Some brave late-autumn lilies fight the herbaceous clutter, their deep-pink petals haemorrhaging colour into the monochrome. A wrought-iron table and two chairs loiter in the corner, dead leaves piled on their surfaces. The sea air is heavy, thick with salt and the promise of rain. The saline breeze rattles the shrivelled leaves on the trees. Overhead, seagulls wheel like bits of discarded paper, screaming at each other.

Adam opens the door before I have time to knock. 'Come in, come in,' he says, kissing my cheek before hugging me. We were not a family of embracers, and even now the practice sometimes leaves me self-conscious, awkward in the uncertainty of how exactly I should react. Not so with Adam. The hug returned, I smile at him, handing over a bunch of lilies. Gorgeous flowers, they were my mother's least favourite. Flowers of death, she called them.

Adam ushers me inside, closing the door behind me. 'My God, it's freezing.' He is wearing a slightly more relaxed version of his weekday clothes. Still academic-looking, more of a handsome professor than a secondary school history teacher. 'Too early to be so damn cold.'

Adam inhales the lilies. Wine wouldn't have been a good choice of gift. Plenty of alcoholics don't mind buying alcohol for other people, but I've never been one of them. If I'm buying, I'm drinking. And that's no good.

The house is warm, and very different to what I'd expected from the exterior. It's almost completely open-plan, all white walls, high ceilings, and huge windows letting in the grey afternoon light. The tidiness strikes me. Chairs are neatly stowed under the long rectangular table; dishes are stacked in piles according to size on the island. The only clutter discernible is a magazine rack, which overflows with newspapers and current affairs publications.

'Cleaner comes on Fridays,' he says, catching me looking around. 'Best money I spend.'

'It's a lovely house,' I say, following him into the kitchen.

Adam splashes water into a tall glass vase, then dunks the whole bunch of flowers into it. 'Thanks. I'm happy with it.' He peers into the oven. 'Just as well, because I'll never be able to move now, not with the way things are going.' He uses a tea towel to remove the square ovenproof dish. 'They couldn't give me enough money when I did the renovations.' He blows on his fingers. 'Throwing it at me, at everyone. The fools.' The square dish is placed on the table beside another similar one. 'Now look at them. Bastards.'

My new coat is too warm for indoors. Soft, navy, and a blend of cashmere and wool, it will suit winter either here or in New York. I fold it over my arms and put my bag on the floor.

Adam pulls a chair out. 'Sorry, Eva. Sit, sit.' Then he whisks my coat out to the hall, hanging it on an industrial-looking piece of metal studded with coat hooks.

I am like a novice on a nervous first date. Adam asked me over for lunch with a couple of his friends. Instinctively, my first reaction was to refuse, but I'm rarely asked anywhere, and this past week has been particularly quiet. Maude is hosting her own party today, a bridge gathering for four. Cards were piled neatly on the felted bridge table when I called down to her this morning. She shuffled across the floor to me, her slippers making swooshing sounds in the quiet room. On the sideboard, the radio played a roundup of the week's events.

'Stay and join us, Eva,' she'd said, as I dried the few dishes stacked in the kitchen and took out her bin. 'You'd be very welcome.'

I demurred. I have no wish to talk about my mother with Maude's bridge friends, don't want to hear anything about her. Lately I've tried to keep her at bay, filter out her face with its perennial expression of dissatisfaction. Sometimes I wonder if my mother is all I can think about, as though focusing on her, analysing her, could work things out for me, get her out of my system. I picked up the phone and rang Adam, belatedly accepting his invitation to lunch.

There are photos on the white walls, Adam in various and recognisable places. Smiling on the Great Wall. Shading his eyes at Machu Picchu. Holding chopsticks and laughing in … Vietnam? Thailand? I can't tell. His beautiful child appears with regularity in the pictures. Her smile catches me. I want to look away, but I'm drawn back to the photos of her.

'And this is Annalie. The photos don't do her justice.' Adam stands behind me. He smells of cotton and fabric softener, layered with something more male, woodsy. Or maybe it's citrus. He leans his hands on my shoulders, then reaches to point to a picture of Annalie standing with him at the top of a mountain, both of them wearing red T-shirts. He laughs, with that pure and simple joy I've witnessed before in parents of children who amaze them. 'She's incredible.'

Annalie's mother is Swedish, Adam tells me. Adam had some sort of relationship with her that ended amicably. The child spends two months with her father each summer, as well as Easter and midterms. He describes a situation so perfect in its simplicity that I wonder if he's being truthful. I've heard the raging, intractable bitterness of divorced parents separated from their children, seen how threadbare the line between love and hate is. There is nothing of their anger in Adam's cool poise, his relaxed confidence in his shared parenting.

As he divulges an anecdote involving Annalie and the day he brought her into the school last year, I tug at the cuffs of my shirt. Would my child have been blonde like that? Would it have grown into a person of strong convictions? Would it have had my eyes? My hair?

There are questions I try to avoid asking myself. Questions about my child are among them. There's no answer to any of them, only the pain of blankness, a dark carpet rolled out before me. It stretches to infinity, and I am incapable of taking the first step towards examining it.

The doorbell drills into the quiet. I slip into the kitchen as Adam greets his other lunch guests. An opened bottle of white wine stands by a large bowl of salad. I pour and swallow an overfull glass in less than the time it takes for the new arrivals to shed their coats. I wipe the glass dry on the abandoned tea towel, place it back in its original position and move to look out the window. The tricks of the alcoholic never fade.

There are only four of us at lunch, and my apprehension is eased by the buzz of the wine and the affability of Adam's two friends. David, the journalist seated next to me, fills my glass twice without asking. The wine glugs under his generous pour. Adam places a restraining hand on David's arm, shakes his head, but I wave Adam's concern away. Obviously, I shouldn't drink anything at all, particularly not after the first large helping I dispensed with in an instant, but it's been weeks, and it slips me into the conversation, disperses the cloud of anxiety I am often shadowed by. David is working on a piece about zombie banks, an addition to our lexicon that has eased itself seamlessly into dialogue. Zombie banks. Ghost estates. Austerity. What a chasm in our society.

'The thing is,' David says, 'it's not the reckless public spending that's to blame for this mess. That's all we're being told, but it's these banks who loaned money to speculators.' He says that fifteen customers each owe five hundred million to one bank. He is excited by his research, by the incomprehensible figures that he's throwing into the conversation. David has a contact in the government, a dissatisfied man who wants the whistle blown. Despite repeated requests, he refuses to divulge his source.

'Come on, you can't not tell us,' says Sally, Adam's friend from their undergraduate years in Trinity. She is a research fellow there now, working on something to do with literature and the curriculum. I wonder if we know some of the same people. Sally is Adam's age, a few years older than I am, but academia in Dublin is a small world.

David ignores the coffee Adam has placed on the table and empties the last wine bottle into his own glass. 'Not a chance. But I'll tell you what.' He leans into the table, making stabbing motions with his index finger. 'This government is on its last legs. No question. And I'm helping to bring it down, column by column.'

Adam grins at me. 'You'd never guess he's won national journalist of the year twice, would you?'

'Get lost,' David says. 'It'll be three times by the time I finish with this. With a bit of luck it'll be the end for the soldiers of destiny too.' He finishes the wine and bangs the glass down for emphasis. 'Any more of this? It's actually not bad for a change.'

'Sorry, we're out. Tesco is around the corner if you want more.'

'Still supporting the multinationals, then?'

'Fuck off.'

Sally raises her eyebrows at me, smiles, shakes her head. 'They're always like this, Eva. You'll get used to it. All part of the homoerotic bonding they so desperately need.'

The men laugh. 'You'd love that, wouldn't you?' Adam says.

Sally sips her coffee.

It's like watching a game of table tennis, observing them, the conversation springing from topic to topic, punctuated by insults and shouts of loud laughter.

'Well, if you've no more wine, and only an evil corporation in which to obtain more, you're going to have to break out the weed.' David darts a glance at me. 'You're cool with that, Eva, right?'

I nod. 'Fine.' The three large glasses of wine have loosened my brain. My shell is slipping away, the thin membrane of confidence has reared its temporary head. I smile at Adam as I raise my glass to my lips, straighten myself in the chair. He raises an eyebrow at me. I'm drunk, buoyed by the booze. Adam knows. I've told him bits about my drinking, prided myself on not consuming anything more than water when with him. He knows I'm trying, and can now see that I've fallen again. I haven't drunk anything in weeks, and my tolerance has slipped. If I were at home now I'd finish another bottle. But weed sounds nice. It's been a while. Suddenly, I'm desperate to be high, to be even more mellow and benevolent than I am now. It feels so liberating to be rid of my angsty self-consciousness, even though I know the freedom is temporary. I wonder what Adam's friends think of me. They have included me easily into the conversation, haven't prodded me to speak, haven't delved too deeply.

Adam rolls a joint with one hand and passes it to Sally. She waves it away. 'No thanks. I'll end up inside on your couch listening to Pink Floyd, and I've a thing on tonight that I need a clear head for.'

Adam hesitates, but I grab the proffered joint, light it and inhale. I keep my eyes on Adam's as I suck at it. The tip glows and the paper crackles. The smoke, thick and yellow, travels my airways. I keep it in until my lungs feel like they're about to explode. I repeat it, then pass to David. I feel the edges of the day finally smoothe themselves out, caress me. I drain my glass. The weed is bitter on my tongue. Adam gets up and changes the CD. John Coltrane's twisting tenor sax floats out of the speakers in the ceiling, round black discs that look like eyes to my stoned mind.

Adam and David continue their talk of banks and politicians. I tune out. It's too much for my overloaded brain to follow. Their weed-thickened voices rise and fall. I allow the music to drown them out.

'I have one of your books,' Sally says.

I blink. I'd forgotten about her. 'What book?' I haven't met her before, couldn't have lent her anything.

'The second one.' She pinches the bridge of her nose. 'I can't remember the title. It's been a long time.'

My skin prickles with shock. I glance at Adam, but he hasn't heard. My poems. I haven't had anyone reference them in years. No one in New York is familiar with my poetry, another reason I found it so easy to work there. I tell Sally the title, quietly. The words feel strange on my lips. *The Circus at Night.* My God. It's been a lifetime.

'That's it. Sorry, I shouldn't have forgotten. Great title.' Sally puts her elbows on the table, leans over. 'I actually tried to trace you last year.'

Trace me?

'I rang your old publisher.'

I raise my hand. 'Why?'

'We were debating putting a few of your poems on the course.'

Course? What course? She sees my confusion, smiles. 'The Leaving Cert course. It's up for a change, and I suggested adding you to the syllabus.' She gets up and fills the water jug. The tap gushes. Ice rattles as she empties a tray of cubes from the freezer.

I'm not sure if it's the weed or the shock, but for a second I think I'm going to be sick. I don't want to have to think about my poetry.

Sally refills my glass as she sits back down. 'I don't know what'll happen, so don't worry too much about it. It'll be ages before anything is decided.' She checks her watch, then slips her arms into the cardigan she left draped on the back of her chair. 'Adam, I have to go.' He stands up, but she shoos him back into his chair. 'I'll let myself out. I'll be in touch.' Sally riffles through her bag, producing a notebook. She tears off a corner and writes her numbers down. 'That's my mobile, that's work. Give me a ring if you can. I'd really like to shoot the breeze about your work. I'll be pushing for you to be included.' She wraps a scarf around her neck. 'If I don't hear from you, I'll get your number from Adam.' She smiles. 'I'm not letting this go.'

I put the scrap of paper in my pocket. I'm not going to ring her. How could I?

'Oh, and Eva, listen.' She leans towards me. 'Not a word, okay? I need to keep it all under wraps for now.'

Keeping this a secret won't be a problem. It's not as though I have anyone to tell. Except Maude, of course, and I'm not telling her because she'd be in favour of it. John Coltrane tumbles from the ceiling, pulling me towards the sound. It's so easy to lose yourself in his music, all those double helix cadences unravelling in the darkening room. I'm definitely high.

Sally squeezes my arm as she leaves. Adam pulls away from his conversation with David. 'What are you two chattering about?'

'We're talking, Adam. We don't chatter. Remember talking? It's what grown-ups do.' She winks at me. 'Goodbye, all.'

I invent an excuse to leave soon after. It's too much, the wine, the weed, the poems, and I need to get out, walk, get cold air on my face, hear the sea move in the dimming light.

In the hall, Adam holds my coat for me. Manoeuvring my arms into the sleeves is difficult, and we both laugh at my repeated attempts. Then, when I'm finally buttoning it up, Adam stops laughing. 'Listen, Eva, I'm sorry. About the wine.' He shakes his head. 'To be honest, I didn't even think of it. That's terrible, I know, but it's the truth.'

'Don't worry about it.'

'But I do. I want you to like being around me, and you won't if I produce the hard stuff every time.'

He really is so very handsome. His glasses have slipped slightly and he pushes them back up his nose. I read somewhere that that gesture betrays self-consciousness, that negotiators must never do it for fear of being exposed as weak, uncertain. On Adam, it simply adds to his charm.

The street lamps have already been lit, and a weak light glints through the glass panels in the door. Adam's face is mottled by the shadowy glow. He leans his shoulder against the door.

I put my hand on the door handle. 'Thanks for lunch. I like your friends.'

'They like you too.'

As though on cue, David's voice booms from the other room. 'Christ almighty, man, would you ever let her leave?'

We smile at each other. Adam reaches out, pulls a strand of my hair and tugs on it. I put my hand to the clip that secures it at the back of my head. It's too tangled to let him loosen it. He catches my hand, squeezes it. Then he kisses the backs of my fingers, one by one.

I could do this. I could stay here, in this spot, spinning the moment out. The light would fade further, David would change the CD inside and forget about us out here. I could maybe put a finger to Adam's face, to those fine cheekbones, that thick auburn hair. How easy it would be. It has been so long since I last spent time with a new man that I've almost forgotten how inviting it can be, like falling into feathers or wrapping myself in silk.

Isaac isn't coming back, no matter what fantasies I cultivate. It's pointless keeping my body as some sort of forlorn shrine to him, rerunning over and over the same dark hurts. My hands are still full of grief; it spills over and soaks everything I touch.

I finger the ends of Adam's shirt, the pale green-and-blue stripes of soft washed cotton. The last button is undone, and I can see his stomach, the skin, the line of hair that disappears into his jeans.

'I like you, Doctor Perry. I like you a lot.'

I shake my head.

He puts his fingers under my chin and lifts my face. His green eyes are dotted with amber. 'I do like you. And I want to know why you look so very sad at times.'

'I don't look sad.'

'You do. And you don't have to tell me, because it's none of my business, but I'd like you to tell me, because you want to.' His voice softens. 'We've all been stamped on at some point in our lives.'

This isn't where we were supposed to head. Lunch with his friends, that's what he said. Not wine, weed and confession.

'You're great,' I say. 'Really.'

'But this is the point where you tell me that you just want to be friends.'

'No, nothing as prosaic as that.'

'No clichés, Eva.' He polishes his glasses with his shirt tail, revealing more of his skin. It's smooth, olive-coloured. I touch my fingers to it.

'I don't peddle clichés.'

'No, I know you don't. Sally told me about your poetry.'

Without warning, the high is gone. That gorgeous, mellow calm has evaporated, and all that's left is the headachy nausea of an imminent hangover. No poetry. I don't want to talk about it.

Again, he tilts my chin. 'No pressure. Not yet, anyway. But I want you to tell me what makes you tick.'

'I will. But not now.' I move away from him to the door. 'Right now, I just need to go.'

'I'll see you on Monday,' he says.

The door closes softly behind me.

CHAPTER 16

The miniature cars are in an old trunk. My mother must have moved them back into Andrew's room at some point. His room is almost exactly as it was when he died. His old nameplate is propped up on a shelf, *Andrew's Room*, and a picture of a red vintage car illustrating the white ceramic tile. I trace it with my fingers, the black letters raised and bumpy.

I haven't been in his room since I left Dublin all those years ago. On the day of Andrew's funeral I'd sat on his bed, alone, shaking, my heavy winter coat doing nothing to chase away the chill. The door now creaks open, air spilling into the room. It is as it was all those years ago. Accessories dated, posters faded. A much younger Bruce Springsteen sulks on a promotional poster for his 1985 tour. Black Sabbath scowl at me, their hair and clothes laughable, hopelessly out of date.

I struggle to open the sash window. Years of being closed seem to suit it, and I break a fingernail before finally heaving it open. Outside it is starting to rain, the vague pattern of drops decorating the sill, disturbing the cobwebs in the wooden corners of the window frame. Traffic passes by in waves. I stand in my brother's room for the first time in many years, yet the world turns as usual. Traffic lights change from red to green, the church bell chimes the hour, drivers switch on their windscreen wipers, and no one knows that I am here, loosening the sediment of years of loss, trying to blow it away, stop it clogging my lungs.

I think of my mother, touching her dead son's things, old folders and notebooks from school that still bear his name, graffitied with band names, his books still on the shelves, his clothes still in his wardrobe, and I wonder how she bore it. I can hardly tolerate it, and I've lived thousands of miles away for years. Did she make his bed, wash his sheets? Did she keep the clothes that still hung in the wardrobe clean and pressed? I wondered if she played songs on his guitar, the pale Epiphone she'd bought him for his sixteenth birthday. It sits in its black case in the corner, the shroud that has kept the music from being played, the faint remnants of stickers in tacky circles around it.

I open the case, the catches rigid and old. The guitar has one broken string. It spirals downwards in a stiff curl. Without lifting it out of the case I strum the remaining strings, their discord matching the powdery gloom of the room. My brother would have hated the sound, would have covered his ears as he winced. He was extraordinarily fussy about music.

At his funeral a single trumpet soared from the balcony. Mahler's Fifth, the opening trumpet tattoo, the intensity almost military. It had none of Wagner's joy through tears, just plain sorrow. Exactly as it should have been. Andrew would have been pleased with my choice.

The priest read from the Book of Wisdom. *But the just man, though he die early, shall be at rest.* I'd closed my eyes. There would be no rest for me. No rest, only years of broken nights.

My mother, a day later, still numbed by Valium, put her hand on her heart. 'Thank God that went well.'

Thank God? In my rage and my sorrow I forgot how I feared her. 'Don't be so stupid, Mother. It has nothing to do with God.' I slammed out of the room before she could respond.

The rain patters on the floorboards. Reluctant to stem the flow of new air into the untenanted room, I half shut the window. The sky spills dingy drops down the panes, distorting the world beyond.

Slowly, I work the wire hangers out of my brother's shirts, fold his jeans and put them all into bags. His two ties, kept for the rare occasions that required them, are rolled on the shelf. I finger the navy and green stripes on one tie, the red and grey of the other. Each went with his one suit, now hanging under cellophane in the corner of the wardrobe. Andrew had had little interest in clothes, would never have bought new ones if the old ones were still wearable. I loved that about him, his disinterest in the accumulation of possessions. Without examining the suit, I fold it in its covering and drop it into a bag. My instinct is to linger on his clothing, remembering times he had worn each one, but I'd never get anything done that way. His books and awards I stack in boxes for the attic. Pulling out my new phone, I call the St Vincent de Paul. I'm in luck. The pickup van is in the area and will be by this afternoon. Getting rid of everything quickly will leave no room to change my mind and hang everything up again. Two hours after I started the room is denuded, the bed stripped. The wall is cold against my back as I lean against it, surveying my work. My brother's room is a shell, only the shelves and the bed remaining. It's good to purge. Maybe I'll even begin to move on, perhaps something will be dislodged and breathing will suddenly be easier. So much of Andrew has wedged itself within me, its awkward shape taking up too much space. Instead of dealing with it, I've simply accommodated it, allowed myself to grow around it. It's been easier that way because I've been a coward. Not facing things head-on has allowed me to turn away. But everything catches up eventually. How much quicker my recovery would have been if only someone had told me that all those years ago. Deal with the pain. For my own sake, I must start to let him go.

I can only imagine my mother's reaction to my disrobing of her house, the inky blackness of her outrage, her monotonous diatribe of the same tired grievances.

I don't care any more.

CHAPTER 17

S ean is standing at the bar. I peer at him through the
throng. It's definitely him. I am about to turn away, but
it's a small venue and he's tall. He spots me. I salute him, and
he pushes his way through the scrum.

'Aoife!' He bends to kiss my cheek. It's something else
I can't quite get used to, this kissing I see people do here in
social situations. New Yorkers do it, but it looks all wrong
somehow when Irish people try it. It's out of place, forced,
just like the mid-Atlantic accents and fake tan that surround
me. 'What are you doing here?'

For a second, I panic. Am I too old to be here? Is
he mocking me, the older woman, out on her own? I
touch my hair, braided in an untidy plait. *Deconstructed*,
a fashion magazine, described a similar plait, something
sexy and hurriedly thrown together. Who knows, maybe
mine looks sexily dishevelled. Isaac loved my hair, its
darkness, its curls. Like clearing out my brother's room,
doing something about my hair is a necessity. I take a
huge swallow from my glass, allow the warmth of the
whiskey to dampen the rising anxiety of being here alone.
Alone and old. Another swallow and it recedes. *My name
is Eva and I'm an alcoholic.*

'I hadn't taken you for a jazz fan,' Sean says, tipping his glass in my direction. 'You're more of a classical fan I'd have thought.' He glugs his beer. 'Classy lady, classy music.'

He is drunk. He is gorgeous. An untidy row of friendship bracelets circles his wrist, coloured strips of leather, rubber, braided threads. His shirt is fitted, grey, with a geometric pattern that makes my head hurt to look at it. 'Who're you with?' He searches behind me for friends.

'No one,' I say. I dig my elbow gently in his ribs. 'And it's Eva.'

Sean nods. 'Right. Eva. Sorry about that. I've had a few.' He takes a drink, then points at me, his finger not quite straight, the beer sloshing around inside the glass. 'Hey, I lost your number.'

I laugh. 'Of course you did.'

He points at me again. 'I actually did. Thought about dropping in to your house, but then I realised I didn't know where you lived.' His smile is blurred with drink. 'I actually did.'

I pat his arm. 'Of course you did.'

'But here we are.' He gulps at his beer. 'And you're looking good.'

I acknowledge the compliment with raised eyebrows.

'Hey, don't give me a look.'

'What look?' I sip again at my whiskey. The need for another already pulls at me. Slowly. I must take it slowly.

'That female look. The one that says you know I'm bullshitting you. Even when I'm not.'

Another pat on his arm. 'Don't worry about it, Shane.'

His offence is almost comical. 'It's Sean. The name's Sean.'

The club is packed, more of a bar, really, and a small one at that. The band is an underground New York avant-garde jazz ensemble, all wild improvisation and punk inflections. I used to see them play in lofts, huge industrial spaces dotted around Downtown. Isaac never got it, this crazy offshoot of jazz, but once or twice he came with me because I loved the music. He pretended to like it so he could seem more with it, less of a fatherly figure with his younger lover. Avant-garde in New York is a druggy scene, full of experimentation, the clubs awash with pills and anything else you might look for. Little separates it from the rave circuit. Looking around this small, crammed bar, nothing could have been further from Manhattan.

A girl jostles me. 'Sorry!' she says, her beer spilling on my arm. She mouths something else, but it is drowned in the noise of the band testing their instruments on the tiny stage. I wipe at the spreading wet patch on my sleeve.

'You okay?' Sean asks.

'Fine, fine. It's just a splash.'

'What?' He leans closer to me. I can smell liquor on his breath. I think of all the alcohol that surrounds me, the countless bottles on display behind the bar, the pints in people's hands, the glasses on the tables. It's not what those in recovery would call a supportive environment. For a second I wonder if I should leave, just turn around and walk out, but then the band starts tuning up, and I remember how much I love this music. So I stay. Sean remains beside me. He seems to have come alone too. It's too loud for conversation now. The band launches into something fast, hot, intense. Some people dance, more continue their conversations as though nothing were happening on the crammed stage in front of them.

The crowd thickens, swells. The music sears the packed club. I finish my drink then fight my way to the bar, where I order two more, and a pint for Sean. I down the first, a double, catch my breath at the strength, then wend my way back to where Sean is nodding his head in rhythm to the insane beat.

His eyes widen as I hand him the glass. 'Thanks!' he shouts above the screech of a saxophone. 'You didn't have to.'

I sip my drink, wave away his thanks. He is intoxicated. It's obvious in the wet look his eyes have, the way his rhythm is slightly off. I wonder about leaving him here, finding another spot on my own, but the club is too small, and it's quite nice having someone to stand with who doesn't appear to expect much in terms of conversation.

I brought Isaac to one session in an old firehouse, in an industrial zone down near the river. The building was let go sometime in the seventies, and had been squatted in by artists and musicians looking for a base. I knew from the moment we entered that bringing him had been a mistake. New York mixes generations much better than Ireland does, and it's not unusual to see people of all ages at concerts or parties, but Isaac had only gone out of a desire to be with me, and much as he tried, he couldn't get it. The trippy music, the flickering strobes, the intensity of the jazz itself, he hated it all. It wasn't even the drugs, and there are usually enough drugs at these events to get you high just from breathing. Isaac was no prude, and had dropped enough acid in his youth to swear him off drugs forever, but he couldn't get the music, the scene.

'I'm too old,' he kept saying. 'I want to be in a nice quiet place, talking to you.' He wasn't sulky about it, just honest. He was in his late forties, fifteen years my senior. Initially it hadn't seemed like much because we were so crazy about each other, but when it came to music and partying, the gap was undeniable. At least we both loved jazz, but Isaac had stuck with swing, bebop, the older forms, and hadn't bothered to let his tastes evolve. I listen to it all, every type. Jazz is rich, a bitter liquid that flows all over me any time I listen to it, filling my mouth, my ears, even my eyes.

In the end, we'd left and gone back to my place. I hadn't objected, hadn't minded because being with him was what I had sought from the night. Having Isaac on a Saturday night was such a precious commodity that I left my heavy partying for the too numerous Saturdays when I was on my own.

The band is manic, all wailing brass and frenzied rhythms. I'm wasted. The bourbon slides around in my bloodstream, pulsing, racing. The club has darkened but the pace is quicker than ever. Sean grabs my arm, hustles me to one of very few tables in the place. I'm too drunk to resist, and it's only when we sit on those small round stools that I realise how tired I am. Not sleeping well is a given, but lately I've been waking early, unable to fall back asleep. It happens more on nights when I haven't had a few drinks, and this past week even when I have. I rest my elbows on the table, pushing empty glasses to the side and dropping my chin onto my hands. My eyes close.

The band breaks for a while. Sean drains his pint, slams the glass down. He glances over his shoulder at the bar.

'Another one?'

I shake my head. It's too intense, the music, the alcohol firing through my system. If I have any more I'll be sick.

When the band strikes up again, it's different. Slower. An old Gershwin standard, not instantly recognisable because of the trumpet, its long drawn-out notes, then the piano winding itself around the chords as the song builds. The music swells as the tenor sax picks up the tune, joined one by one by the double bass, the drums, the guitar, until the whole band is playing, led by the wail of the trumpet, building into a wall of solid sound. It transports me. This is jazz. No other music can do this to me, can capture me so completely. Isaac would change his mind about this band if he could hear this one song. Where is he now?

I sit up. Gershwin segues into another languid, protracted piece. A singer comes on. She is tall, red-haired and voluptuous, wearing a green satin dress that trails on the floor behind her. She moves slowly, keeping the beat with her hips. Her voice when she sings is warm and full, toying with the rhythm, and she smiles at the musicians as she leans into the microphone. She sings about adding initials to her monogram, her face a picture of sincerity.

In this instant I miss him more than I have at any point since we left each other. It's been almost a year, but I'm appalled at how fresh the wound is, how it still bleeds when I poke at it. But I'm better off this way. Isaac bailed on me when I needed him. He bailed on our child. He cannot be in my life.

When the band finishes, Sean nudges me with his shoulder. 'You asleep?'

I grope under the table for my bag and coat. When I stand, he stands too. 'I'm off,' I mutter, dragging on my navy coat. My fingers fumble with the buttons. A splash of something wet trails down one sleeve. My lovely coat. Cashmere and light wool. What was I thinking, leaving it on the floor to be trampled by careless feet?

'Do you want to share a cab?' Sean shrugs his arms into a black jacket. We are the only ones leaving. Two people stand behind us, waiting for our table.

'I'd rather walk.' A craving for cold air grabs me. A long walk, a clearing of my head, a glass of water. These are things that matter for now.

Sean accompanies me. We walk mostly in silence, both of us inebriated. My hands I keep deep in my pockets.

Some generous soul kindly decided on a cashmere lining in each pocket. I run my fingers over its velvety softness. Sean offers bursts of conversation, to which I reply, but the bad part of being drunk is setting in now, leeching warmth from my bones. Nausea hints at what is to come.

It is freezing, like breathing icicles instead of air. Christmas parties spill out onto the streets. Girls in tiny dresses and bare legs, screaming with laughter, totter in jagged lines along the paths. Their huge platform shoes, bizarrely orthopaedic against the wispy dresses and furry jackets, cause more obstacles to staying upright than the bottles of lurid drinks swinging from ungloved hands. Everyone demanding their right to have a good time. Christmas lights are looped around street lamps, across buildings. They wink in shop windows. The wind is sharp, bowling litter along the paths. A cluster of stars is visible above the buildings. At the canal, we stop. Muffled music radiates from anonymous buildings. The weeping willows trail their empty branches in the blank water.

'Will we get a last one?' Sean gestures towards a pub. Its customers have disgorged themselves out onto the dark street. Cigarette ends glow, taxis are hailed. Under a street lamp a girl sits alone on a bench by the canal, her hair spread fanlike around her bare shoulders. She attempts to light a cigarette and fails, her blue lips shivering. Her enormous shoes lie discarded at the curb. Fake tan is streaky by her ankles. But for the ridiculous clothing, she could have been me at any time in my past. Alone, drunk, frozen.

'I'd rather not. But you go if you want.' The cold air is sobering me. I touch the girl on her arm. 'Are you okay?'

She peers at me, suspicion in her drink-fogged eyes. 'Fuck off.'

'I only asked if you were okay.'

'And I told you to fuck off, granny.' Beside her on the bench her phone buzzes, a large, expensive rectangle of light. She answers it, dismissing me.

'Come on,' says Sean, draping his arm on my shoulder. 'I'll walk you home.'

An empty beer can floats on the corrugated surface of the canal. A refugee from the pub relieves himself into the water. Sean shouts at him, but the guy is too wasted to notice. The tinfoil moon sits right above us in a sky so clear it looks washed.

We walk on.

The house is in darkness. I dig in my bag for my keys. I forgot to leave the hall light on when I left earlier. Sean waits beside me. Our breath billows white clouds around us. Frost has already settled on the grass, thousands of diamonds winking in the half-light. My fingers are arthritic with cold. Suddenly, I don't want to be alone in that house. It's pulling me into its sticky web, enveloping me in its shadows. Impulsively, I turn to Sean. 'Come in for a drink.'

I make hot whiskeys. The spice of the cloves and the warmth of the glass in my hands chase away the vestiges of cold. Sean takes the glass appreciatively. We sit in the tiny kitchen because it's the only room that is not freezing. Of the five ancient storage heaters in the house, three have packed in, and I don't have the money to replace them, or install proper heating. I turn on the oven and leave the door open, not caring if it makes me look like an eccentric. I have to do this or Sean would go home to his own heated house.

'Any plans for Christmas?' He fiddles with the dial on the radio. A twenty-four-hour Christmas station floods the kitchen with seasonal music. I assume he'll change it, but he fixes the volume and leaves it.

I catch a clove between my teeth. 'Not really. You?'

'Just the usual. Parents, sister, that sort of thing. I'd better enjoy it, because with any luck I'll be in Oz next year. No more cold winters for me.'

Maybe I should go too. Not with Sean, but somewhere. I don't know if I can do New York again. I miss it more than I could have thought possible, but I can't go back to what I had before. Too much has happened. I can't creep around the English department, avoiding Isaac, blaming him for everything that went wrong. I want more than that. But my job, my lectures, my papers, everything I've been working towards.... I could move on, find another university. The States is packed with top-notch colleges, and Isaac would give me a reference. I wouldn't have to start from zero again. It's easy to leave. You just take one step, one foot in front of the other, and keep repeating until where you're coming from is only a blur and where you're going to is yet to be revealed.

Sean spreads his hands at the open oven. He is laughing. 'This is mad! Haven't you heard of central heating? It's all the rage, you know.'

I find myself laughing with him. Santa Baby leaves convertibles under the tree on the radio behind us. It's ridiculous, of course it is, warming our hands at the oven. Andrew and I used to do this also, and once we realised how silly it looked it never failed to amuse us. I still miss him, miss my brother. Something in the laughter, the way it breaks up the shreds of reserve inside me, echoes with all the booze in my system, changes things. I have a vision of myself at Maude's age, deep in my eighties, sitting here in this house, this wretched keeper of unhappiness, with my hands spread out in front of the oven, and I don't like it. Not one bit. I see my books in piles, my papers everywhere, half-finished and long-forgotten poems floating around the rooms, empty bottles punctuating the stillness.

I can't do it. There are many things I've got wrong in my life, but I can't keep on getting them wrong. I can't grow old here, in this mausoleum, my mother's ghost keeping me in line, imprisoning me.

I take Sean's glass from him, take his oven-warmed hands in mine. Maybe it's the whiskey, possibly it's fear of what lies ahead, but I have no problem kissing him, kissing this beautiful boy in my kitchen one week before Christmas, and not allowing myself to feel bad about it.

CHAPTER 18

I thought it would be strange, being with another man after all those years with Isaac, and in a way it is, but it's good too. Sean undresses me slowly, not asking if I want this or that, just assuming that I do. And I do want it. I need it, need to erase all of Isaac's fingerprints on my skin, all over my body. For a young guy, Sean knows what he's doing. He slips his jacket off, pulls his shirt over his head without undoing the buttons, gathers me to him. The kitchen is too small for this. I take his hand and lead him upstairs.

'Christ, it's freezing,' he says, as we climb the stairs, me leading him by the hand. This strikes us as funny, and we convulse again. It's good to laugh.

I take him to my room, and we lie down on my bed, kissing. He curls into me, dragging the bedclothes over us. His fingers trail my spine, coming to rest in the hollow below my ribs. I'm conscious of how thin I am, how visible my bones are under my skin. Since it got cold I haven't run as much, but weight hasn't added itself to my frame. I hope he doesn't compare me to girls of his own age, all of them still smooth with that post-adolescent plumpness to their skin and bodies.

I force myself back to the moment. Sean props himself up on one elbow. His hair falls over his face, still long and surfer-blond despite the time of year. A tattoo marks the skin on his left shoulder, loops over and down his back. I touch my fingertips to it, follow the curve of ink. *Tread softly because you tread on my dreams.*

'Yeats,' he says. 'It's a total embarrassment.'

It's corny, certainly, but he's so young, so perfect, that it doesn't jar.

'I got it done in college.' He rubs the words, pulls a face. 'One of my friends was training in tattoos, and I offered to be his guinea pig. I liked the poem in school, and it seemed better than a heart or a skull or whatever.'

'You could have got a rose,' I offer.

'I know. With someone's name.'

'Exactly! Or maybe just "Mother" printed underneath.'

He pinches his inked skin. 'Yeah, I really missed out there.'

I trail my fingers once again over the lettering. 'I like it.'

He shouts with laughter. 'No you don't, you're just saying that.'

I grin at him in the faint light that leaks through the window. 'Probably.'

'Wait, you're an English teacher, right?'

I shrug. 'Of sorts.'

'Of sorts? You either are or you're not.'

'I am. But usually in a university.'

Sean's groan is theatrical. He rolls over on his back and puts his hand to his head. 'Even worse.'

I prod him. 'Why the drama?'

He lowers his hand. 'The drama, my dear Aoife, is that you know your shit. You know poetry. I'm hoping to impress you with my prowess, and now I'm here, naked, all this stupid poetry all over me, and you, you're probably laughing at me.'

I shake my head. 'I'd never laugh at you. Judge you, probably. But I'd never laugh.'

He kisses me again, crushing our laughter. He is a surprising lover, gentle, considerate, all the things I'd assumed were pushed aside in boys his age in the race to accumulate numbers, add notches to bedposts, scalp their female victims and hang the trophies on their walls. Afterwards, we lie in a tangle of sheets, the moon spilling though the uncurtained window, painting our skin several shades lighter. I am the colour of milk, Sean a tint darker. His hands soothe me. I wrap my white limbs around him, afraid he might disappear. I push Isaac away, put him into the locked box that he needs to be kept in. Contortionist that he is I know he'll be out before dawn, mocking my foolishness for thinking I could ever be rid of him.

I watch Sean's chest rise and fall through the bars of light that stripe the bed. From where he lies, half a pillow away, he trails a finger over my cheek, my lips. I bite his finger gently. He taps my nose. We are crushed together in my single bed. I can smell the whiskey on his breath, the lingering notes of his cologne, spicy and warm. He pulls on my hair. I feel his fingers getting caught in the tangles and I put my hand up.

'Don't.'

'Why not? You've great hair.'

I inch away from him, reclaim my hair, my self.

I'm embarrassed by the state I've allowed it to get into. I'm aware of the metaphor I've unwittingly created in letting my hair become so neglected. I'll get it cut soon.

Sean's fingers snake across my head again. 'Hey, relax. I can fix this. It's just a bit tangled.'

Great. The first time someone shows any interest in me in a long time, and he ends up offering to fix my hair. I pull away. 'Another time.'

'But why wait? It could be so much nicer.'

'What are you now, a hairdresser?'

He laughs. 'Trust me. I know what I'm doing. Have you any olive oil?'

I do. The cold-pressed, expensive kind. Not something I want to pour on my head. Sean disappears downstairs, and reappears with the bottle in his hands.

'How did you find that?' I reach for the bottle.

He lifts it out of my reach. 'It was on the table. Now sit up.'

My instinct is to say no, but I have nothing to lose. My hair is a disaster. I obey, and sit with my back to him, the duvet wrapped around me. Sean pools the oil in his palms, rubs it over his fingers and then over my hair. Two handfuls later, the resistance in my hair buckles. Sean's fingers eventually begin to trace paths through the impossibility of my tresses.

I allow him to unravel the chaos, the rhythm of his hands lulling me. Maude had often brushed my curls for me as a child, the strokes of my old paddle brush as hypnotic as drugs. My mother had rarely done my hair, except to yank it into a ponytail when it exasperated her.

'There,' he says, kissing my bare shoulders. 'Finished.'

I touch my head with tentative fingers, rake them through the slippery locks.

'I had a girlfriend with dreads. I helped her with them, so I know a bit about managing difficult hair.'

'Thanks.' I can't quite look at him. It's like I'm a naked grub, wriggling under his microscope. Self-consciousness is suffocating me, and I do what I invariably do when I'm in a situation that makes me uncomfortable: I reach for a drink. My second hot whiskey is still on the bedside locker, cold now, but necessary. I swallow it in one gulp, close my eyes, wince at its strength.

'Hey, some for me too!' Sean wrestles the glass from me. 'My God, you know how to drink.'

Embarrassed, I turn from him. I hate having attention drawn to my drinking. I'm not that sort of alcoholic. Even at meetings, I find it difficult to stand up in front of everyone, wave my boozy flag in the air and declare myself. *My name is Eva and I'm an alcoholic.*

Sean attempts to turn me to face him, but the moment has gone. It's too much, my hair, the remark about my drinking, the way Isaac keeps edging his sneaky way into everything. I am cold, exhausted. The whiskey, instead of blunting things, is sloshing around in my stomach. I didn't eat much today, just a sandwich at noon, and the night has closed in on me.

Sean hefts the bedclothes up over us, attempts to snuggle up to me.

I thump my pillow. 'We should sleep.'

'Have you a sweater or anything you could give me? It's freezing in here.'

'Try the drawer.' I pull a long-sleeved top over my head.

Sean puts on a sweater, an old one I keep for reading in. He clambers back into the bed and touches the insides of my thighs. He kisses my back, then runs his hands over my oily hair. 'It's fucking sub-zero in here. How do you survive?'

'Hot whiskeys.' I inch my back into the curve of his body. My head hurts. 'I need to sleep. I'm exhausted.'

'I think I've a bit of marching powder in one of my pockets.' His voice trails off, hopeful.

This is where a large age gap gets in the way. If he thinks I'm going to stand chopping lines of coke on the bedside table at half past five in the morning the week before Christmas, then he is definitely with the wrong woman. 'Not a chance. In another lifetime, definitely. But not tonight.'

'It was worth a shot.' Another kiss to my back.

'It was.'

Sean is asleep before I am, his sweatered chest pressed against the ribbed cotton of my top. It takes an age to get warm. I drag on socks. That helps. Then pyjama bottoms. I wriggle against Sean until I'm comfortable. I can't help it. He's so warm. He moves, and in sleep drops one arm over me, his hand resting on my stomach. I tighten my abs, then let them go again. He's asleep. He won't notice. I touch my hair, the slippery strands running easily through my fingers. The bed smells of olive oil, but I'll change the sheets in the morning.

Downstairs, the clock chimes the hour. Six. I hear it again an hour later. Sean hasn't stirred. My eyes itch with exhaustion, but my mind turns cartwheels in the frozen darkness and I cannot sleep. My thoughts betray me, find their way to the coke in Sean's pocket. My credit card, a crisp twenty rolled into a tight tube, the hit of bitterness at the back of my mouth. But I resist, because, really, what would be the point? Gradually, I feel the whiskey leaving my system, taking with it all moisture from my cells. The requisite headache nudges at my skull. Sleep somehow captures me, but not before dawn quietly silvers the sky.

CHAPTER 19

It is early January before I hear from Sally, that murky time of
year when the sky seems to begin at shoulder height and the
entire colour spectrum consists of varying hues of grey. The
electronic beep of my phone slices through the silence of the
morning. I am working on a paper that I've been earmarked
to deliver at a conference in Columbia next month. At the
last conference I attended I delivered the keynote speech on
imaginative literature of the early twentieth century. This year
I won't be there, but I want the paper published. I've been
putting it off, filling hours marking essays and Christmas tests,
wasting my time with the trite minutiae of grading instead of
using my brain and producing something of worth. French
schools outlawed homework years ago. I support the ban.

Isaac's assistant emailed me a week before Christmas,
asking me if I could still write the paper. 'Emotion in
Modernity'. So here I am, outlining the abstract, barely a dent
in the required 7,000 words, my phone trilling loudly on the
table. I don't recognise the number, but I answer it anyway.

'Eva?'

The voice is friendly, but unfamiliar. 'Yes.'

'Hi, this is Sally. Adam's friend,' she adds, when there
is no instant reaction from me. 'Sorry if this is a bad time.

Adam gave me your number, and I thought I'd try and get you before school starts again.'

I remember her, and her wish to include some of my poems on the school English curriculum, although I have since wondered if I heard her wrong. Besides Maude, no one has mentioned my poems in a very long time.

It appears that I didn't imagine it all. Sally wants to meet me to talk about the poems she has bookmarked for inclusion. We will get together in two days, for coffee. My palms are suddenly clammy with apprehension. I itch for a drink. What if she decides she doesn't want my work after all? Or, worse, she requests new poems and then wonders why I don't have any? What will I tell her?

If I stay in the house I will drink. It's only eleven o'clock. It's a dry day. Cold, but dry. Gritting my teeth against the desire to flood my brain with numbing alcohol, I change into my running clothes and flee the house before I succumb to the open arms of temptation.

The air is so cold it feels as though I am breathing needles of ice. My face numbs against the switchblade of the wind. The sky is the colour of bone, picked clean and held up to the midwinter light. I pound the footpath, no destination in mind.

I've allowed my running to slide, and I'm in pain. At the canal I pause, leaning on the wooden lock for support as I catch my breath. Farther down the canal, the Luas thunders overhead. I'm still not used to seeing this toylike silver tram sliding through the city. The water is still and dark. A swan hisses as it floats past.

Running is a habit. An old habit. It soothes me, and its aimlessness clears my head. When I started running, back when Andrew was sick, I used to leave the house in whatever I was wearing, and just run. I learned quickly that the very least I required was a decent pair of running shoes. Just to the canal and back, I'd promise myself, but as I got better and fitter I found that I couldn't stop. I ran until I was so exhausted that I had no choice but to return home. I kept running from that house full of dark shadows, from my anger-shattered mother, from my crazy brother. Weight melted off me, I grew thinner, leaner, and still I couldn't stop running. After my first stint at giving up drinking I picked up my running shoes again, and each time the urge to drink bit me I flattened it with a destinationless run in a New York park.

I want to stop drinking again. I can't keep on doing what I've been doing since I got back to Dublin. I can't live a healthy or productive life if my principal objective each day is to count the minutes until I allow myself a drink. It's starting to show on my face, in my body. My legs scream at me to stop running, my breath is shorter, raspier than before. I don't want to be that woman, alone with her books and empty bottles. I actually don't know what I do want, but I don't want that.

Coffee. I promise myself coffee when I'm finished running. It's not the same, but it's a pretty good substitute. Lots of espresso, so strong it makes my hands shake and my nerves jump. Maybe if I drink enough of it I can even pretend I'm high. I retie my ponytail. The difference in my hair since Sean detangled it is still a novelty. I haven't heard from him since he left the following morning, but I don't mind.

The pavement is icy at the edges. I pick up the pace. I keep to the centre of the path, the well-worn part. I allow myself to be guided by the pounding of my feet. I empty my mind of thought, a trick I learned all those years ago when I ran to escape home.

CHAPTER 20

It's been years since I was last in Trinity. I gave some lectures here, ran poetry workshops for students. I don't know it as well as I know UCD, but I like it a lot more. It's cold again today, with a flinty wind barrelling between the buildings, killing the noise of the buses on Nassau Street and the self-righteous anger of motorists blaring their horns. I head for the arts block, an ugly example of failed 1970s' architecture, all damp cement and cheap windows. There are few students outside, and those that are there are fighting the cold with coats clenched tightly across chests, hats jammed low over ears. Bicycles lean against railings and posts. A paper bag filled with air drifts high above me. Tourists stand in line for *The Book of Kells*.

The café is the same as university cafés the world over: long rows of tables, plastic stackable chairs, canteen food. Food servers wear hairnets and latex gloves along with their striped uniforms. Mostly they speak with foreign accents, a big change from when I was a student. Back then it was mainly older women who worked the food counters, with the odd student thrown into the mix.

I am early. I order a double Americano and a croissant and carry my tray to a corner table. Scanning the large space, I do not see Sally. The high ceilings make for very poor acoustics, and the sharp clatter of dishes and cutlery rises higher than the drone of voices. I flick through the newspaper, check the clock on the wall ten times in as many minutes, and wonder if I could possibly leave before Sally gets here.

This is ridiculous. My poetry isn't for dissecting in a classroom.

How I miss it, miss writing.

My mother had taught me to read to keep me occupied before I started school. Too much of a nuisance around the house, she spelled words for me and gave me paper to copy them out on. Anything to keep me from pestering her while my brother was at school. She gave me the alphabet, but it was my father who sat with me, honing my new skills. Day after day I wrote words, reading them aloud in whispers. Progressing to Andrew's discarded school readers, I devoured them so frequently that soon I no longer needed to keep my finger under the words as I read. I even forgot about my sullen mother in my efforts to make my gentle father smile. It was the beginning of the shell that I would carefully construct around myself. Poetry hardened the veneer, kept me solitary and self-sufficient, became the varnish that deflected the curiosity of strangers. When I wrote I had the ability to reach outside the shell, write myself into an ordinary life. When the ink dried, I hid my head again. Poems kept me alive in the face of maternal rejection, through the bewilderment of a fatherless childhood, gave me something that most people never find. Without it, my sadness caved in on me, pushed me from the ledge of familiarity and sent me plunging to turbulent depths I hardly dreamed existed.

Somewhere along this lightless abyss, I learned to accept the loss of my words. Now, I can talk about it. Here, in this garish university cafeteria, with its appalling acoustics and mediocre coffee, I can meet with someone and allow the possibility of my poems to be studied. Somewhere, I crossed over into acceptance. The air is clearer there.

I'm finishing my second coffee when I spot Sally, pink-cheeked and flustered. She plonks her bag and folders down onto the table.

'Sorry, Eva, I'm so sorry. I couldn't get away.' She rummages through her bag, retrieves her purse. 'I couldn't even text you because I was in a bloody meeting. Hang on.' She disappears and is back in minutes, a coffee mug slopping its contents onto the tray in her hands. 'Sorry,' she says again, tearing a sachet of brown sugar apart and dumping the granules into the mug. 'First day back and it's already mad. No such thing any more as easing yourself back in.'

I wait as Sally drinks half her coffee, breaks her toast into pieces before buttering it. 'How's Adam?'

The question sounds casual, but carefully asked. 'Fine, I think.' I've barely spoken to him since Christmas. He's been busy with his family, his visiting nieces, his New Year spent in Sweden. And I've actually missed talking to him. Tomorrow school starts, and I'm looking forward to seeing him. Jim Collins has extended my contract until the end of the school year. It's a good thing.

Sally looks at me closely. 'He's a good guy.'

I fiddle with a sugar sachet. 'He is.'

'He likes you.'

It's so unexpected that I laugh.

Sally laughs too. 'Don't tell me I've surprised you.'

It's not that it's a surprise. I met her to talk about some of my poems, not to whisper about boys. We're practically 40, and I don't know Sally well enough to be having this conversation with her. Awkwardness makes me fumble for words.

Sally grins. She picks up one of her folders. 'Don't mind me. I'm just poking my big nose in where it has no business. Adam would kill me if he thought I was sitting here with you, having a cosy chat about him. Forget I said anything.' She pulls some sheets of paper out. 'Here we are,' she says, handing me a few pages stapled together. 'This is what I've been working on. It's more or less final, and I'd like you on board, with your agreement.'

I scan the pages. It's just names of poets, some Irish, some international. With each name, Sally has included five or six possible poems. In the margins are handwritten notes and queries. My name is on the last page. Five of my poems are proposed.

For a while I was used to seeing small articles about myself in literary publications, and for my last book an extensive piece in *The Times*. But it's been so long now that it's almost as though it never happened, and to see my name, neatly typed in bold alongside all these poets of note, is daunting. Something stirs inside me and I recognise it. Excitement. It is quickly doused by reality. What's the point in having my work picked over, rehashed, if there's nothing new to replace it with? It's fine for the other poets on the list. The dead ones are free of all expectation, and the living just keep on producing work of incredible magnitude and depth. To see my name on the same pages as Billy Collins, Seamus Heaney, Adrienne Rich, Sharon Olds and others has lent the moment an unreal quality. These are my gods. Not rock stars in glittery make-up and tight leather, but these poets, their genius stretching far beyond the page.

'What do you think?' Sally asks.

I'm not sure what she wants me to say.

'Are you okay?' She leans forward. A girl collects our trays, and we wait in silence while she wipes the table clean.

'Look, I know this is probably the last thing you were expecting, and let's face it, the school syllabus is hardly the place for radical poetry, but it gets your work out there, gets people talking about it again.' She sits back in her plastic chair, tucks her hair behind her ears.

I spread my hands on the table. My skin is chapped in places. I must put cream on them. The table beside us fills up with students. Undergraduates, no doubt. They talk loudly, American inflections heavy in their otherwise Irish accents. When I was their age, it was the west-Brit accent that staked out social territory. Now, everyone comes from California. London is old-school. The west coast is in. Sally rolls her eyes.

'Yours?' I ask her.

'God, no. I'm not lecturing much this year, thankfully.' She checks her phone, which has beeped three times, then puts it aside. 'So, what do you think? Are you in?'

'Don't you have to run this by some people?' It's too sudden, and I feel under pressure to do something, say something, and I'm not sure what.

Sally waves a hand in the air. 'I already have. We've been working on this for six months. It has to be decided on pretty soon.'

I run my finger down the page. God, it's been a long time. 'What about copyright?'

'That can be a problem, but I think we'll be okay. I contacted your old publishers. The man I spoke to was new, but they still have you on the old files, said there shouldn't be a copyright problem. Nothing we can't sort out at least.'

I put my hands to my face. 'I'm not sure. I haven't written in years, and I've nothing new to offer.'

She places her elbows on the table. 'It doesn't matter, Eva. It has nothing to do with that. It's to do with the poems themselves. They're fantastic, and worthy of inclusion in any anthology.' She checks her watch. 'Shit, I have to go in a minute. I'm giving a tutorial to third years. So, are you on for it?'

'Can I think about it?'

Sally starts to gather up her belongings. She glances again at her phone. 'You can, but don't take too long. This has to be in by the end of next week.' She hoists her bag onto her shoulder, stands, and looks down at me. 'Think about it and ring me in the next day or two. It's a good thing, Eva, really. I'd do it.'

I watch her stop to talk to three people before she finally leaves. My hands are shaking, whether from caffeine or nerves I can't tell. It hits me that this proposal of Sally's, this possible inclusion of my poems on the course that I'm currently teaching here gives me a deadline. I can't teach my own work. I couldn't. How would I talk about those poems, read them aloud in class, listen to the sighs of boredom, or worse? I will either have to find another job entirely, or move back to the States. At least it will put an end to this lack of clarity that I feel about my life right now. I have an out.

I pick up the newspaper she left behind and read about the day's occurrences. Unemployment, cuts in public spending, developers in court, even more scandals in the Church. Nothing much changes in Ireland.

CHAPTER 21

A dam's daughter is coming to visit him for the midterm break. He wants me to spend a day with them while she's here; he is determined that I will. I'm not as sure.

'The poor kid will need a change of scenery from just having me around her all the time.' He looks over his shoulder as he manoeuvres into a parking space that opened up just as we arrived. We exit his vegetable-oil car, which always smells faintly of doughnuts. He gets his oil from a doughnut and coffee chain in Rathmines. Once a month, Adam pulls around to the rear of the premises, and used oil is siphoned into the car's tank. I admire that in him, the determination to do things properly. Adam cares not for the jibes about his car. 'I'm above that' is his usual reply. And he is. We are going to the National Gallery. A touring exhibition of Picasso is on for a month, and Adam has two tickets. There is a school rugby match on today, and we finished classes at lunchtime. The teachers are expected to attend the game, support the students, but I slipped out the side door as everyone assembled in the hall. Adam caught up with me minutes later.

'Right.' Again, that doubt, all those plaguing questions I ask of myself. *What should I do? What do I want? Was it the right decision?*

'We can go to the zoo, or whatever. She's easy to please.' Adam is casual in his tone, but he's thrilled at the prospect of an unexpected week with his child. Her mother, a biologist, will be in Moscow for a week's conference, and Adam has agreed to take Annalie while she's gone.

'Does it affect her? Not having you around, I mean?' We walk through the square. It is cold today, and I wrap my scarf around my neck, tug my hat down over my ears. Most of the trees are bare, pared back for winter. They wave their cuttlebone branches in the slight wind. The flowerbeds have been recently turned, but nothing is visible in the brown earth, not a hint of anything to come.

'I don't think so, not really.' Adam's shoes echo on the stony path. We pass the Oscar Wilde sculpture. Tourists in bright jackets take photos beside it, taking it in turns to put their hands on Wilde's marbled legs, his feet, smiling despite the freezing air. I feel sorry for them, being here at this time of year. Dublin is grey and unwelcoming in midwinter, despite its upgrade in wealthier times to a city on everyone's wish list. The hotels may be glitzier, the shops plentiful, but in late January a curtain of dampness clings to every surface, lending the city a bedraggled air that no money can dispel.

Through the shrubbery, pieces of the children's play area can be glimpsed, flashes of red and yellow, all the bright, primary-coloured equipment. The playground, when we walk through it, is a big disappointment, the swings rusting and chipped, the slide in need of repair, more like the playgrounds beside the public housing on the Lower East Side than one in this beautiful park.

'I'll bring Annalie here,' Adam says as we pass. 'She still loves swings, and long may it last.' He coughs. His breath is a cloud on the freezing air. 'Can't abide the thought of her getting into boys.' He pulls a packet of tissues from his inside pocket. 'You ever think of having kids yourself?' His tone is casual, throwaway, but I know the barely veiled curiosity behind it. This question is the one most asked in offhand terms, but overloaded with meaning and hidden judgement. Women ask it mostly when they don't know you well enough to ask such a personal question, and men ask it to see if it's worth pursuing you. There is no right answer. Say yes, and the men run a mile, while the women quietly pity you. Say no, and men will only date you so they can sleep with you, secure in the knowledge that you won't try and trap them. Everyone else thinks you're cold.

Or so I've been led to believe.

Isaac never wanted children. That is what he told me every time the issue arose, and in the past couple of years it arose quite frequently. His wife couldn't have them, and didn't wish to adopt. Isaac happily fell in with her. He loved me partly because it was easy to be with someone who saw life in intellectual terms, who didn't equate happiness and fulfilment with reproduction.

Except for me it wasn't quite that easy.

Everyone goes through a phase of wanting children, even those who avowedly don't want them. I never dedicated much time either way to thinking about it, until one day when a colleague brought her baby son into the faculty lounge. All my barriers vanished. I had a turn at holding that beautiful tiny boy, and something clicked inside me, some airless tunnel finally let in some light and air, and instead of turning from the emotion, I faced it head on. Out of nowhere, I wondered about having a baby. It wasn't a sudden, gasping need that grabbed me by the throat and demanded me to breed. It was more subtle than that. I noticed things. Baby things. Like the number of them I now observed on my runs, the nannies pushing big prams around Central Park, the toddlers wobbling on unsteady feet, plump arms windmilling. It was new for me, and at first I was taken in by the novelty of it all. I wondered what it would be like to be called *Mother. Mama.* That sort of thing. Very gradual.

'Do you?' Adam stubs out his cigarette.

I shrug. 'Not much.'

When I found out I was pregnant, shock and fear, but mostly shock, exploded in my head. I kept it from Isaac for three weeks, unable to bring myself to say the words over the phone. It was supposed to be something I'd planned, not the result of a long weekend with my married lover, who, it turned out, was the most commitment-phobic man I'd ever been involved with.

I was in Los Angeles, on a research project for three months. Isaac had visited me at the end of January, and by mid March I knew that something wasn't quite right.

I didn't need a test kit to know. I just knew. And it made me sick. It's terrible to admit that, I know, but from the safe distance of one year I can look over my shoulder and be honest with myself. I felt sick. All the time. When I wasn't throwing up, I was a nauseated mess. I could barely focus on my work, was unable to eat, and all I wanted to do was sleep. The tentative imaginings of having a baby faded to nothing in the face of the reality I was in. Who would help me? Where would I live? My shoebox in the East Village was hardly large enough for me. And I didn't want to sandwich my child between the sounds of bottles smashing late at night and screaming in Spanish. *Hijo de puta! Te odio!*

My mother slithered into my thoughts, silent as a ghost. What if I turned into her, mothered the way she did? What if my brother's madness festered in those microscopic dividing cells inside me?

I spoke to Isaac every day, but stalled at saying anything to him. We spoke at length about work, about my research. The secondment to LA had been offered to me, an extension of the research I was doing in New York into cultural responses to poetry. The English faculty in UCLA had a small but thriving modern poetry department, and I settled in quickly. Work was busy, with little time for procrastinating. Due to the individual nature of research, I was largely left to my own devices, an arrangement that suited me fine. Daily briefings and casual meetings kept me in touch with my new colleagues. I found the experience refreshing after the intensity of New York. I enjoyed the freedom of being away from the familiar. If I am honest, it was nice to be away from Isaac too, just for a while. Lately, I'd begun wondering if that was all I was ever going to be in, a relationship on the side, the supporting act while the main attraction continued onstage. For the first time since we started seeing each other, I had to ask myself what I wanted, and what I thought I was going to have in the future.

Except now this had happened.

I was in LA, busy writing notes on how different groups in American society respond to poetry. Our research was ongoing, with feedback from the sample populations providing the backbone to our work.

Then Isaac came to visit.

LA was hot, hot in that late winter way that the west coast has, hot in a way that New York never is except in July. Coming from the unimaginable cold of a New York winter, it was like plunging into a furnace, the air dragon's breath on my heat-parched skin.

I'd been drinking. It was a holiday weekend, and the extra day off work sent me scurrying into corners of my head that I preferred to keep sealed shut. Isaac was late, something I'd noticed happening a little too frequently, something that I had chosen to ignore because I didn't like the thought of what challenging him would bring. It was one thing to question myself about what I was doing, but another thing entirely for him to have doubts too. And he didn't say he was having doubts, I just knew he was. Call it intuition, call it low self-esteem, but my radar was beeping like crazy and I dulled the sound with a myriad of So Cal cocktails that were never less than marvellous at intoxicating me to the point of oblivion every time.

I'd been waiting for him for hours. His flight had been due at noon. He had a lunch meeting with someone from USC, some man he shared research with, but had promised me he'd be at my place by four. Afternoon dissolved into evening, the light fading quickly as it did at that time of year in southern California. On the tiny balcony of my borrowed studio apartment, I finished my third margarita, then poured another from the blender. Below me, Sunset Boulevard wound its way to the ocean, a shimmering thread of sluggish traffic and street lights. The heat made zigzags in the humid evening air, the scent of eucalyptus and gasoline omnipresent in the noisy city evening. The palm trees rattled their fronds like bones. A miniscule lizard scuttled up the wall. The insane excitement of LA palpitated. Tourists screamed from rented stretched limos, kerb-crawled in convertible Porsches, roved the streets in packs, their oversized bodies and extra-large clothes branding them different no matter how hard they tried to fit in. The real Angelenos were far away, tucked in corners of dive bars, eating on patios, being discreet in the Chateau Marmont. I longed to be out there with Isaac, sitting in a cool bar, getting a table in a trendy restaurant, ordering lobster or whatever was in season on the LA dining circuit.

Finally, Isaac rang the bell and I staggered to the door to buzz him in. Salt congealed on my fingers and cheeks, and I was too drunk to care. I swayed to the huge white bed. A book lay face down beside where I fell, but I didn't bother turning it over. When alcohol swamps my brain, words swim into each other, turning pages into an inkblot of incoherence.

Probably it was the booze, but I allowed myself a moment to be critical of my relationship with Isaac. The criticism usually remained below the surface, nudging me regularly, always ignored. I loved him. It shouldn't have been so complicated.

Yet I was so easy for him, a convenience, a takeaway girlfriend to whom he had no obligation. What other woman, with any level of self-respect, would allow a man to behave thus? I was the green virgin, stretched on the rack, waiting for him to bestow the love I greedily coveted. He, the alpha male, held all the power clenched in his hands because I allowed it to be so.

He stood at the foot of the bed, unknotting his striped, preppy tie, dropping his jacket onto the chair. 'I see you haven't wasted any time.' The judgement in his voice stung me, hurt my feelings. 'Fuck it, Eva. You're a bit old for this.'

I flopped over onto my back. I wore a voluminous shirt, nothing more. The heat forbade it. 'I missed you.' I reached for him. 'I miss seeing you.'

He ignored my hands, splashed whiskey into a tumbler. 'That's because you're out here. What did you think it'd be like?' He wiped his forehead with his wrist. His shirt was damp, wrinkled with the unseasonal heat. 'No one sent you here. It was your choice.' His mouth open, he poured the whiskey into himself in one go, like I'd seen men do in films from the fifties, the sixties, when reaching for the cut-glass decanter straight after work was the height of sophistication, of glamour. Except this wasn't decades past, and Isaac was wearing jeans and a creased linen shirt, not a Brooks Brothers suit and Hermès tie. I hadn't seen the shirt before. All those years with him, and he wore a shirt I had never seen. What else did I not know, not witness? Who gave it to him? His wife? Another lover? Was there another lover? The questions made me nauseous, sloshing around inside me with the margaritas and the salt. I closed my eyes. The room began spinning, and I forced myself to open them again, focusing instead on a crack in the plaster, like a child's crayon drawing, running the width of the room. The ceiling fan revolved slowly. The hot air barely stirred. 'Christ, Eva. Look at you.' He wiped his mouth with the back of his hand, refilled his glass. Shaking his head, he stalked to the balcony door. From the bed, I could see the empty blender lying on its side. Isaac stood framed in the open doorway. Outside, Sunset swarmed with traffic. The sky glowed lavender. To the east, the hills were black ridges in the darkened evening. I fancied I heard a coyote barking, but this far down in Hollywood, and with so many people around, it was probably just a dog.

We were like a disgruntled married couple. That couldn't have been what he'd signed up for when he fell in love with me, to have to have his excuses carefully thought out before he faced my dissatisfaction, my gaping need. I'd fought my battles with booze, had been sure that this time I'd won.

'You're a fucking disgrace.' He kept his back to me. 'Have you any idea the planning it took to get out here, the pretence?' Isaac turned, rested his back against the sliding door. 'I was actually really looking forward to seeing you. But not like this.' He swallowed the last of his whiskey. 'This is not what I need at the end of a long week.'

Crickets made scissory sounds in the shadows outside. The hot night air seeped into the room. The sky was purple with heat, the quarter moon levitating above the low-rise streetscape.

Isaac tossed a tissue-paper package in my direction. 'This is for you. Although I'd kind of hoped you'd be sober enough to at least see it.'

Struggling to sit up, I unwrapped the gift. A soft grey cloud fell onto my bare legs. I held the garment to my face and started to cry.

Isaac sat down beside me. Putting his arms around me, he removed the cardigan from my hands. He lay me down on the bed, kissed my face, smoothed my hair on the pillow. With his thumbs, he wiped the salt from my face. 'I'm sorry, Eva. I just don't know what to do any more.' He kissed my shoulders, my neck. 'I love you, but you need more than I can give you, and I want less.'

Adam puts a hand to the small of my back as we enter the gallery. Ushering me inside, he keeps his hand on me. Even as we rove from picture to picture, devouring Picasso's women, his sadness, his starving families, Adam finds some reason to touch me. Once it is to move me to the side to allow a German tourist room to view a painting of a blind man reaching for a bowl. Then he taps me on the arm to show me five women, their faces and bodies moving on the canvas. When he pulls me to stand in front of him, he leaves his fingertips on my waist. As we admire a still life, he pulls me close to whisper his interpretation.

'See that?' He points to a blue musical instrument, all cubed angles and pitched sides. 'This is where Matisse comes in.' Adam circles his forefinger in front of the painting. 'This design, the colours, it's all Matisse.' He drapes his arm around my shoulder, casually.

I've loved Picasso since my brother brought me a poster of *Guernica* from a school trip to Madrid. I like to think I'm knowledgeable on the subject, but Adam's enthusiasm is burning so brightly that I don't wish to dampen it by blurting out that I already know what he's telling me. I'll let him know another time. Right now, in this packed exhibition, boxed in by eager viewers and overlooked by a stern supervisor who regularly steps forward to request more distance from the paintings, it's nice to have Adam's hand on my arm, his voice in my ear.

I've seen a lot of Adam recently, but it's been strangely platonic. Since the day I went to lunch in his house, he has been as friendly to me as he's always been, but he hasn't again reached for a lock of my hair. We have gone to the cinema a few times, to a play in the Gate, we've eaten in other chichi places where they take your number and text you when there's a table. But it's as though Adam has drawn back from me. That one time he tucked my hair behind my ear in the fading light of an autumn Saturday in Sandymount, and I responded by ducking out of the house, has not been repeated.

Afterwards, when we have exhausted Cubism and ourselves, we sit in the café. It is packed, and we squeeze ourselves into a corner. Beside us, a child sets up a wail.

'I'll bring Annalie here. She'd love it.' Adam uses a tissue to wipe away crumbs left by the previous occupants. 'She's very creative.'

I idly wonder if there is anything his child can't do. But I'm being mean, and maybe more than slightly jealous that he has her.

'They do art classes.' I'd read it on a poster on the way in.

'Really? Brilliant.' He sits back in his chair, pleased. 'I'll bring her in. I'll have to get some new paints for her. The old ones have probably dried up by now.'

'Adam! What are you doing here?' A large hand slaps Adam on the back. He chokes slightly on his coffee. It is David, the journalist. He is amused.

Adam is less gregarious. 'Hey. Remember Eva?'

David's handshake is strong and manly. 'Eva, good to see you again. How did you drag this philistine in here?'

Something witty and clever is expected of me, but spontaneous humour evades me. I smile, say hello.

David is waiting to interview a politician. One of the identikit suits that are responsible for the yawning chasm the whole country is tipping into.

'The place is fucked, completely fucked. If it was anywhere else but Ireland, heads would be on platters.'

'So why are you here if you're waiting to talk to him?' Adam asks.

'Location, dude. It's just around the corner, and the coffee here is great.'

David's coffee is black, and he drinks it quickly. He checks his phone. 'Shit. I have to fly.' He grabs a bag, throws it across his chest and settles the strap over his jacket. 'Good to see you, Eva,' he says again. He slaps Adam on the shoulder. 'I'll see you soon.'

Adam shakes his head. His hair has got longer. There is no grey among the reddish brown. 'I'm always running into him. No matter where I go, he's there.'

'I like him.' I do. He's clever, he brims with energy. David has enthusiasm for life, which I admire.

'Women always do. He thinks you're beautiful.' Adam taps the back of my hand with his finger. 'Eva.'

I look at him. 'What?'

'I said, David thinks you're beautiful.'

Embarrassment stains my face. I can feel it, spreading. 'Stop.' Never have I learned just to say thank you to compliments. My laugh is short, intended to chase away the moment.

'Well, actually he does.' He leans closer to me, drops his voice. 'And he's right.'

I should respond to him, say something, defend myself, but I fail. Adam's thumb grazes my lower lip.

I'm saved by a voice announcing the imminent closing of the gallery. Reluctantly, we stand, pull on our coats.

'Will we get dinner?' Adam asks as we drop coins in the donation box. 'It's too early to go home.'

Since the Saturday in his house, Adam hasn't offered to go for a drink. Nothing about it has been mentioned, just a quiet understanding of the problem I have with alcohol. My addiction is something I've preferred to keep private. Others' awkwardness in the face of it makes me awkward, and that makes me want to have a drink, and the cycle spins forth. Avoiding alcohol by all means is the only way I can be sure of not drinking. It's too difficult now for me to be around it and stay sober. It's the oldest cliché, but it's true. I must avoid it.

Adam holds the door for me.

Offices are in the process of disgorging their occupants onto the streets. A splatter of rain darkens the path. Umbrellas pop open, the only splash of colour in this grey late afternoon. Cars are beginning to turn on headlights. The wind has picked up and great gusts propel us along. Merrion Square is locked now, so we walk along its perimeter. Adam puts his arm around me, hugs me to him. I sneak a sideways look at him. His hair is blowing over his eyes and he rakes it back. He catches me watching him, and smiles.

The Merc is parked at the far end of the square. Adam opens the passenger door with a flourish. 'Madam, your chariot.'

I laugh. The interior is strewn with test papers, ragged schoolbooks, old coffee cups and bags of recycling. The contents seem to have multiplied during our few hours with the paintings. 'Do you ever clean this car?' I ask as I put my bag on the back seat, pushing a box of paper to one side.

'Never,' is his reply. 'My father likes to have a go every so often, but that's about it.'

Adam is still standing at the passenger door. His hands cup my shoulders. The wind blows my hair across my face. He pushes it aside, then thumbs my bottom lip again. He starts to say something, then thinks better of it, and puts his mouth to mine instead. His kiss is surprising. Warm mouth, firm lips, vague taste of coffee. I don't know what I had expected. Pupils widened, black with lust, mouth slack, maybe? What I get is quite the opposite, but it thrills me, properly, not in same way as being with Sean, but more, and in a different way. Adam appeals to my mind. That sounds terribly pretentious, but I don't mean it to be. An intelligent man is a beautiful man.

Before I can react, return the kiss, trace his face with my fingertips, do anything, he is gone, not saying a word, just opening the driver's door as though the kiss never happened. He starts the engine, leaving me still half in, half out of the car.

Darkness has thrown a blanket over everything by the time we reach his house in Sandymount. Adam offers to make dinner. I accept. Truthfully, I wouldn't have minded a restaurant, the pleasing anonymity of ordering food that I don't witness being prepared, the distance the table would force between us, the comfort of other diners preventing any more surprise kisses. I need time to process the kiss, the hand-touching, the arms draped around my shoulders. It all has an endpoint, this I know. The fact that suddenly I'm thinking about birth control defines the point in itself. With Sean, things happened and I allowed them to. With Adam, it's different. He's older for starters, but it's more than that: I like him.

By accepting dinner in Adam's house, I am complicit in this dance. And I'm not taking any birth control. Since last year, it hasn't been something I've needed. Sean had provided his own, two square packets of foil wedged behind a twenty euro note in his wallet. I had peeked when he went to the bathroom. I prefer to be in control of my body myself, don't trust anyone to take care of things in the way that I do. The pill doesn't suit me any more. It bloats me, makes all my clothes uncomfortable around my waist. I feel slightly dulled when I take it, as though my mind is too tired to absorb all the information it needs.

Adam negotiates rush hour traffic. The Merc insulates us from the cold.

The sea hangs heavy on the air. The tang of salt and seaweed is slightly nauseating. I'm not sure I could live in Sandymount, with its dampness and smells, the coating of salt on every surface and the vague feeling of being on the edge of the world. I shiver. The rain is pouring down now, hopping off every surface. It skates along the road, runs into the pavement cracks. A discarded chip bag disintegrates in the gutter.

Adam kills the engine, and in the silence that follows all we hear is the rain drumming on the car roof. A seagull screams in the distance.

He turns to me. 'Will we make a dash for it?'

I follow Adam inside.

CHAPTER 22

A dam lights a fire, if it can be described thus. What he actually does is touch a match to a wrapped log in the grate. Blue flames instantly swarm. Small pieces of wood are stacked neatly to one side. He places some on top of the flaming log, then sits back on his heels and admires his handiwork.

I slip into a seat near the fireplace. The house is cold, and I keep my coat on.

Adam stands. 'I'll stick the heating on. You'll be warm in a few minutes.'

A mood lamp leaks muted light into a corner of the room. The table where we ate lunch the last time I was here is covered with papers. Adam starts to clear them away.

'Working on something?'

He spreads his hands. 'Sort of. A piece for *The Times*. A book review. Just some historical tome.'

'Impressive.'

'It's not. I know the editor, and I do him favours from time to time when he's stuck.' He moves things to bookshelves, to the coffee table, then turns back to me. 'Now, some tea? Water? Or I can squeeze some juice if you'd prefer.'

'Water is fine.'

'Still or sparkling?'

He doesn't have to go to this much effort. I know what Adam is doing, have seen it before, that shrouding of alcohol, offering every drink possible except the one that I really want. He is a kind man, and I don't resent him for mentioning everything except the liquor-soaked elephant looming large in the middle of the room.

I wander into the kitchen. Adam is chopping and peeling and sautéing. A hot, smoky scent fills the space. He hands me a knife. 'Here, chop that, will you?'

I remove the seeds from a chilli pepper, then slice it finely. Adam slides the pieces into the pan. There is a sudden sizzle. I tear coriander leaves, crush lemongrass, then leave the knife aside and lean against the counter. The house is extremely tidy and clean.

He catches me looking around. 'The cleaner was here today. I'm not responsible for all this.'

'I didn't think so.' His car breeds rubbish, paper and books. Finding space to sit is an achievement, but the smell of doughnuts makes it worthwhile.

'I just don't see things till it's too late, then there's a huge mess, and it takes me days to clear it.' He wipes his hands on a tea towel. 'I'd pay ten times the amount not to have to think about it.' He twists the lid on a bottle of Italian lemonade. It fizzes open. The music of fizzy drinks is also the symphony of beer. Sweeter than any other sound. I clench my fists. I want a beer so badly I can taste it, taste those microscopic bubbles in my throat, feel the wet cold of the bottle in my hands and the eddy of exhilaration as the alcohol hits my bloodstream. I ignore the faint hiss of effervescence as Adam puts the plastic bottle down. My hands shake as I raise my glass of water to my mouth. The ice cubes chill my lips.

Plates are taken from the cupboard. There is a clatter of cutlery. Adam nods towards the table.

'Let's eat.'

Something electronic and mellow flows from the speakers in the ceiling. Our empty plates have been pushed to the side. A small tin with a scratched picture of a Christmas tree on the lid sits on top of a notebook near my plate. I fiddle with it. The lip flips open. Inside are four small joints, tightly wrapped.

Adam laughs. 'Confiscated from one of my sixth years.' He leans over, puts his finger to my lips. 'Not a word.'

The smell of the weed is sweet. I run my finger down the length of the paper wrapping. God, I'd love some.

I know it won't kill me, but having kicked drinking to the kerb for now, getting high isn't exactly how I should be celebrating my tentative sobriety.

Isaac liked to smoke weed sometimes. His brother grew it, and a couple of times a year Isaac was the recipient of a bag of Humboldt County's finest. I'd never bothered with it much before I moved to New York. Crumbled pieces of hash, wrapped in a cigarette and furtively passed around at the back of the student bar, was never my idea of fun, and it tasted disgusting. But weed is different, and I crave something that could replace the gap left by booze.

Adam notices my hesitation. 'Here, I'll put them away,' he says, reaching for the tin. 'Will you have some tea? Coffee?'

What I'd actually like is a hit or two off one of those skinny little joints. Just a quick hit. It wouldn't hurt me. Drugs have never been my issue. Which student, I wonder? How did Adam intercept them?

To distract myself, I look at a series of pictures on the wall opposite the table, an uneven line of photographs in square black frames. Nothing much appears to be happening in any of them. I count them. Seven. Strange number for a sequence. A prime number. Adam follows my gaze.

'My sister took those. She's really good. I tell her all the time she should be doing more of them, but she doesn't believe me.'

The photos are intriguing, if indecipherable. I turn back to the tin. 'Maybe we should just try one.'

He gives me a look, one I've seen many times before. It's a don't-you-know-what-you're-doing-here sort of look, a you're-an-alcoholic look. And that's the thing, I'm an alcoholic. *My name is Eva, and I'm an alcoholic, not a bloody drug addict.*

There are matches beside the fire. I light a joint, straighten the crude filter, then inhale.

I take three hits and hand it over. That's enough.

The weed kicks in within minutes. Whatever strains they're growing these days, they're strong. I shouldn't have taken more than one go at it. I look at Adam, but it's hard to focus. The electronic music that seeps from the ceiling swirls around me. I want to laugh, but if I start now, this early, I won't be able to stop. I know myself, and I will laugh and laugh and laugh before I sink into a stoned semi-coma. No. The urge is stifled. Adam moves to throw more sticks on the fire. His movements are slow, deliberate. He shoves a fat log into the flames. Sparks shoot up the chimney as he adds another. Instead of resuming his seat at the table, he settles on the floor by the hearth. I try to lean into the high, into the mellow calm of being stoned. Negativity must be kept at bay or it will swamp me, ruining everything, and I'll spend the rest of the time fighting panic and warding off thoughts of my mother and how she must have hated me to have treated me as she did.

159

'Eva,' he says, arranging cushions. 'Come over here. It's warmer.'

I wait for him to pat the floor beside him, but to my relief he doesn't. Instead, he leans back against the cushions, cradles the back of his head with his hands and closes his eyes. I hate when men pat the floor, inviting you to sit with them. It's cheesy, unoriginal. If done to me, I ignore it. For some reason I am absurdly glad that Adam's eyes are closed, that for now he prefers to listen to the music and be inside his own head.

Standing up, I place my hands on the table, almost knocking a framed photo of Adam's child over in the process, then pick my way across to the fire. A beer bottle is on the hearth. I hadn't noticed it till now. One glance at him. Eyes still closed. The bottle is warm on the side that faced the fire. A centimetre of liquid lies quietly at the bottom. I raise it to my nose, inhale its scent, that intoxicating, addictive mix of malted barley and fermented sugar. The fizz has long since subsided. I shake the bottle gently, watch the pale liquid within slosh around. The need to drink, that drive to consume at any cost, fills me.

From somewhere outside my stoned head I observe myself, halfway between sitting and standing, a near-empty bottle of beer in my hand, while Adam stretches out on the floor beside me. I look ridiculous, a thief caught mid-plunder. Self-consciousness, that old enemy, creeps over me, the weed making it acute.

'Do you want that?'

I jump at his voice. 'What?' I turn.

'If you want one, I'll get you a cold one.'

I thrust the bottle at him. 'No. I told you, I'm off it.'

He twitches the hem of my skirt. 'Come on, sit down.'

I don't move. The logs crumble sootily and rearrange

themselves in the grate. The rain has picked up again, and it hops off the window panes. Upstairs, a door slams.

Eventually, I fold my legs under me, lean my back against the armchair. Within minutes, pins and needles seize both legs, and I stretch them out in front of me. The toes of my new boots are pointed and my legs appear elongated, elegant. In the fireplace, the flames wind themselves around each other. My face warms in the heat.

'Eva.' Adam's voice is unexpected. I jump slightly. He laughs, a slow, ponderous sound. 'Sorry.'

I pull my gaze away from the fire. How much time has passed since I sat down? Adam's eyes are pot-reddened. His glasses are nowhere to be seen. His face is closer to mine than I'd realised. His hair hangs over one eye. I want to push it away, but my hand feels too heavy. I think of the line of hair on his stomach, how it disappears into his jeans. I think of it, but I do nothing. If I were to do something, touch him, put my cheek on his shoulder ... if I did these things to him and he pulled away, how would I cope with the shame? So I imagine it instead, imagine myself pushing that lock of reddish hair out of his eyes, rubbing my fingers along his jaw, now stubbled with end-of-day shadow. I imagine myself slipping my hand inside his shirt and splaying my fingers, starfish-like, across the warm expanse of his skin. I think these thoughts, and I do not act on them. Let him make a move, if there is any move to be made.

'If the sixth years could see us now,' he says, laughing. 'Stoned out of our heads on confiscated weed.'

'If Jim Collins could see us,' I say, joining him in laughter.

'He wouldn't know what we meant. He thinks getting high means jumping for the ball.'

'Or winning the lineout.'

'Or kicking a penalty.'

'Or getting good marks in exams.'

'Or taking off in a plane.'

I'm laughing so hard now that I can't stop. Adam tries to say something, but laughter prevents him, which makes it all the funnier to both of us. Eventually, ages later, we subside into exhausted mirth. I don't want to look at Adam or I'll be off again.

We are both now leaning back against the armchair, side by side. Unseen, the music has changed to something else quiet, a soundtrack to some film I haven't seen.

'In New York they'd consider you a hipster,' I tell him.

He shifts to look at me. 'I'm flattered. A 43-year-old hipster. Imagine.'

'No, seriously. You read the right books, you've seen all the cool films. You're the only person I've ever seen here with a vegetable-oil car.'

'Bio fuel.'

'Whatever, you're still the only one who seems to drive one.'

'Does this mean you like me, Doctor Perry?' He taps the tip of my nose with his forefinger. 'Do you approve?' His mouth is full of amusement, and I can't tell if he's joking or flirting. I want him to flirt with me. He's good at it, subtle. Moves in and moves back again quickly. Pulls on my hair and lets it drop just as easily. Kisses me at his car and jumps into the driver's seat. I don't answer him. His fingers move to my cheek, to my temple. He winds my hair around his fingers, draws me closer to him. His brown eyes widen slightly. The fire flickers orange on their surface.

The first time Isaac kissed me, it charged through me like a laser, jerking my body towards him. It was one of those kisses that go on and on and on, and still you can't stop kissing, can't pull your mouth away. Kissing Adam isn't like that, but I don't want to pull away. It's different to the kiss at his car, more insistent, more demanding, and maybe it's the weed that's making me dizzy, but he manoeuvres me to the floor and somehow manages to divest me of my top and my cashmere cardigan without my even noticing.

'Eva, Eva, Eva, you're so sexy,' he mumbles into my neck. He props himself up then, and looks down at me. 'I don't know how I've managed to keep my hands off you till now.' Adam slides his body on top of mine, pins me to the floor, erases me with kisses. Minutes later, I open my eyes, and I'm shocked to see the room is still the same; the hardwood floor, the long dining table, the shelves of books, the uneven line of black-framed photographs. The kisses I return are urgent, greedy, insistent. I pull away but Adam brings me back into the embrace again. When finally we break apart, Adam rolls off me, lies on his back, turns his face to mine.

I put my hands to my flaming cheeks, don't meet his eyes. He tangles his fingers in my hair and forces my chin towards him.

'Eva. Listen.' A log explodes in the fire, shooting an ember onto the rug, where it burns like a tiny bomb. My head is still stuffed from the joint.

The music has stopped. As though to give himself something to do, Adam gets to his feet, goes to the stereo to rectify it. It's not really a stereo, just one of those things that an MP3 fits into, more of a rectangular speaker than anything else. He presses some buttons and the music starts up again. I wonder – and this is the stoned part of my brain pondering, because normally I don't worry about things like that – I wonder what the name is for the speaker. *Can you put something else on the speaker?* doesn't quite have the same ring as *put some music on the stereo.* I'd ask Adam; he certainly knows, but I don't want him to know how ridiculously out of touch I am with the digital revolution. Email and a mobile phone are enough for me to deal with.

He brings a bottle of sparkling water, a proper glass bottle, the expensive kind of water, and a glass for each of us. My mouth is dry, cottony from the weed. The bubbles burst on my tongue.

Adam leans towards me again, kisses my cheek, my jawline, my neck. He winds and unwinds a lock of my hair around his finger. 'Listen, I'm not going to push you into anything. I like you, I actually really like you, but I'm not about to jump your bones just for the hell of it.' He refills our glasses.

What do I say? I concentrate on a thread that curls from the seam in my skirt. I'm hopeless when confronted with men who like me. It's easier when they just let things happen before analysis sets in. I'd been out with Isaac five times before the subject of his wife arose, and by then it was too late to do much about it. But confronted with this, now, with Adam sitting in front of me, his face a sketch in earnestness, I'm hopeless.

The thing is, I do like him. A lot, in fact. He's intelligent, funny, extremely attractive. He is interesting, he reads and writes, likes music, so why am I hesitating? Most women complain that there aren't enough men like Adam to go around. He's obviously a good father, seems to have few neuroses, and he's been more than tolerant of my quirks, which I know are legion.

His foot nudges my leg. 'So?'

It was much easier to sleep with Sean. There was lots of whiskey involved, plus Sean's lack of years, which kept everything on a lighter level.

Adam could be someone. I can't believe I'm actually saying this, only one year after Isaac walked away from me and everything threatened to come undone. Came undone, for a while. If something happens with Adam, it's not something I will leave lightly. And I believe I will leave, eventually.

I've been gone too long. They say two years is enough to make you a stranger, five years a stranger forever. I don't know if I can be here, in Dublin, living here, inhabiting this space I vacated so long ago. Sometimes it feels as though I'm skipping along on the surface, expecting something to change. Waiting for the a-ha moment that will clarify everything.

I suppose it could be Adam who clarifies it all, but somehow it needs to be more. I need more.

'Everything okay?' He shifts. His shirt has all its buttons undone. Did I do that? His skin is tawny in the firelight, smooth, except for the tangle of hair across his chest. I touch my palm to it. He catches my wrist, kisses the white skin on the underside. I push against him, slip his opened shirt off his shoulders, kiss his skin. No, it's not like it was with Isaac, but this isn't Isaac. I'm also older now, and the fact that Adam already has more possibilities, fewer complications than Isaac, adds to his appeal. He unzips my skirt. I trace the line of hair on his stomach, open his jeans in a rush. We shed the rest of our clothes, but in what order and how I do not know. For once I am enveloped in the moment, self-consciousness swamped by the glorious, thrilling fact that a man, a gorgeous, clever man, wants me. Even the first time with Isaac was clouded by how concerned I was about myself, about how I looked to him, whether I could ever measure up to the myriad lovers whose spectres ghosted my thoughts. Now my mother is absent, her mocking smile no longer bothers me. I don't want a drink. I don't even think about needing a drink. For the first time that I can remember, I'm fine as I am. I haven't felt this liberated since I discovered the boost an early morning vodka can bring to a dark day. Maybe it's Adam and how gorgeous he is in the flashes of firelight. I am wrapped in his attention, reassured by his presence and the appreciative sounds he whispers over and over. A raised ridge of pink scar disturbs the smooth plane of his shoulder. I press my lips to it, run my tongue over its uneven surface. Damage is unbearably endearing. The fire is hot against our skin, but we pay it no heed. Maybe the rug is less comfortable than it could be, but we do not notice. The rain pounds so hard against the windows that it sounds as though the glass will surely break, but we ignore it. Time is ripped out from under me, and everything else ceases to matter.

Adam is a shockingly good lover. Maybe it's the last vestiges of dope in my blood, but something about this is much, much more than I'd expected. Afterwards his arm is draped across me, and I kiss him. My smile is foolish as I snuggle against him. The vague promises I invariably make to myself at moments of utter contentment such as this gather as one.

I won't mess this up.

I will be good.

I won't let him slip away.

I will be good.

I won't destroy everything like I usually do.

I will be good. I will. I will.

CHAPTER 23

This room is bigger than mine. The open curtains allow a thin stream of street light to trickle in. The window is mottled with rain. It splashes from the gutters onto the path below. From the village of Sandymount there is little to suggest activity, nothing more than the muffled sounds of distant drunks, wheeling around the green long after closing time. It's a couple of miles or so from Ranelagh, but another world entirely. Every night from my bed I hear cars swishing past, the drunken screeching of students on their way to a party in someone's flat, trucks making late-night deliveries. Down here, the silence lies heavy upon the night. I can hear the sea sucking at the sand, a swishing sound that seems only to come out at night, when everything else has quietened down to rest.

Adam is on his side, facing away from me. Asleep, I think. The duvet is bunched around his waist. I touch his back with my fingertips. His skin is warm. I turn once more to the window. Outside, the rain is starting up again, its intermittent patter shutting out the sounds of the sea. The patterns the drizzle is making as it rivers down the glass shift and disappear as quickly as they are made. Adam snuffles and shifts around. When he settles on his other side, his mouth at my shoulder, he kisses me.

I should respond in some way, but I prefer to watch the rain. There's something calm about the noise of it outside, as though it magnifies the silence in the room. I'm also not good with intimacy this early on with someone new. I can't help it. I want to be affectionate, to stroke skin, drop insubstantial kisses on whichever body part is nearest to me. I know the expected moves, and part of me yearns to make them, but I can't. Rejection horrifies me, and worse than that is the fear that I'll be found out, discovered for the phoney that I am, playing the part of a satiated lover. I'm no good at acting.

Adam's hand snakes onto my stomach. He splays his fingers on my skin, absent-minded in the rhythmless way he caresses me.

'Great skin,' he mumbles into my shoulder.

'It's just skin,' I say, moving so that his hands falls away. Men love to admire skin, whether or not they even notice it. I mean, it's just skin. Maybe it's because skin is easy to compliment, unlike hair (are you serious? It's horrible, you're mad) or bodies (God, I'm so fat) or even clothes (this old thing? I've had it for years).

'Never underestimate the power of good skin.' He pulls me in close to him. He rubs the pad of his thumb up my ribs, over my collarbone, then into the dip between my breasts. I give up and allow him. It feels too good not to. It's all so new, so unexpected, yet I can't relax. I wish he'd fallen asleep and left me to my contemplation of the rain. That way I could have become accustomed to being in a different bed, would have had the night to come to terms with the fact that the even breathing on the next pillow is not Isaac's, won't ever be Isaac's again. Adam draws me to him, and I empty my head of Isaac. When it is over, his fingers smoothe my face, my hair, my shoulders. I compare him to how Isaac used to be after we'd made love, how Isaac invariably plunged into sleep, like a stone, heavy and unaware.

'Eva.' Adam's voice is sleep-thickened.

'Yes?'

'Go to sleep.'

'I will.'

'Give all those thoughts a rest and just go to sleep.'

I tug the duvet up to my chin. I'm cold. I don't think I'll sleep, not in this strange bed, but maybe it's the weed that claims me, maybe it's the violence of the rain against the window as the wind picks up, possibly it's just plain exhaustion, but not long after Adam drifts off, I too succumb. It's probably the weed, but I sleep better on this rain-sodden night than I have in a long time.

'Have you ever been pregnant?'

The question is a shock, opening up the cold freeze of morning more effectively than any bucket of iced water to my face. Blindly, I feel my way along the rock wall of my grief, hands splayed, fingers twitching for something to grip. Adam is circling his fingertips on my stomach again. The clock says half past eight. Too early by far for such a question.

'What kind of a thing is that to ask me?'

Adam rolls onto his back. 'Shit. Sorry, you're right. That was way over the line.' He leans over to his bedside locker and takes a drink from a glass. Did he go downstairs during the night to get that while I slept?

'Why do you ask?' I shift, my back still to him. What is it about parents, this right they seem to acquire by reproductive osmosis, the right to assume that everyone else wants children, or has children, or spends their lives yearning for them?

'Just curious, I suppose. About you, your history.'

'Why?' I check the clock again. There is over an hour left before we need to leave. We have the first two classes off this morning, something to do with the computers being upgraded. 'Do you think I'm hiding my child from you?' I am aware of a rising edge to my voice. This is territory uncharted for me.

Adam shushes me, attempting to flatten the hackles his question has raised. 'Sorry, Eva. I don't even know why I asked.' I push the bedcovers to the side, thankful for the gloom of winter. Adam must have drawn the curtains during the night, probably when he fetched the glass of water. Then I notice a similar glass sitting by my side of the bed. Thoughtful. That was a thoughtful gesture. I elbow another photo of his daughter. Annalie, her name is Annalie. I shouldn't forget, because her photos are everywhere. Annalie, blonde and fantastic, strong and confident, smiling the same smile from every frame. I don't know how he can stand to live so far away from her. If she were my child, I'd wrap her in the softest blankets, crush her to me. Keep her safe.

I ward off Adam's apologies because this is something I will not discuss with him, with anyone. 'It's fine, no problem. I just need to get ready.' He points me in the direction of the towels.

The drive to school is quiet. Political discussion on the radio plugs the gap left by Adam's unprovoked question. It washes over me like sea foam, numbing in its repetition. The lies, the accusations, the nonsense about the imploded property market, as though property were the only thing wrong with this country. As though politicians and cute hoors hadn't been ripping Ireland off in every guise imaginable since the dawn of independence, and now, when they're still at it, people are somehow required to be surprised, shocked that any of this could have happened. I want to switch it off, all of it. I want to point the finger of blame at them all, the bankers, the politicos, all who allowed this to happen, with their mock shock, their disbelief that this could be happening to Ireland. Poster child for neo-liberal economics. Celtic Tiger indeed. Who actually believed that all Ireland needed was houses built on every cubic centimetre of land, badly constructed rubbish that would disintegrate with the arrival of the first heavy storms? Public money plundered for private gain, and now the public money will pay the private losses. A headline from the newspaper sometime in the past week said it all: privatise profits, nationalise losses.

I switch to a classical station. Vivaldi cuts through the strain in the air, kicks up its heels and mixes everything in its wake. Adam reaches too late to stop me.

'Hey, I was listening to that.'

'I've heard it all before. So have you.'

'That's not the point.'

I face him. His profile is in the shadow thrown by the visor in the sudden burst of late-winter lustre. The sky is water-washed, clean, uncertain. 'So what's the point, then?'

'If it's important, it needs to be said enough times to sink in.'

I sit back. 'Rubbish.'

Adam takes his eyes off the road for an instant. 'You're joking.'

'I'm not. Everyone knew what was going on here was ridiculous. I even knew it, and I haven't been here for a decade.'

'So you just ignore it now?'

This isn't what I'd expected so soon after being asked if I'd ever been pregnant, a political argument about the collective blindness of an entire nation in the face of sudden and inexplicable wealth.

'I didn't know you were political.' He pokes me in the soft part of my side. It tickles more than it hurts. I twist away. He does it again.

'Bugger off, Adam.'

He laughs out loud now. 'What's this? You're feisty?'

With laughter, I pinch him. The atmosphere has softened again. 'Leave me alone.'

'Seriously, I never had you down as political.'

'Why not? Because I don't talk endlessly about it?'

'Who did you vote for?' Adam pulls into the staff car park. He hauls the car into a narrow space between two SUVs. 'One day, I swear I'm going to leave notes on those fucking cars.' His leather bag is on the back seat. He grabs it. 'Who drives those things anyway? Idiots, that's who. The bigger the car, the bigger the asshole driving it.' He gropes under the sea of paper and homework notebooks on the back seat and pulls out a tatty history textbook and another even rattier anthology of war writing. 'Go on, McCain or Obama?'

I pull a spare scarf from my bag, rummage for my classroom key. 'I won't dignify that with a response.' I slap his hand away as he reaches to poke me again. His laugh is a shout in the empty air of the car park. The morning is one of those bright, cold affairs, all colour drained away by the heavy banks of cloud that are gathering again. The smell of rain hangs heavy about us, in puddles, on the wet shrubs, the leafless trees. It is both clean and tainted, a metallic edge to it. I breathe it in deeply, then twist my scarf around my neck in the hope that it will look as though I am not wearing the same clothes as yesterday, the day I did not attend the rugby match.

We drift apart before entering the school. I wonder if he has noticed the sudden change between us, how things seem lighter, easier, despite his intrusion. The word I am searching for is intimacy. Things are more intimate between us.

Further meditation is impossible in the swarm inside the building. I watch Adam's head bob among the boys, the high fives and greetings that he bestows, the shouts from the students that he never fails to respond to with wit. He fades into the crowd, swallowed by the mass of grey uniforms. I settle my skirt, smoothe my hair. The school day closes over my head like water.

CHAPTER 24

Aelita's child sits on the bottom step of the staircase, a picture book on his lap. He is absorbed by the colours, and doesn't notice me watching him. His name, I've learned, is Seamus. 'Beautiful Irish baby,' his mother proudly announced when I asked her about him. He accompanies her each week, and I assume to every job she does. Seamus doesn't seem traumatised by his mother's occupation with her work. He seems, in fact, to relish being close to her. He's quiet, but happy, and radiant when he glances at her. I observe him, observing her, and again there is that catch, that unnamed well of longing, its depths dark and unplumbed.

'Seamus?'

He stills the fingers that stroke the page of his book. His answer is silence.

'Would you like something to drink?'

Now that I have his attention, I'm not sure what I can offer him. A half-bottle of Russian vodka, procured in a discount German supermarket, and which I am avidly avoiding, is the only thing I can find besides coffee. A clutch of oranges languishes in a bowl. These I squeeze, then present to him on the stairs. He refuses to come into the kitchen, a shy shake of his head the only indication of his desire to stay put.

The child swallows the juice quickly, wipes his mouth with the back of his hand and hands me the glass. He does not leave the step.

'Seamus, you are behave, yes?' Aelita struggles down the stairs, a bucket filled with bottles in one hand, hauling the vacuum cleaner behind her. I take her cleaning supplies from her and deposit them on the hall floor.

'He's perfect,' I say. And I mean it. A perfect child. I wonder if Aelita knows how fortunate she is. My brother was perfect in that way in his baby pictures, all that smooth skin and plumpness, the huge eyes and fluffy hair. I sense him sometimes, here in the house. I don't mean his ghost is here; nothing as prosaic as that. It's more of a feeling, traces of him in rooms, behind doors, on creaking stairs. It's impossible to be here and not think of him. Death takes the physical person, but everything else is left intact, so much so that in the aftermath of Andrew's death I lived as though he were still alive. I brought him news from school, the remnants of fights with my mother, snippets of conversation, books I read. I brought them all, and more, to my dead brother, and I recounted it all to him, not forgetting he was gone, but not allowing it to get in the way.

And so the strangeness that had always been in our family, in this house, grew up around me, like grass in a neglected garden. My mother retreated further from me, and it suited me just fine. I wrote poetry, read books, studied for my exams and finished school. The strangeness stayed with me through university, but I was used to it. Like a parasitic limb, it became part of me. In the aftermath I took to wandering the house at night, after Maude and my mother had turned in. I walked through each room, touching things. A shawl Maude had crocheted, itchy, rough mohair that I couldn't tolerate against my bare skin. Cushions, curtains.

The wooden banister with its polished balusters. I bumped my fingertips along the wallpaper, the heavy flock velvety and unpleasant. In this desperate Braille I found little in the way of solace, but I kept on seeking proof of my own existence, waiting for something to reach out and touch me back, but nothing ever did.

When I ran out of things to touch, I took to sitting on the top step at the front of the house. I witnessed the slow change of summer to autumn, smelled the first fires of the season. Night fell easily and early, and my mother, mummified in her own private sadness, took to hibernating earlier and earlier. We never spoke of what we were going through. I was aware of her writing countless letters, watched her slip a memorial card of my brother into each envelope before sealing it, but I wasn't consulted or acknowledged. He was mine too, but it was as though I'd faded away.

In this way I let the shield harden, allowed it to become unmoveable. It was easier that way. I studied harder, got better marks, and eventually applied myself to my work with a dedication that I know I couldn't have mustered had there been distractions in my way.

Aelita wears a cross around her neck. It sits on a heavy silver chain, and she zips it from side to side when she looks out the window or stares into the middle distance. Maybe she prays. A priest I studied with asked me once about God. He was a kind man, with a brilliant mind. We developed a rapport based on mutual interest in each other's field. Dan was his name. He's a professor of poetry at a university in Vancouver now.

'What about God, Eva? Is there room for God in there?' His index finger tapped my temple gently.

There is no God for me. God's face remained stubbornly hidden when I was at my lowest. I'd never given him much thought before Andrew died, but afterwards he evaporated. Having no faith in a place like Ireland is difficult, especially when all around me people bathed in religious radiance. I waited for a sign after I found my brother, but none came. Eventually, what little belief I'd had petered out and expired. My mother had never wanted me; why would God be any different?

At Dan I had shrugged. 'It's a bit crowded in there, to be honest.'

'Just don't close off the possibility,' he'd said. And I had liked that. No dogma, no screaming insistence, just a gentle reminder.

Seamus tugs on my shirt tail. He holds out his book to me. 'Can you read?'

Aelita grabs the book from her son's hand. 'No!' Her other words are in Polish, but she lowers her voice in admonition. I know what she's saying. *Don't annoy her. Don't do anything but sit quietly. We need the money.* She puts the book in her bag by the door. Seamus sticks his lower lip out and sits back down on the stairs.

'It's fine,' I say to Aelita. 'I'll read to him.'

'No. He fine.' She pulls a yellow duster from her bucket. 'He like read with himself.'

'Really, Aelita, it's not a problem. I'd like to.' She doesn't believe me, but she shrugs and starts spraying polish on the hall table. I wait a second, then retreat. She is displeased, but she will never say so. I pay her, so she'll allow her son, albeit grudgingly, to have a book read to him by me.

Seamus retrieves the book from his mother's bag. He slips his small fingers in mine. Dry baby skin, warm softness. I want to squeeze his little hand, never let it go. The urge overwhelms me, catches me unawares. 37. The longing is only growing.

For someone my age, I've spent a surprisingly small amount of time with children. I'm almost nervous of this quiet child, with his solemn face and his big eyes. He sits on a chair, swinging his jeaned legs. I pull out a chair and ease myself in beside him. He shifts on his seat, moves closer to me.

The book is something bright and simply drawn, a story of a pig and her family. I finish reading in minutes, and Seamus sits on his chair, his face expectant. The clock hums on the wall, the same old electric clock from my childhood that I've always hated. It may have come from the farmhouse where we lived before my father died; I actually have no idea how it ended up on the wall in this city house, big, ugly thing that it is. I hate it because it's so old and unstylish. It's like something I remember on the walls in school when I was a child, functional and unsightly. The glass has been cracked down the centre of the face for as long as I can remember, and my mother never had it fixed because she couldn't get it off the wall. It's too high up, and Andrew was the only person who could reach it, standing on a chair. I mean, who even has electric clocks any more? It reeks of institutional living. I will hire a handyman and have it removed.

'Again,' Seamus says, patting the cover of the book. 'Read it again.'

We read the story of the cheerful pig three more times, until I finally close the book and place it face down on the table. When we have drawn and coloured on some paper that I had left on the table for making notes, I wonder what I should do with the child now. He does not get off his chair or call for his mother. Aelita has moved into the front room now, the vacuum cleaner muffled by the closed door.

I move to the fridge. 'Would you like something to eat?'

Seamus shakes his head. He looks up at me. 'My dada,' he begins, then breaks off. 'My dada.'

Where is his father? Aelita wears no ring. Is the man in Latvia or Poland? Somewhere far away, unreachable to this small boy? Do they talk to him, about him? I was a child with no father, and his absence was keenly felt. I was 4 when we left, 5 when he died, and we never spoke of him. We weren't allowed to.

The night we left was a warm one. My parents had been fighting all day. Mostly it was my mother fighting, hissing at my father so we wouldn't hear, her anger a rattlesnake in the quiet confines of the small farm, her face an abstraction of fury. Andrew and I were sent out to feed chickens, play in the fields, anything that would keep us out of the house. The day was hot, the mute dryness of the midland air rendering it difficult to amuse ourselves. When we weren't chasing hens in the yard or letting the calves suck our fingers with their rough black tongues, we sat in the shade and made up games and willed the time away, the cornerless sky stretching beyond us and our sheltered, rural world. We hid outside the kitchen door, beside the boot scraper, and listened as words we didn't understand drifted to us. *Degrading, demented, disgraceful, damnation.* I stored their alliteration in my alphabetic mind, their sounds washing me.

Later, Andrew and I were ready for bed, our pyjamas too warm in the sullen heat. The order to go upstairs never came, and we sat in the living room, our father's jazz records strewn on the floor, the volume on the television turned up high. Tension filled the small house.

I was asleep in the overstuffed armchair when my mother woke me, roughly jostling my shoulder. She ushered Andrew and me into the car. We were going to Dublin, she said, to the place she was from.

Like a sleepwalker, I stumbled to the car, loose gravel sticking to the soles of my bare feet.

'Ow!' I hopped, my foot punctured by a sharp stone.

'*Get in the car.*' She brooked no argument.

'And Daddy?' I asked her, fretful of leaving him behind. He was such a gentle soul, his feelings often hurt by my mother's abrasiveness.

Her face was obscured by a box she carried. 'He's busy. Don't start arguing with me over this.'

But it was dark, and there was no work to do on the farm when it was dark in summertime, unless a cow was calving or there was some other emergency. My father wasn't around as my mother stuffed our things into the boot of the old Hillman Hunter, her movements frenzied.

The red leatherette seats were still warm from the day's sultriness, the pattern of tiny holes textured under my hands.

'Why isn't Daddy coming with us?' Andrew wanted to know.

'Because he isn't.' My mother started the car, swearing when it didn't turn over the first time.

'But I want him to come too.' My brother started to cry.

My mother leaned over and slapped his pyjamaed leg. He howled louder. One of the farm dogs barked into the quiet night. I stared at our house, the grey brickwork matte black in the overwhelming darkness, perfect as an illustration. All the lights had been turned off except the small lamp in the corner of the kitchen. The windowpane threw the muted light into the night.

'Stop that this instant. Daddy's busy. He's not coming with us.'

Eventually, Andrew stopped crying when my mother let him sit in the front with her. I was pleased to have the whole back seat to myself. The seat was shiny and slippery, and I could sit where I pleased. Kneeling up, I gazed out the back window at the thumbnail moon, curving in the carbon paper sky, the stars scattered like glitter.

We left sleeping towns in our wake, the indifferent landscape swallowing them whole. My mother kept the radio on, nothing but the white noise of static as we passed through long stretches of countryside. She didn't speak to me once during the journey, and I was glad.

Dublin, when we arrived, was another world. Its strangeness was unlike anything I could have imagined at 4 years of age. We passed traffic lights, their lollipop colours changing before my eyes. I begged my mother to wait so I could watch the lights change again, red to green to orange to red. She tutted with her habitual impatience and told me not to be such a nuisance. Traffic lights weren't for admiring. Yet they were. I'd never beheld them before, and they stood to attention in the metropolitan landscape, coloured sentinels in the navy night. Row after row of buildings slipped by outside the car window, railings encasing them in a silent embrace. The river was dark, unmoving, the street lights in their curlicues reflected imperfectly in the glazed water. I poked Andrew to wake him, to show him the hugeness of the sleeping city, its bizarre components, but he mumbled thickly in his sleep and turned away.

Seamus traces a hairline crack in the table's surface. It leads nowhere. 'Would you like to draw something else?' I ask him. Again, that childish shake of the head, side to side, his fringe swinging. I am exhausted. It's been possibly ten minutes, and I'm spent. How do people do this? What spurs them on, allows them to keep on asking and offering, coming up with new things to suggest and proffer? Adam's daughter arrives next week. He has made me promise to spend at least one day with them. Where will I find the resources? I place my hand on Seamus's. Surprised, he looks up at me. His smile splits his lovely face in two. With his free hand, he pats my cheek.

'Eva.' He pronounces it *Ava*. 'Eva, more book.'

As we finish the book again, Aelita appears, summoned as though by magic, at the kitchen door. She is shrugging on her raincoat, pulling her ponytail out of the collar. 'Is all finish. Mrs Maude she is finish too. Next week same, yes?'

I say yes and pass her an envelope with her pay. All cash. No cheques, ever, just hard cash.

She holds Seamus's coat out. 'Come now, Seamus.'

With a nod at me, she turns. The door closes behind her.

In the silence that follows, I remain in the kitchen. I can hear Maude's door open, then close. Back from bridge. Then the muffled sounds of her at home, the dulled noise of the television, the creak of ancient plumbing. I will visit her in a few minutes, bring her something to eat and the day's paper. Maybe next time Aelita comes I'll bring Seamus down for a visit. Pretend to myself for ten minutes that he's mine.

CHAPTER 25

Leafing through a book, I find the photograph. Isaac and me. Summer three years ago. All photos of us were deliberately left behind in New York. Those that I didn't destroy.

Holding it is a shock. His face, so handsome. Those angular cheekbones, the brown eyes. The linen shirt. His arm encircling my shoulders, holding me close, as though I mattered. As though he loved me.

It is my face, though, that amazes me the most. My face, that laughing, smiling, happy person. My eyes on him, all my attention focused on the man holding me.

A day trip to Coney Island. Crushed on the subway with the tourists, the beachgoers and the Brooklynites, on the hottest day so far of that summer. A child near me cried the whole way, his mother holding him on her ample lap while fanning herself with a magazine. It had been my idea, one that Isaac had scoffed at, but I wanted to go. Seven years in New York and I hadn't made it as far as the end of the subway line. We had a good day, a very good day. A stroll on the boardwalk, hotdogs, the freedom just to be with him and not have to consider our moves in case we ran into someone. Not that bumping into acquaintances is a common problem in New York City, but Isaac was careful. New York is a city so busy with itself, so self-obsessed, that it doesn't notice anyone else. There is a relief in that, something that doesn't exist in Dublin, although there is something nice about seeing a familiar face when I'm out and about here, a sense of belonging to something whole.

I stroke his face in the photo.

The end came quickly, as it turned out. The decision was mine, but I can't say that Isaac objected.

I'd gone back to Manhattan for a week from LA. I was due to give a paper at a seminar in NYU, and despite the fatigue and nausea that swirled around me at a constant and astonishing pace, I managed to deliver the paper, answer questions, and appear to all concerned as though I were one more busy academic, flying in from one big city to another, a whistle-stop tour, and the end of a fragile hope that I'd foolishly allowed myself to be duped by.

The heating in my apartment building was broken. The Salvadorean super was sick, and for three days I baked in an abundance of calefaction. Added to the nausea, it was too much. I called Isaac.

'We need to talk.'

'Sure, sweets.' It had never irritated me before that he referred to me as *sweets* when he wasn't about to do what I wanted, but now I positively raged.

'I'm pregnant.' This, delivered before he had taken his coat off or shaken the early spring rain from his hat. This, thrown at him as he dawdled in the doorway of my third-floor apartment in the East Village, where the heating was broken and the Dominican neighbours screamed at each other over the blare of television. *Te odio! Cabron! Puta! Te voy a matar!*

'You're fucking joking.' The professor of English, swearing. It wasn't something I was used to hearing. Next question: 'How long?'

Deflated, I turned from him. 'Oh, don't worry. I'm well within the limits.'

'Thank God.' He followed me and sat down in the tiny kitchen, at the table barely big enough for two people. The window looked out over the fire escape, a jigsaw of rusty ladders at diagonals up and down the building. I leaned on the sink.

'Don't you even want to talk about it?' I asked.

'And say what? I don't want a child. You don't want one either.'

But had he asked me? The question was too big to discuss in a miniscule kitchen, amid potted plants and shelves buckling under the weight of books. It needed space, light, air to breathe. Room to change minds, if that's what was required.

'How would you know what I want? Have you ever even asked me what I want?' I hadn't meant to scream at him. This was supposed to be a dignified conversation. 'Do you think I want this, this tiptoeing around, this constant pretence when everyone, absolutely everyone knows exactly what we're up to?'

Isaac's head shot up. Something sparked in those brown eyes. 'What do you mean?'

It took a lot of effort not to throw something at him. 'I mean that everyone knows I'm fucking the star professor. Or maybe that he's fucking me? In every possible way.'

'Don't be childish.'

It was meant to be a dialogue between two adults discussing this new fork in their road.

It dawned that I was on that road alone.

Isaac pinched the bridge of his nose. 'Jesus, Eva. We're not 17.'

'What does that have to do with anything? You're 52, for Christ's sake! *52!* A rush of despair jangled my nerves. I'd thought that maybe things would be different after his disastrous trip to LA. I'd even stopped drinking.

'I'm too old for a child.' And suddenly he looked it, as though something had veiled him up to this point. A sprinkling of grey in the cropped hair. A huddle of wrinkles at his eyes, the slight sag under his chin.

I was alone. I was thousands of miles from home, with no one around me. He'd become my family, and like families always do, he'd let me down.

'Then you have to leave.'

His fingertips rubbed at a worn patch on the kitchen table. Despite the white walls, the pale floor, the tasteful photographs and my shelves of books, my apartment looked like the shoebox it was. Who was I kidding? I was a 36-year-old washed-up poet, with a job in academia that I enjoyed, but it was still only a job. I was fooling myself if I thought it was any substitute for writing. I earned a good salary, I had tenure, I was a regular on the publication circuit. There was plenty to be positive about, and I was proud of my achievements, but little about my life appealed to me at that instant. And I had no one to share it with, not really.

'Eva.' His voice tripped over the syllables. 'Eva. What should we do?'

My elbows throbbed from leaning on the cold porcelain of the Belfast sink. I turned to face him. 'What do you want to do?'

'Not this.' The words were soft, his voice gentle, measured. If I hadn't been involved in the conversation, had I been merely eavesdropping, I would have thought myself an intruder on lovers' whispers.

I picked up an uncorked wine bottle, left over from God knows when, splashed the remaining wine, stale now and vinegary, over him, and threw the bottle at his head. I missed and it smacked off the cupboard behind him and smashed into a thousand pieces. '*I'm* sick, *I'm* pregnant. *You're* the one who's supposed to do something.'

'What can I do?'

'Go fuck yourself.' My hands shook. They itched to slap him as my mother had slapped me, numberless times.

'But you need help.'

I almost felt sorry for him, his ruined shirt and lack of comprehension of what it was to be me. All that time together and he didn't know me at all.

'Get out, Isaac.' I slumped back into the chair. 'Just go home to your wife and your childless life and leave me the fuck alone.'

He didn't go. Instead, he lifted cups from the draining board, filled the kettle, rummaged for teabags in the caddy. While the kettle boiled, he swept up the glass shards. The pieces clinked as he put them in the bin. 'I'm not going anywhere. You can't be alone and I'm not leaving.'

My burst of energy seeped away. I slumped in my chair, gazed at the free world outside the tiny kitchen window. The sky was the colour of tin, the beaten metal of a cold spring in New York. The roosters on the roof of the next building protested, their squawking even more irritating than it was at dawn each day. I cursed the person who'd put them there, some Puerto Rican who thought they reminded him of home. I was sick of Manhattan, of the great divide between rich and poor, its litter and noise, the filthy human carousel that I needed to get off.

'I'm sorry, Eva.'

His apology fell into the abyss. There was, quite simply, nothing left to say.

When Isaac finally departed, I wrapped myself in the huge wool blanket he'd bought for my birthday. Soft, finely woven, outrageously expensive cashmere in the palest blue. Baby blue. Stepping onto the fire escape, I unscrewed the bottle of Jameson I'd bought in the Irish shop in the village and drank it straight from the neck. A police siren shrieked down in the street. Homeless people slammed dumpster lids, scavenging for yesterday's scraps.

I finished the rest of the whiskey. The cold darkness gathered and swallowed the activities in my neighbours' homes. The other apartments rang with someone's laughter, a handful of cracked notes on a trumpet, an old piano playing ragtime.

A child's mitten lies on the hall floor. Hand-knitted in chunky wool, it has a piece of elastic with an open safety pin at the top. It probably fell off as Aelita hurried her child into his coat. I inhale it, the wool scratching at my nose. Whatever it is I'm searching for it's not in this piece of childish apparel, with its smell of fabric conditioner and bubble gum. What I search for cannot be found.

Isaac accompanied me to the clinic, a discreetly private oasis of pale carpets and walls, good prints of Impressionist paintings and uncrumpled magazines. He paid in advance with his credit card and left before I saw the doctor, because I insisted. I insisted because it was the only way I could convince myself that I was doing the right thing. We'd barely spoken since the wine throwing. Turns out our love was brittle after all, dismantled by the unwarranted entrance into our lives of unplanned upheaval. The disappointment that he was just like everyone else was grinding. Love conquers little in the end. I stood at the reception desk and watched his tall figure disappear through the automatic doors.

I haven't seen him since.

Maude's name appears on the screen of my phone. 'Eva?'

She invites me down for dinner. It's nice to be asked. I offer to cook, which she accepts readily. I suspect she just wants company.

A nurse brought me into the examination room. I clutched the positive lab slip in my sweating hand, held onto it while she placed my shaking legs in stirrups, covered me from the waist down with a white paper sheet. The table was cold beneath me.

'You're absolutely sure you want to do this?' she asked, smoothing the sheet, then transferring her stroking fingers to my arm. I wanted to lie there forever, pretend she was my mother. I could have cried just from the kindness of her touch. She was about my age. I felt decades older.

I'd been through it all, the questions, conclusions, the scenarios I'd run ragged through my aching brain. I nodded. 'I'm sure.' Isaac hadn't probed, hadn't wished to break the thin membrane of relief that he was getting off so lightly. If I said to the nurse that I wanted to come back another day, I knew I wouldn't return.

She touched my hand, her fingers cool and dry. 'It's not as bad as you think.' Her smile was the most real thing about that room, with its scrubbed white walls and sterilised steel equipment. Her shoes squeaked softly on the tiled floor.

In the kitchen, I begin to make dinner. Nothing too complicated, just some chicken and rice. Maude loves rice. The water boils in the saucepan, and I cover it, the steam hot on my skin.

I wished Isaac had offered to marry me. Abandon his Upper West wife, with her trench coats and expensive shoes, and come and live with me. Even lying on that cold steel table, in the moments before the anaesthetic claimed me, before the doctor scraped my insides clean, I hoped he would come back, do everything I thought was mainstream and predictable, and carry me out of that expensive, hushed necropolis.

The sadness had an iron fist, and it gripped my soul in a vice. Afterwards, when I was empty, lying in recovery, I watched the light change shape on the white ceiling. Afternoon, mid afternoon, evening. I was staying the night. I hadn't wanted to, but Isaac insisted. The nurse recommended it. Isaac said it was the least he could do.

It was the only thing he could do. A private room in a private clinic would have cost him, the bill a stain on his credit card account. He would quickly expunge it with justified self-assurance, seek solace in his wife's inheritance, which allowed such extravagances to pass invisibly by.

They used words in the clinic. *Procedure. Operation. Excision.* Or what I had, dilation and curettage. The removal of that which remains. All spoken in the language of denial. I was as guilty as anyone who worked there. I described what had taken shape inside me as a foetus, an embryo, a zygote. Anything but baby. Never baby.

They filled me with pills, and I slept like a body buried. The cold blue light of my mind extinguished temporarily, the whirling regrets put to rest for a while. I departed the next day, the tablets leaving me with a head that felt stuffed with sponges. Physically, I felt fine. Inside, I was as far removed from the streets of New York City as it was possible to be.

It was one of those April days in Manhattan, when the sun was so bright against the windows that it hurt my brain.

The city gargled dust trapped between its buildings. Sirens split the metropolis open, its wounds gaping and bleeding for anyone to see.

On the subway back to my apartment, I observed everyone go by, all of them cheerful and young. The train window resisted my finger as I wrote a word on it. *Mother.* I quickly wiped through it. No one had seen me. Not a mother any more. I hadn't allowed myself to think about it, but I already missed what I was not going to be.

Not *Mother.* Not *Mama.*

What deluged me, brimmed inside me until I thought I would melt on the subway floor, was too much to be called grief. I kept expecting to cry, but how could tears help? Sorrow as deep as the dark doesn't allow for tears. It freezes them, sends them scuttling to a fathomless place, never to be found. In the abyss, tears have no function.

I hardly knew who or what I was. I offered up thanks for the lingering remains of the medication. At least my mind only functioned at its most basic level.

I craved obliteration, instant obliteration, but I had no energy to throw myself in front of a car. I desired anything that would release me from the endless breathing and moving and grieving that constituted living.

I understood how my brother had killed himself. The sirens had sung too sweetly to be ignored, preening themselves on their chilly rocks, waving their arms in invitation to those undone. The promise of a land not ruled by despair, that gelid god.

It would be so easy. Just a mouthful of vodka and a fistful of pills.

But I didn't have the courage to do it.

Spooning rice onto plates. Stirring chicken in a dish. These small tasks keep my mind from straying too far into the darkness. They moor me, vessel of sorrow that I am. It is easy to do this, to put rice on a plate and take it downstairs to where my great-aunt waits, her swollen leg raised on a footstool, the day's paper on the sofa beside her. These are the things that can keep the night at bay.

I have no choice but to keep afloat.

CHAPTER 26

Andrew's anniversary is marked by a brief notice in the *In Memoriam* column of today's paper. Maude must have put it in; it has never occurred to me that this is what should be done. I suppose she is following what my mother most likely did each year at this time. I have remembered my brother constantly, but most especially on this day of days.

The sky is blocked by ravaged clouds the colour of molten lead, and the wind rattles the windows and doors. Cold air slips through every gap, sending the temperature indoors lower than it has any right to be. It is one of those Irish spring days, a day when it seems as though winter will never leave, as though we are condemned to inhabit for eternity a world of razor-toothed winds and shining sleet. Ice frosts the grass, makes the daffodils bow their heads in sorrow. People scurry by outside, bent into the gusts. This is the second wave of morning people, fewer now, their hurry less urgent than those who thronged the path two hours before. These are the less employed, perhaps, the elderly, the housewives, the students. Their time is more elastic than those who cram onto buses, into cars, pack the bike lanes between the hours of seven and nine.

I'm not going to school this morning. I didn't offer an explanation for my absence, nor was I asked for one when I rang the office two hours ago. My coffee cools in its cup as I sit in the chair by the window, the same chair in which my brother slowly unravelled. The paper is folded on my lap, the deaths column open. Hatched, matched and despatched, my mother liked to call the announcements page in what must have been a rare occurrence of humour. I wonder if many will read the notice, its careful wording. Irish people love death, though, and its offshoots: removals, wakes, Masses, flowers and cards, not to mention the funerals themselves. Nowhere else would people travel great distances, take time off work, rearrange entire days because someone has died. In New York, invitations are issued to funerals. There is no question of merely turning up at the church. Americans aren't interested in death the way Irish people are. They don't drive for hours to attend a removal, or wonder who will tend their grave when they themselves are gone. Most of the Americans I know would be happy to have a quick cremation and for their ashes to be scattered in a place beloved by them. Funerals are bigger than Christmas here, and they last almost as long. Not for the first time, I feel the distance between the life I've lived in the States and what I ran from here.

My phone squawks beside me. Maude. It's time to leave for the church.

Since Andrew died, his funeral and that of my mother are the only occasions that have lured me to Mass. Religion is not something that intrudes upon the diurnal arrangements of my life. It's not even that I despise it, or rail against its injustices and elitism. I simply don't care about it. I find it, at best, an irritation, something to be avoided. Religious people are not counted among my friends, and if pushed, I admit to a yearning for a time when religious discourse is no longer in the public arena.

Maude would disagree with me were I to air my opinions. She walks beside me now, her hand linked through my arm. She requires neither walking stick nor help; she simply enjoys the physical contact, and I am again guilty for not spending more time with her.

The church's spire rises above the surrounding houses, a pleasing mix of pre- and post-war architecture, where red brick dominates. The money of the past decade or more is visible in the renovated houses, the skips outside, the huge cars, the security cameras on the widened gateways. It's all so ridiculous, so redolent of money easily gained that it leaves an aftertaste of nouveau riche lingering in the air. We battle with the wind. It gnaws at our cheeks, stings our eyes and whips our clothes into an insane dance of coat-tails and scarves.

The service is as it always was, and I slip into the automatic responses to prayers and psalms. I feel hypocritical, standing and kneeling, murmuring dormant refrains, remembering cast-off snatches of benediction. The priest reads notices, reminds his flock of active retirement meetings, AA groups, flower-arranging classes and a talk on local heritage that will be given by a well-known journalist.

I'm waiting for the names of the dead to be read out, and suddenly there they are, several names, Billy and Bridie and Molly and Willie, all those old names, old people's names, and as I wait for my brother's name I hear it, but it's wrong. Anthony Perry. The priest stumbles, corrects himself. Andrew Perry. And the moment is gone, replaced by more names, more Marys and Johns, Bridgets and Josephs.

I glance at Maude to see if she's noticed the glitch, but her eyes are closed. The priest has moved on to other things. He glides around his altar, king of his territory, green robes swishing as he moves.

I realise that my grief, this steel cage I've inhabited for over twenty years, is just someone else's mispronunciation, a name on a list among others' dead. Grief has claimed such a huge part of me for its own. It has blunted me, stolen some element of me that I didn't even comprehend was being taken until it was too late. And I have been the loser.

Is there a choice for me? Will I be the same each year I mark my brother's death, a year older, but still stuck inside, still 16 and finding the body of the one person I loved, looking for all the world as though he had just slipped into sleep?

My mother may have been the same, but she had her whole life up to Andrew's death to be whomever she wanted to be. Was it the same for her? Was she the object of pity, the one others shook their heads about, secure in their conviction that she never got over her son's death? She didn't; this I know for sure. I know it because I never got over it either. Since Andrew left us I have been aware of a certain detachment that has grown up within me, something that often keeps me present in flesh only, while my spirit lingers outside the window, observing all that unfolds in my life.

The priest speaks of earthly flesh, of its return to dust at the closing of day. Where does it all go to, all this earthly flesh, this human substance? Where does the knowledge go, the bits of ourselves we have given to others, and the parts of those others we retain after they themselves have left us, we who are the repository? The air in the church is heavy, ponderous with absence, with loss, the loss of the Marys and Johnnys, the Jims and Annies. Who are the bearers of them?

Incense thickens the still air. The priest mumbles over the consecration. The sparse congregation kneels and stands like puppets on invisible strings. Maude pats my arm and I place my hand on hers and hold it there.

Outside, Maude thanks the priest by name. I linger by the gate, not wishing to be drawn in to questions I can't answer. The priest, his green robes gone now, replaced by plain black and the white flash at his throat, glances my way. I lift my eyes to the sky. It is the colour of ash.

'Will we go to the grave?' Maude asks, as she tucks her hand in the crook of my arm.

I shake my head. 'No. If you don't mind.' I've been there once, and for now that's enough.

Maude doesn't ask again. This time we are blown from behind as we make our way home, our path eased by the wind at our backs. We pause for Maude to rest at a low wall. She eases herself onto it, rubs her knee and then her hip.

'Let me tell you this, Eva.' I turn to her. 'There is nothing glamorous about getting old. All this,' she gestures at the offending body parts, 'this pain and discomfort. It's awful.'

I want to say something, to offer some sort of comfort, but Maude busies herself, standing and brushing her coat down with her gloved hands. Instead, I give her my arm again, which she squeezes as we begin again our walk home.

CHAPTER 27

Inotice a man a few mornings later as I leave for school.
He is standing at the bus stop a couple of houses down,
but the bus arrives and takes off again and still the man
lingers. Something about him catches my attention, but I'm
not sure what it is. Maybe it's his coat, an expensive city coat,
all navy wool, single breasting and immaculate tailoring,
or maybe it's the similarity in his age to my father, to how
old he would be if he were alive today. The man brushes
early cherry blossom off his shoulders, fallen in a flurry as
a sudden gust of wind shakes the branches of the trees.
Already, too many blossoms lie banked along the footpath,
turning brown at the edges. Indifferent feet trample them in
the early morning rush.

I should think about my father more than I do, and
maybe I did, once, when I had capacity for other deceased
members of my family. Sometimes I'm aware of how much
headspace my brother occupies, yet I have no choice but to
return to him, the original source of my sorrow, and touch
every pouch of pain, feel every throb. There's no doubt that
it is worse here than it is in New York. There, somehow,
none of it seems as real as it does in Dublin. In Manhattan
I can think of Andrew at a remove, without having to

live in our childhood home, without having to be around reminders of him that keep tearing strips of skin off the buried wounds. Pain changes shape, moves around, slips to the back of my mind on good days.

Today I'm more rushed than usual. Sean shuffles behind me, his finger hooking the back of his shoe, pulling it on. His hair is flattened by his beanie, absurdly blond against the black wool.

'Wait up, Eva,' he says, his breath pluming in the early morning light.

'Can't,' I say, eager to be gone. 'I'll be late.'

'Well, drop by later. Or call me.' He puts his thumb to his ear, his little finger to his mouth, the universal gesture of staying in touch. It makes his youth ridiculous, even more pronounced than it should be. That's when the man at the bus stop catches my attention. He is much older, late sixties at least, yet I think that I probably would have more in common with someone of his age than I do with Sean.

I return the gesture, feeling more like Sean's mother than his accidental lover. 'Okay.' Happy, he ambles off in search of coffee, or more sleep.

There had been no intention of sleeping with Sean again, and it happened by accident more than anything else. Another chance meeting at the café, followed by a pizza in one of the eateries in Ranelagh that has managed to stay afloat in the midst of the wreckage. He is leaving for Australia in a month, so it was an easy decision. No strings, no chance of it leading anywhere. I kept all thoughts of Adam firmly out of my head, and even now, watching Sean's shoulders hunched against the cold and the cruelty of an early wake-up call, I don't feel guilty. Proud, maybe, of having nabbed such a beautiful man for a fling, slightly sorry that he's going away, and secure in knowing that I won't hurt him. He is moving on to bigger things. This interlude I will remember with pleasure.

The sky is flinty, coated in a jumble of silvered clouds. I wrap my scarf tightly around my neck. Jesus, this climate is unforgiving. New York is cold, and the snow can be relentless, but I'd forgotten how the damp in Ireland gets into your bones, settles in deep. The east wind shreds my skin. Apart from the blooming trees, there is barely a hint of the spring we should be in. The budding branches are spines against the opalescent sky. I blow on my hands.

A bus arrives, and the man steps back. He looks out of place here, slightly lost. I pass him, my book bag heavy on my shoulder. When I glance back he is watching me, but he turns away before I do.

Adam plonks coffee down beside me. It slops and splashes the book I am trying to read. I brush the offending liquid away. The mug is staffroom standard issue. In black lettering is printed *I love spreadsheets*, with a red heart substituting the word *love*. Whose job description is it to come up with such phrases, such corporate jargon? Maybe there is irony somewhere in there, but I can find no evidence of it, and I have essays that I need to return to the boys that I just can't get started on.

I make room for him at the table. The stack of essays sits in a pile. I move them to the windowsill. The radiator pumps out heat. I remove my cardigan, smoothe my shirt. Tom Ford, bought in a sale in Manhattan, a fraction of their original price, and I love wearing them. I understand the attraction of expensive clothes, the quiet power that wearing them imparts.

'So, Annelie's arriving on Saturday,' he says, his cheer exposed, shining.

I sip from my spreadsheet mug. 'Great!'

'You won't back out, will you? From agreeing to spend a day with us?'

Sean's nakedness presses itself to the fore of my mind. He is full of youthful swagger, a bravado that anyone could puncture with one misplaced word, one careless swipe.

Adam and I are not a couple. I must remind myself of that fact each time Sean cavorts in my head. We've yet to have that discussion, and I find I've been waiting to have it, am anxious to know what Adam thinks of me beyond conversation and sex. Lately, when he is absent, I think of little else: Adam in his car, Adam at the Picassos, Adam in his house, Adam sharing my pillow, his hair over his eyes, a half-smile playing about his lips.

And, my God, the sex is so damn good.

Outside the staffroom window, thick drops of rain start to fall. The fluorescent ceiling lights are yellow in the reflection. It is mid morning, but it looks like early evening. This was the kind of day my brother died on, cold and wintry, the daylight leeched by an overhang of cloud and sleet.

Adam nudges me. 'So?'

Of course I'll meet his child. 'Sure.'

'Great! Want one?' He offers me an unwrapped piece of wax paper, in which are squares of brownies. 'Left in by a grateful mother.'

'Grateful for what, you dirty old man?' Pat, the PE teacher is sitting behind us, listening to every word we say. 'I know what you're like around those mothers.' He slaps his thigh, hoots with laughter. I roll my eyes at Adam.

'Yeah, yeah, you just wish you had my gifts.'

Pat slaps Adam on the back. 'I might even be as lucky as you with the good doctor there.'

My eyes widen so far that for a second I think they'll never close again. 'What did you say?'

Pat stops. 'Jesus, Eva. Sorry about that.'

'Don't tell me. It just came out of your mouth before you had time to think, right?'

He looks abashed. Adam laughs, winks at me.

'Come over later,' Adam says as he leaves the table. 'I missed you last night.'

I shake my head. 'Can't.' Two men in two nights? I mean, I could, of course, but I'm already regretting slightly last night's encounter with Sean. If anything is to happen with Adam, if we are to make anything out of this friendship-with-benefits, it can't happen if I'm sleeping with someone else. I've wondered about a future with Adam, and each time I erase it from my mind before it's had time to take shape. Adam will stay in Dublin. His first responsibility is to his child. As it should be. That's how these things work. Annalie comes first.

Before the bell rings for the next class, the rain has turned to hail, the slush piling up quietly outside, gathering on the granite windowsill, on the teachers' cars, on the front playing field. Fat, wet granules stick to the glass beside where I sit, pausing as if in shock, before melting slightly and zigzagging down the pane.

Jim Collins strides into the staffroom, rubbing his hands together briskly. Surely he cannot be cold? The school is ridiculously overheated today. Something to do with the thermostat getting stuck. A handyman was being sought when I arrived in this morning. The elderly caretaker is unable to fix it.

'Eva,' he nods as he passes. 'No matches today, I'm afraid.'

I murmur my sorrow at such news.

'So,' Jim announces to the few teachers in the room. 'If this keeps up we'll have to close a bit early. I'll have to get the whole system shut off. Terrible waste of money, all this heat and the windows open.'

'There'll be no coming in to make up the lost class, will there, Jim?' A geography teacher, Bernie, looks up from the newspaper.

'I'll have the parents on the phone within minutes,' Jim says, ignoring him. 'Anyway, decision taken. We'll close before the last class.'

A mild cheer goes up in the staffroom. Jim Collins sighs.

Bernie shakes his newspaper. 'Better hope it doesn't snow, right, Jim?'

'Don't even mention it, or we'll be in over Easter making up the days for sure.'

I slip out as soon as the bell has rung. The boys are milling around the corridors, shouting, high-fiving each other, throwing books around. It's only an early finish, nothing to get too excited about, but the air is giddy, festive with the elongated afternoon. They really are only kids, and I envy them their youth, their ability to still be excited by a missed class. I want to tell them to slow down, to stay young for as long as they can, but I know they wouldn't listen to me even if I could say such a thing to them. They're in too much of a rush to get somewhere else, when really all they're doing is running frantically into the future, eyes blindfolded, hands tied behind their backs. They need their hands held, they need help with all the big decisions that lurk ahead. Probably, they just need their mothers.

I see the man again, the man in the expensive coat. He sits in the window of the café, a newspaper open on the table in front of him. I push the door in, order a double espresso, and for a second our eyes meet before we both look away. We do not affect recognition from this morning. Probably he does not remember seeing me.

I don't know him, but I could. He has a look that I've seen many times before, an aura almost. Money gives you that, that confidence, and so too, sometimes, does age. He is quite like how I imagine Isaac will be eventually, older, confident, assured.

I sit behind him, finally able to open my book. A copy of today's paper is folded on the table. Someone has filled in half of the crossword and all of the sudoku. I read a few pages, but my attention wanders, drawn to the street outside and the melting hailstones gathered in soft drifts at the kerb and along the windowsill. Insanely, it is starting to snow. There are early blossoms on a few trees, and blunt flakes of snow are whirling past the window.

When I step outside, traffic is crawling along the main road. The street is hushed in a way I do not recall having witnessed before. How white it is becoming all around me, how white and silent and thick. The web of snowflakes thronging the air parts for me as I make my way the short distance to the house. My face stings from the cold. My lungs drag in ice with each breath. The stillness is clean, devoid of anything that could blemish the as yet untainted transparency. It was on one such day that my brother left us for good.

CHAPTER 28

It is late when I wake. The Roman blind is half up, and the brightness of morning has edged its way into the bedroom. I check my clock. Half past eight. If school isn't closed, I'll be late.

Outside, the garden is suffused with white. I make my way to my mother's room and look out the front. The main road is thronged with cars, all of them stalled, going nowhere. Footprints darken the paths, inches deep. A blackbird hops across the snowy front lawn, a smudge of jet against the pillowy mass.

I dutifully check the school website. Closed, due to unforeseen weather. I ring Maude to see if she needs anything, then lay a fire and heap blankets on the couch.

Andrew, our lost boy, sat by the window in this room, and slowly allowed the pandemonium of his inner life to consume him. I suppose we shouldn't have been surprised by his death, but we were. It shocked us to the core. My mother, of course, blamed me for it. *You knew!* she shrieked at me, when the doctor had been called and she and Maude had finally returned home from bridge. *This is your fault! You knew he was going to do this and you didn't stop him!* Did I know? Had I known what waited for me behind the door of his room that cold day? Sometimes I imagine Andrew's ghost is around me, a wisp, an ethereal presence upon hushed air. Insubstantial. I have questions for him, answers I still seek all these years later. What could I have done to save him? How did I fail him, our beautiful, lost boy? The density of these questions weighs on me now as the fat snowflakes swirl from the platinum sky. Jesus, yesterday there were early cherry blossoms on the wind; today, I'm piling sticks and peat to ward off a freeze.

What could I have done to stop it all? Time has accumulated like dust, and like dust it runs through my fingers whenever I try to hold it.

Then, as now, it was March, a month so cold it hardened and froze any warmth that tried to filter through the leaden clouds. A week's worth of bad snow lay dirty in the streets, piled up and icy along the walls and in the gutters. Andrew was calm, had been for a few days. He sat by the window, his head turned to the outside world, which carried on regardless. We had come to an arrangement, Maude, my mother and I, that he would always be within our sights. We agreed that it would a discreet observation, that whichever of us was in the room with him would be engaged fully in a task other than minding Andrew in his chair by the window.

It was a long weekend, and I was compiling poems for a small poetry press that was interested in reading some of my work. My mother and Maude were playing bridge, an afternoon game, one of those competitions that go on for hours. It wasn't until I needed to contact them that I realised I had no idea where they were even playing. Andrew had taken his meds and was quiet in his chair. A music magazine lay open on the coffee table, but he did not touch it. I read and reread my poems, then rang the editor who wanted to publish them and spent half an hour talking to him. I remember being enthralled by the possibility of a book of my work being in print. I was 16, and it gave me a foothold in a world yet to be imagined.

At some point during my conversation in the hall, Andrew went to bed. He touched his fingers to my shoulder as he passed me sitting on the bottom step. I moved to allow him by.

'Are you okay?' I placed my hand over the receiver, whispered to him.

He raised his hand languidly. In farewell? I won't ever know. The phone call ended. I went up to my brother's bedroom. He lay on his back, his breathing shallow. A water glass sat by his bedside, his bottle of pills still three-quarters full. I remember that detail, the bottle of pills, the relief I felt that they were all still there. I reached over and removed them. The hospital had warned us to keep them from him, but Andrew always managed to find them. I moved to the window and pushed the sash window down. Outside, the world was the colour of dead water, the cold freezing everything into silent submission. I left the door open and went back downstairs.

Now, of course, my question is still *why did I leave him on his own?* That was the rule, the one we had agreed upon. I know I was 16, and leaving a mentally ill person in the care of someone so young was beyond anything that could be deemed acceptable nowadays, but I wasn't some silly teenager with no thoughts other than meeting boys and listening to music. I was a poet, for God's sake. It had to mean something.

By late afternoon I was finished. The poems were due by the end of the week. Outside, snow had started to fall, proper snow this time, falling thickly, wrapping everything in a layer of white.

I prepared a tray and carried it up to Andrew's room. He had turned on his side, no longer snoring. The silence in the room lay over everything, an aquarium of cold bedroom air. Burnt sage leaves littered the windowsill. That was Maude's touch, burning dried sage to keep evil spirits away. My mother called it hocus pocus, but I suppose we would have done anything.

'Andrew?'

Silence.

Settling the tray on the desk under the window, I stood by his bed. After all those years of living alongside Andrew, I understood his illness, knew of its intricacies and winding paths, but the unpredictability frightened me. I was alone. And I was in charge of minding my brother.

'Andrew.' I nudged his shoulder. He didn't move.

His skin shone bone-white in the dull afternoon light. How pale he was. His hair, always longer than my mother liked, curled over the collar of his pyjamas.

I touched his forehead. Smooth as stone, and almost as cold.

What was wrong with him?

Gently, I cupped his face, brought it around to meet mine. His eyelids lay at half-mast. He wasn't breathing. No pulse fluttered in his neck, or at his wrist, the places I knew to check.

'Andrew, come on, please, come on. Wake up. Come on.' I rubbed my finger on his cheek. It was colder than it should have been. 'Wake up. *Wakeupwakeupwakeup.*' I shook him slightly, but there was no response. His head flopped back to the side when I took my hand away.

Something bloomed on the sheets. Something terrible and dark. Something that wet my fingers when I touched it.

The blood. Oh my God, the blood. It couldn't be possible that one body contained that much blood. Seeping and bleeding and flowing and gushing and soaking and staining and dripping and draining. All over the bed. All over the blankets, the sheets, his body, my hands, his pyjamas, the blood, oh God, Jesus help me, the blood. His blood. *Stop the flow.*

In one sweeping motion I ripped the covers off him, shrieking like something inhuman. The contents of his shelves, the tray on the desk, the books on the bedside locker, all caught in the slipstream of the whirling covers, crashed to the floor in a spinning frenzy of books, cups, paper, magazines, a blur of sound and flying liquids, and I screamed and screamed and could not stop.

And my heart broke, simply smashed into jagged splinters.

I sank among the bloodied sheets, buried myself in the clammy coldness. I lay there till evening spilled itself like ink into every corner. My brother lay on his bed, a dead king still on his throne. The appalling twilight gathered me into it, but I couldn't move. I knew I had to do something, phone someone, but all I was able to do was stare through the dullness at the devastation in front of me.

My phone beeps. Adam. *Gr8 news! Will I bring the cappuccinos?* I smile. I text him back. *I'll call you in a few hours.*

The envelope is a cream oblong, and it drops onto the floor with a slap. My name, typed, looks up at me. The solicitor's address is printed in the corner. A snowflake has smudged the ink of my name.

Dear Eva. I wonder if there's a problem with the house, with my mother's estate. *I have been instructed by Goldberg and*

Co., of Lexington Avenue, New York, to inform you that there is an outstanding matter in relation to your late father's estate.

My father died after we moved to Dublin. I didn't know until after the fact. I don't know his anniversary, or what he died of. He had no brothers or sisters, no relations that I knew of, and my mother refused to be drawn into conversation about him. He's been dead for over thirty years. Why a matter about his estate now? And what estate? But most importantly, why is a firm of Manhattan lawyers writing to my mother's solicitor? My father had probably been to Dublin a few times in his life. He most likely never even possessed a passport.

The letter reveals nothing more, except to say that my father's executor wishes to meet with me, and would I please ring the office to make an appointment with Mr Bergin.

I leave the letter beside the phone and lie down on the couch. The snow has eased off, but the cars are still jammed in a rigid line all the way up and down the street. A red car has been abandoned outside my neighbour's garden. A bus has broken down farther up the road. People are walking, many of them already carrying supermarket bags. Stockpiling in case of emergency. There are a few inches of snow on the ground. Hardly cause for a national crisis. New York keeps going, labouring away under feet of snow, winter after winter. Weather is not a reason to shut down there.

I am aware that I've settled into a rhythm of sorts here, but already I can feel the dissonance unravelling again, that sense of still being a stranger here, no matter what happens. I don't want that for myself, don't want to find myself in ten years' time lurching from term to term, always longing for the holidays to give me a break. I saw it in New York, and I see it in the staffroom here. The counting of days until the next day off, the number of Mondays to get through until the next school holiday. That mindset sits well with its bedfellow, dissatisfaction. I don't want it for myself. My apartment will be mine again in June. My hiatus from work can be extended, but I need to get back to it, do something more with myself than teach literature to schoolkids who only ever want to know what might come up on the exam paper. Even the sweetness I encounter in so many of my students here can't disguise the complacency and downright laziness that drags so many of them down, keeps them from true success. American students, with only half the ability of some of the boys I teach here, and little of their charm, would claw over dead bodies to reach their goals. I miss that, working with decisive people, students who don't need me to spell out every word for them, predict questions that will appear on their public exams just so they can rehearse answers. My research can't wait forever, and my patience is wearing thin.

Slow, it's been a slow process, but I'm becoming anxious to leave.

I venture outside only for milk and bread. The snow has eased, and according to the radio report will probably not fall again, apart from the odd flurry. It is perfect weather for sitting indoors with a bottle of whiskey, some cloves and a lemon. I force the thought from my mind. A drink would be the perfect addition to this day of freedom. In another life, I would have spent the day writing. Now, the hours are empty before me, vacated of words I could twist into cadences and rhythms. A drink would fill all the gaps. Better, then, to walk, however aimlessly.

A group of children pelt each other with snowballs. A crude snowman sits in the middle of the footpath of a small residential road off the main drag. He has stones for eyes, and as buttons, and stick arms wedged at different angles on either side of his misshapen torso. Someone has stuck a paper coffee cup on top of his head. The screams of the children echo in the quiet morning, the omnipresent racket of traffic silenced by the snow. A small child is making a snow angel on her own. I glance about for her mother, but there are no adults to be seen. One of the snowballers shouts a name. *Sophie!* I think he says. And again, *Sophie!* The child gets to her feet and immediately slips, her feet shooting up in front of her, cartoon-style, before she lands in a heap on her back. I anticipate a tantrum, or at the very least tears and injured screams, but she laughs, and her laughter is as clear as water and full of joy. Without dusting off the residue of snow that clings to her, Sophie runs, shrieking, over to where the older children are stockpiling snowballs.

I pick up a prescription for Maude, and on impulse buy her some flowers and two newspapers. I wonder what she will do if I leave. *When* I leave. I don't allow myself to think of her on her own in that house. I don't want to wonder about what she will do if her leg gives her trouble, or if she's sick in the middle of the night. Plenty of old people live alone, and anyway, Maude already lives alone. She just always had my mother upstairs if she needed her. And now she has me. Except I want to leave. I walk briskly back to the house, deliberately keeping the pace up so my mind is distracted from thoughts of Maude, old and alone. It's a chore, making sure I don't slip on the ice underfoot, and it keeps self-reproach at bay. The sky is sallow and unmoving, and despite what the forecasters say I doubt the last of the snow has fallen. As I approach the house, a tall figure with a black beanie is leaning his back against the front door.

'Sean!' I fumble through my reusable shopping bag for my key.

'Hey, I was just passing and thought I'd stop in and say goodbye.'

It is more relief than anything else that fizzes through me. He hasn't changed his mind about me and decided he wants a relationship. He's leaving for Australia. Sooner than I had thought. I invite him in for coffee. I even have croissants.

His shrug is fluid. 'Sure. Why not?'

It's not that the sex isn't good. It is. Better than it should be, actually, but there isn't much else to do with him. We cover ourselves with the blankets I left on the couch earlier. The fire I lit before I went out has subsided to a tangerine glow. An ember spits itself out and burns redly on the hearth. Maude's radio filters through the floor. My book lies unopened on the armchair.

Sean twists a piece of my hair. 'So, I'll write.'

We both laugh. 'No, you won't.'

'Course I will! Long, scented letters.'

We laugh again. It's nice, this easy farewell. I trace my fingers over his Yeats tattoos. He squirms.

'What?'

'These stupid things. First thing I do when I make a bit of money is get them lasered. That's it for me and ink.'

I follow the loops the words make. 'I think they're nice.' And I mean it.

As he leaves, Sean kisses me. 'Be good. And go back to New York. There's nothing happening here for any of us.'

I watch till Sean turns the corner, and that's when I see him. The other man. The one in the navy coat. He's leaving Maude's garden flat, the coat buttoned to the neck, a tweed cap pulled down on his head. He spies me, salutes, then climbs the steps towards me. Fear rumbles in some distant region of my insides. Something – intuition? – has instructed me to be wary of strangers who lurk in the wings, then present themselves as this man is doing now, with broad smiles and an outstretched hand.

Whatever it is he has to say to me, I don't think I want to hear it.

'Eva,' he says, those hands reaching for mine. 'My name is Peter Mahoney.' The accent is unmistakable New York, the pronunciation of his last name American, with the stress on the middle syllable. 'I'm sorry for just arriving like this, but I'd like to talk to you.'

CHAPTER 29

Anonymity is what appeals to me most about hotels. Isaac and I used to meet in them at the beginning. No one cares who you are or what you do. The huge lobbies, the potted plants and revolving doors all conspire to create a place where identities are shed like onion skins and new circumstances can be invented at will.

Peter and I have arranged to meet here, in this city centre hotel. I walked through Stephen's Green on my way, relishing the sudden change in temperatures. The colours of the green are deceptive, allowing me to think I'm in another, bigger city, where grey does not predominate, and real buildings dwarf the landscape.

The low buildings in Dublin annoy me. Everything here is irritating me at present, from the ridiculous ways of dressing – bare feet stuffed into ill-fitting shoes, even in the depths of winter, fake tan smeared on every conceivable body part – to the shops that are but disappointing imitations of proper stores in proper cities. Everything seems to be a copy of something bigger and better somewhere else. It's as though Ireland has sold all semblance of its own self for a shabby imported version that cannot but disappoint.

I'm exhausted lately.

Peter has something he wishes to talk to me about. After introducing himself on the doorstep, he declined an invitation to step inside. He is staying here for a week. It suits me better this way. Something niggles at me, some vague conviction that all is not right with this man in his tailored coat, who loitered for a day or two before asking Maude where I was.

My guess is that Peter has been sent by Isaac, instructed to run me to ground and drag me back to New York, to my job, to him. Has he shadowed me, uncovered clues to my existence here, biding his time before approaching me?

It is nearly eleven o'clock, our appointed hour. I sit by a window and order an espresso. The place is buzzing. So much for the recession that is crippling Ireland. No evidence is on display here, among the suited professionals and the expertly overdressed. It was almost impossible to get a table.

Peter sits down in the chair opposite me that I've kept my coat on. He shakes my hand.

'This must be strange for you,' he says. 'I'm sorry for the mystery, but I thought meeting you in a neutral spot would be the best.' His skin is smooth, his teeth expertly cared for. It's his accent that gets me the most, that vowel-broadened East Coast drawl. It sounds like home.

'Is Isaac okay?'

Confusion films his face. 'Isaac?'

Disappointment dampens the buzz the espresso has given me. Of course Isaac isn't looking for me. Why would he bother?

Peter orders black coffee in a cafetière. When it arrives he busies himself with pouring it, dropping sugar in, stirring. Again I think that my father would be Peter Mahoney's age now, somewhere in his late sixties. Would he still have all his hair? Would it be white, like Peter's? If he could see me, what would he think of me? After we left him I spent most of my time missing him, pondering what he was doing, what music he was listening to. I sought out my face in shiny surfaces, peering at my green eyes, my dark hair. My mother slapped my hands, retribution for my vanity, but it wasn't my own face I pursued. It was my father's.

'Where are you from?'

'Bay Ridge.' His accent is unmistakably Brooklyn. 'But I live in midtown. Have done for years.' He coughs, pauses. 'Eva, I knew your father.'

Impossible. My father barely left the flat midlands. 'How?'

'I lived here when I was younger. Well, not here, not Dublin, but Ireland. Shanrath.'

My confusion must be visible, for he talks rapidly again.

'My parents were immigrants. You know the story, they left in the forties, spent the rest of their lives longing for the place, then all their dreams came true when I decided to come back for a while, try it out, find a place to fit in.'

There is nothing in his story I haven't heard before from the scores of Irish Americans I've encountered in my years in New York. What I've never understood is this yearning they have for the homeland, the old country. Now, all I can think about is getting out again. It's all illusion, of course, all romance about a place that doesn't exist.

'I met Tom shortly after I arrived. His family farmed the neighbouring land.'

To hear my father's name mentioned so casually, as though he were someone I was used to discussing, is shocking. My mother, when she mentioned him, something she rarely did, only ever referred to him as *your father. Your father.* Her lip curled palpably around the words, as though the taste were too disgusting to bear.

'Did you know my mother?'

'Yes.'

'She died last September.' Has it already been that long? Six months. Something has happened to time since my arrival in Dublin, an undetected slipping away of all those weeks and months. Six months.

'I'm sorry.'

'Don't be.'

Music tinkles from a piano in the corner of the room, a welcome spill of sound. I recognise Liszt, the soft notes of a piano concerto. 'But why are you here now?'

Sunlight suddenly dazzles the table between us. I look out the window. 'Crazy climate, right?' Peter laughs. 'Four seasons in one day.'

I'm tired of it, tired of it all. It's time for me to go, leave Dublin, and probably never come back. I crave consistency, knowing where I am, what kind of day it's going to be.

I live in New York, I tell Peter. His shock is disproportionate to such a small piece of information.

'What?'

I explain about the house, but don't give any details of my sabbatical. I'm going back, I say. This is temporary.

He runs a hand over his face. 'If we'd known,' he says. 'If we'd only known.'

I shift in my seat. Something is off here. There's something unsaid that I can't put my finger on, a whole part of this that is hovering beyond my comprehension. Something, a shadow maybe, lingers, obscuring the finer details. There is a sense of the conversation being waterlogged. I'm missing a component but I have no idea what it is.

The waitress lingers behind us. Peter points to my empty cup, which is wordlessly refilled. He points to pastries on the plates of the people at the next table, and within a moment croissants appear, small white pots of butter, others of jam. This is a man used to ordering. How like Isaac he is in his confident ability to ask for exactly what he wants, barely pausing his conversation.

Peter mentions a new exhibit at the Whitney, construction that's causing huge traffic problems in midtown, a concert hall scheduled for opening next week in Brooklyn, just over the bridge. The New York Phil will inaugurate the new building. Isaac and I went a few times to see the Phil at Avery Fisher Hall. An hour in a cab in the crush of rush hour, the day's work left behind us downtown. Once, the traffic was so bad we jumped out half way and took the subway to 66th Street. Isaac didn't like the subway, and it took quite some convincing to get him underground. But Isaac has no place here, not in my head and not in my life. He belongs firmly in the past.

I lean forward. 'Peter.'

He pauses, sips from his cup. The people at the next table leave and are replaced seamlessly by a couple with a sleeping baby.

'Why are you here?'

He coughs. 'I knew your father.'

A flash of irritation crackles inside me, flushing my cheeks. 'I know. You said. But he's been dead since I was a small child. Why are you telling me this now?'

The baby next to us wakes with a bawl. Her father shushes her, jiggling her on his lap and kissing her. She responds by arching her back and screaming even louder.

Peter shifts in his seat. He looks at his hands. They are good hands, the nails square, the skin smooth.

'Eva.'

A vein throbs in my temple. A drink would be nice, because I realise I don't want to hear whatever it is this man has travelled to Ireland to tell me. I'm in a hotel, for God's sake. There is booze all around me, oceans of it, enough to drown me several times over. Glasses play their tinkling music everywhere, despite the early hour. Ice chinks, soda fizzes, even a champagne cork pops. In this precise moment I think I could murder the man in front of me for a drink.

In the end, after all the pauses, the procrastinating, Peter rushes the words out. 'Your father didn't die when you were a child. There was no heart attack or tumour or whatever your mother told you.' He inhales, a shuddering breath. 'He only died six weeks ago.'

The rest of what he says is a blur. Some words surface through the garbled, bloated mass. My father didn't die when I was a child. He died recently. In New York City. A few miles from where I live.

I sit on my hands. They are shaking.

My father and this man were friends. My mother disapproved. No surprises there. Peter recounts walks in the evenings, pints in the nearest pub, three miles away. Then the marriage, and Esther's cold eye of censure cast over her new husband's friend.

'I don't know what way to say all this to you.'

'Just say it. You and my father rendezvoused in the evenings. What was it, pints of stout and talk of milk quotas?' My bitterness sounds childish. I'm jealous, I suppose. Someone knew my father and I never did.

'We were friends, yes. Good friends. We were both isolated, I suppose, cut off from everything. And I was miserable, missing New York.'

'You could've joined the football club.' Wasn't that what country boys did back then? Played sports, turned up at the local dance blitzed on cheap whiskey and tried to grope the other farmers' daughters. All loud talk, no action guaranteed.

'Do I look like a football player?' He smiles. 'Believe me, I couldn't be further from it.'

I understand my father's loneliness, his need for a friend. His elderly parents were dead by the time he met my mother. No siblings. My mother had to have been the one who moved in on him, because my father was the quietest person I'd known.

I remember his humble collection of jazz records. I remember his hands, rough from labour, dirt filling in the grooves. But mostly I remember the way he treated me, like I was some sort of rare bird. His opaque delightfulness.

My nose prickles, and I wonder if I'm going to cry. I haven't wept in a very long time. There's simply too much to cry over, and I'm not sure I'd even know where to start. After the abortion I thought about stabbing needles in my flesh, stubbing cigarettes out on my thighs, or sticking my hands in fire. I tried to focus on physical pain because the other pain was simply unendurable. There were no tears to cry. That well of release had long since run dry, evaporated by a grief too enormous to conquer.

Something is wrong with Peter's story. Something doesn't gel, doesn't make real sense. My mother had been many things, but one way I couldn't see her was in the role of monopoliser, demanding all of my father's attention for herself. She was too self-sufficient for that, too severed from warmth.

Peter sighed, a huge intake of breath. He rubs his palms on his knees. 'Esther took you and Andrew away. She told Tom that if he went near either of you, or tried to stay in touch with you, that she'd go to the police.' He rubs both of his eyes. 'It was Ireland in the seventies. It was easier to believe such threats, to take them seriously.'

'So, what, he pretended to be dead?' Why am I listening to this man, wasting my morning when I could be outside, running by the canal, reading a book with only fictional people and events unfolding in front of me? I could be preparing a short bio for the new textbook of poems that will include five of mine for the next school year. Anything but listen to this.

'He didn't pretend anything. It was Esther's idea.'

'And he just went along with it.'

'He didn't feel he had any choice,' Peter says, sadly.

'What happened?'

'He came to New York with me. Esther said he'd died, told everyone he was dead, including you and Andrew. We went to New York. He sent her money for the two of you every month, and she never told anyone the truth. I think eventually she'd even convinced herself he was dead.'

Suddenly the hotel erupts into sound. Phones ring at the reception desk, glasses clink in the bar, the piano music crashes in thunderous waves of drama, people's voices scream in high-octane conversation. In my head I sweep the cups and coffee pot to the floor in an arc of liquid and shattered china. In reality, I do no such thing.

My father, alive and in New York. All those years. And me, living nearby. Walking the streets, hailing cabs, sitting at patios, hiding in jazz clubs. Lying in Sheep's Meadow, the buildings a horseshoe around the park. How many times had I come close to him, overlooked him on the street, wandered near where he was?

Did he pass me on the subway as the trains screamed and rattled their way along their endless circling track? Were we seated at the same moment on the edge of the Bethesda fountain, watching children throw balls around? Maybe we both gave money to the homeless man in the Knicks cap who waited, paper coffee cup in hand, outside the deli on Prince Street, day after day. Had we been to the same movies at Film Forum at the same time? Or walked by each other in Washington Square Park, stood watching the same street artists perform or chess games unfold?

'I'm sorry, Eva. I am. It wasn't Tom's wish.'

So why do it then? Why pretend to be dead? Who would do such a thing? Of course, even I could answer that. My mother.

'What does my mother have to do with all this?'

'Everything.'

My mother had been in love with Peter. She wanted him out of her sight because she couldn't have him. She forbade him to call to the little farmhouse, denied him hospitality because she wanted him for herself. Her upbringing, her religion, her own repressed nature would have conspired against her desires, so she put him away from her. It was easier to send my father packing, to spirit her children away under cover of summer darkness, than to have the man she wanted two miles away, single and for the taking, and utterly, utterly forbidden.

'She was in love with you.'

Peter's hands are joined on his lap. He shuts his eyes.

'Wasn't she? In love with you?'

A slow shake of his head. *No.*

No? It's the only thing that makes sense. 'Yes she was. She was in love with you, and you knew it.' Jesus Christ, is Peter my father? Is that what this is about, what he's attempting to tell me through all this clumsy fumbling? My eyes dart about the room, alighting on anything that isn't this man sitting erect in front of me. A bus thunders by outside, rattling the window in its pane. Even though I'm seated, my legs feel wobbly. I might never stand up again.

'My mother was in love with you.' If I repeated it enough times he'd have to take ownership of the truth. I needed to hear him admit it.

Again that slow shake of his head. His eyes, navy with intensity, swung to meet mine. 'Your father was.'

The coffee and the croissants slosh in my stomach. Bile bites my throat, and the noisy hotel drawing room tilts on its side. I expect everyone to slide in one direction, but no one seems to notice except me. They carry on answering phones and mixing drinks, stirring sugar into coffee and laughing at each other's jokes.

My mother knew. She created a story, her own invention, out of it, but she'd known all along. She conjured up a house of silent ghosts and a buried life, never to be unearthed.

Deception, like steel, holds the cold forever.

Suspended above it all, I hover, shivering, my teeth rattling like cups on a silver tray. Peter's hands obscure his face.

Patterns bloom black in front of my eyes. My father and this man. My father and the American. My father and Peter.

The world dims its lights. My mind abruptly blanks, vacates itself, and the floor reaches out, gathering me into an empty embrace.

CHAPTER 30

The new motorway out of Dublin is strangled, even on a Tuesday morning in April. Each tiny town that has been bypassed hosts an unparalleled vista of the barely moving snake of vehicles winding its way, minute by aching minute, along the new road.

How the Americans would laugh at our vision of progress. A road that's been decades in the making has swallowed enough money to fund developing countries, sliced open historic sites and destroyed the countryside, all in the name of getting people to where they wanted to go, faster. And still it crawls.

Adam has loaned me his car, his vegetable-oil Merc. The smell of doughnuts is at times too much, and I have to roll the window down when it threatens to overpower me. The nausea has subsided, though, so it's easier.

This trip is the return leg of the journey I made over thirty years before, aged 4, with my mother driving and my brother asleep in the front seat. Now the small towns are signposts instead of milestones, bypassed and built up beyond recognition. New housing estates have been conjured out of developers' hats, turning everywhere into a suburb of Dublin. Names like *Brook, Manor, Court, Vale* have been tacked on in some misguided attempt to convince people that they're living in the city. The desperate need for uniformity.

What's so wrong with being different? Why is individuality feared? Although I can admit to sometimes imagining my life in a parallel world, one where I don't have to dwell on the inner life, where I'm happy to work in an office job and come home to my suburb each evening, nothing more pressing on my mind than what to cook for dinner. Maybe my golf-playing husband and I would watch television after the children are put to bed, some nonsense singing competition where we could be truly concerned about what the outcome would be. We could read cheap thrillers and romance novels on a package holiday to some overcrowded *costa*, not know a line of poetry or a beat of jazz, name our children after celebrities or obscure Irish heroes.

I've chased the unattainable, and look where it has got me. In a borrowed Mercedes, a plastic drum of used vegetable oil rolling around on the back seat in case of an emergency, returning for the first time to the place of my birth. I should have done it years ago. What have I been waiting for, my mother's permission? Her approval? Other than vanishing after my birth, I doubted there was much I could have achieved that my mother would have approved of.

Traffic inches along the motorway, each lane stuffed with cars and freight trucks. Exhaust shimmers in the air, poisoning the banks of daffodils that flourish on either side of the road. The faces of the drivers I see are blank with boredom. Some yak on phones, other tap their fingers on the steering wheel. Most are probably doing the same journey every day. Welcome to the new Ireland. Let us squeeze you out of the cities and into featureless housing developments, and let's hope you're too fatigued from commuting, too worried about money and your massive mortgage to stop and think that you're being done from every angle.

A listless child waves to me from the car in front. A police motorcycle weaves among the gridlock. Cows graze in distant fields. The sun reveals itself in jagged bursts from behind clouds, an intermittent spotlight on the green surroundings.

I revealed nothing to Adam about Peter, or the trip I needed to take, the inheritance I'd uncovered when I finally dragged myself into Charles Bergin's office, and Adam was enough of a man not to ask. His week with his daughter was a success, and I discovered how interesting it can be to spend time with a child. I need the practice.

My father has left me the farm. When he moved to New York he locked the door of the house and kept the key. It wasn't sold or rented. The land was leased to another farmer until the end of last year. The house is probably in ruins.

Charles Bergin assured me that he knew nothing of my father's recent death.

'I have a letter from a firm of American lawyers, with instructions for you,' he said, as we sat in his office on a bright day at the end of March, and he read me what I owned. The farmhouse, the land, any equipment or animals or crops that are still there.

He quoted from codicils, explained what I needed to do in order to take hold of my inheritance. My father also left me money. The business he owned with Peter in Manhattan was very successful. The money resides in a bank in New York, and requires my signature plus my presence before it can be accessed.

So either way I'm returning to New York. Back to the city of a thousand languages, self-absorbed and consumed, eating itself up in a vortex of around-the-clock noise. The city that never sleeps. What an understatement. The city that never even blinks in case it misses something, some new trend or piece of art, something that hasn't happened anywhere else. How exhausting to be so constantly chasing after the tail of your own reputation, never to be able to draw breath in case it occurs somewhere else instead. I love New York, even though its self-awareness grates at times. All those movies, all the art and stories, none of it comes close to capturing the real city, because a city is a constantly shifting landscape, and to try and pin it down to a few characteristics is to keep its flame in a jar. I understand that much about New York, but I've met few other people who did. Maybe my father felt that way about it. I like to think he did.

It feels like I'm emerging from hibernation, a tunnel that has taken an eternity to crawl out of. The light is still too bright for me after all that time underground, but I'll get used to it eventually. At least I can dig my way out of the buried life. Unlike my brother, who had to leave the world in order to be free. Unlike my mother, who constructed a wall of anger that no one scaled. Unlike my father, who jumped ship and swam to another shore. My soul requires work, but at least I still possess it.

I honk at a woman applying mascara in the car in front of me, holding me up. She gives me the fingers before putting her car in gear and driving on. For all the difference it makes. Five minutes later, another bypassed town, another thousand cars and trucks trying to exit and enter the slip roads. I give up.

A Brazilian girl, all big hair and polished skin, brings me my coffee and sandwich. The small pub is empty, except for the daily clientele of about four men, who probably squander all their days here, checking the horse racing results and making their pints last for hours. Widowers, or bachelors, or maybe men whose wives had run away after they caught them engaged in illicit relations with the neighbouring farmer's nephew.

A barman polishes glasses, and the Brazilian girl swipes at tabletops with her cloth. A radio plays bad country music, but at least the volume is low.

The girl is in Ireland to work. She stayed in Dublin for a month, hated it, then moved with her friend to the midlands. She loves it, she tells me in accented English. She wants to stay. The climate doesn't bother her, she says with a graceful shrug. After a lifetime of the tropics and poverty, there is more to be experienced. She teaches samba in the community centre three nights a week, and already she's booked out.

Samba in the Irish midlands. Motorways, supersized shopping malls, SUVs on every road, and now samba. What a change from my father's youth, when all that was available was the land or the priesthood, Mass and the GAA at the weekends.

I feel very old and very weary. I'm only 37, but it's like I've lived ten lifetimes. I wish I were more like Maria, the frizzy-haired beauty who still has enough faith in the universe to ignore the rain and the monotony of the flat land, to get excited about teaching Latin dancing to the rhythmless hordes. I can just about muster up the energy to teach literature.

I understand how people snap. The line is so fine, just silk really. My brother slicing his skin was just his way of saying *enough*. I could order a few whiskeys now, then get behind the wheel of the Mercedes and fall asleep. It would be harder in broad daylight, easier to do it in the quiet of night, with fewer people around to pull me from the oily wreckage, call for ambulances, do some mouth-to-mouth to get me moving.

I pay for the surprisingly good sandwich. Honestly, I expected a slice of orange cheese on cheap white bread, maybe a bit of ham for good measure, not the olive bread I've just consumed, with feta, tomatoes and tabouli. I drain my coffee cup and get back into the car.

It should only be a ninety-minute drive from Dublin to the farm; it feels like a drive across the outback. The original road, the one we took that night in the old Hillman Hunter, surely would have been quicker than this traffic-clogged Hades.

I check the map. Not too far now. Two more towns to bypass and then I'll be there. I pass an unfinished housing estate just off the motorway. The signage proclaims it to be a place where dreams begin. Nightmares, more likely. The grey concrete, the land stripped of all greenery, the road leading nowhere. A ghost estate. A headache dislodges itself and begins to pulse. My nerves prickle. Dread pools in my stomach. I almost wish I'd brought someone with me, but whom could I have asked? Not Maude, not Adam. Not Sean, already settled into his Australian odyssey. My sad social circle. Regardless, I couldn't have asked anyone. This is one of those journeys that must be made alone.

Finally, the motorway is behind me. I'm back on narrow roads, with verdant hedgerows dividing land, chestnut trees with buds just peeping into bloom. New lambs stagger on spindly legs in fields, beside the woolly contentment of their mothers. The sun skids in and out of cloud cover, the air clear and free of city pollution.

I surprise myself by knowing the farm when I get to it. The road is narrower than I remember, but it's the same. The wide red metal gate for keeping the cows in the field is now black, and in better shape than it had been when I was a child. I recall picking the bubbling paint off it, digging up the rust with my fingernails, then spending ages washing my hands to get the smell of rust off my skin. That metallic taste. I can still feel it on my tongue.

The Mercedes barely fits in the driveway. Blackberry bushes scrape their limbs against the paintwork, the overgrown grass on a level with my eyes as I drive. Two thrushes fly out of the bush, their squawks of fright ringing loud in the empty country air. No one has disturbed this path for a long time.

Doubtless some developer must have investigated the house and land. Charles Bergin said the fields had been tilled until last year, but a thousand houses could have sprung up if the farmhouse had been bulldozed. They built everywhere else, why not here? I could sell it all, and never again have to worry about an income. No more academia. I could pack up and leave. Maude is safe and independent. With a bag on my back I'd be able to go wherever I want, stay as long or as little as I desire. I could keep running, as I've been doing since my brother died, and maybe if I stop thinking, even for a minute, I might just be able to forget it all. Reality has worn me out. One way has led me to another, and I'm further from the starting point than I've ever been, too far even to contemplate returning to zero, if I could even remember what that was.

I kill the engine outside the back door. We never used the front door, from what I recall. The old boot scraper is still there, smaller than in my memory, rusted down to a brittle skeleton. The chicken coop has rotted away, the wire netting oxidised, the wood almost gone. A crow flies out of the cowshed.

The silence is overpowering, deafening in the sounds that are no longer heard. The cows lowing, the hens fighting for grain, the hiss of the cats as they fought over mice, the crunch of gravel under work-heavy boots, all extinguished.

The car door groans when I open it. I palm the house key and step out into the hush of the early afternoon. The last time I crossed this gravel I'd been barefoot, sharp bits making me hop, my mother's hand on my pyjamaed shoulder urging me into the car, her impatience gleaming, transparent in the late June night. Even then I'd aggravated her, my gaping need, her cold failure to fill it. But it was my brother's need that eclipsed all else, and she hadn't had the courage to face it. Far easier to dwell on me, cut off from my father. Impatience with a dispossessed child was an easier repository than the bewilderment of an unhappy boy, whose sadness, left unchecked, grew into the demon that swallowed him whole. His rage and self-abasement sneaked through his cells like the deadliest tumour, gaining momentum from the fear it evoked in others.

Simpler by far to focus on the soft target. That was my mother's knack. That way at least she could be seen to be doing something.

The sky had darkened as I drove the last few miles. Rainclouds now meet and meld, obliterating the spring brilliance. A breeze whips my hair across my face. Dust blows up from the gravel. It mustn't have rained in weeks.

A half-inch of water reposes at the bottom of an ancient barrel near the back door.

The dithering has to stop. There is no reason to stay outside.

The key fits perfectly in the rusty lock. The door swings inwards with a creak that speaks of years of neglect, a longing for oil. Gathering my apprehension in a tight grip, I step inside.

CHAPTER 31

L ike anything from childhood that hasn't been visited in years, reality never matches the memory of things. As a small child, my experience of the world beyond home had been limited. The farm was infinite, the fields stretching to disappearing point on the horizon. The house, with its stone floors and big rooms, had provided untold space for my brother and me to run around in, play our imaginary games on the grand stage they required, with no wish for a bigger house or more room in which to let our young lives unfold.

The house is small. Very small. Even in the murky light, not aided by the filthy kitchen windows, I can make out the proportions. Modest at best. I flick the light switch, but even if the electricity was turned on, the single bulb that hangs suspended from a frayed cord is long expired. Back outside, I knock the debris from the windowpanes as best I can, three decades of dirt, dust, moss, and whatever else travels the currents of air before coming to rest on a solid surface. I then retrieve the torch I'd had the foresight to bring with me. I'd had no idea what awaited me. Possibly a crumbling heap of bricks, or a burned-out shell. Vandals exist everywhere, not just in the marginalised suburban estates. Apathy finds willing hosts in every environment. I can't believe the house hasn't been burnt, or at least used by local teenagers for drinking cider and indulging their clumsy fumblings.

I make my way from the small square hall to the kitchen. The air sags under its heavy smell of decay. Rotting wood, damp stone, powdered plaster, mildewed fabric. In the fireplace a huge pile of twigs has gathered, the detritus of years of nest-building. Old feathers stick to the stone hearth, and two bird skeletons bare their bony breasts where the coal scuttle had been. Had they fallen, dead, into the room, or had they given up hope of ever escaping the cobwebbed gloom?

The muffled squawk of a crow sounds deep in the chimney, the only sound in the bruised silence.

So many years, but I remember some of it as it was. On the table an abandoned cup sits on its saucer. A cracked teapot with a matching jug keep it company. Dust and grime have smothered their pattern, but I can see that they are part of a set. A wedding present, most likely, from a kind well-wisher, a person who could never have dreamed of the turmoil that raged inside the small stone house. My parents' wedding had been a small affair, my mother ashamed of her age and how long it had taken her to find a husband. The guest list had comprised Maude and her husband, girls from the office where my mother worked, and some neighbours from the townland. It had taken place on a Tuesday morning, and lunch had been served in a hotel. It was the first time my father had been in a hotel, and I imagine him, nervous and self-conscious in his new suit, running a finger inside his collar to loosen the shirt. Where had Peter been? Sulking while doing the milking, raking hay with all the ferocity of suppressed temper, pounding the narrow lanes, anything to keep him occupied? My mother had had no idea. Of course she hadn't. She'd probably never imagined that such things between two men were possible.

I open the cupboards. Mice have obliterated anything that had been left, nibbled mounds of what must have been cardboard boxes into small heaps on the shelves. A glass jar with a label faded beyond legibility contains something fossilised, and two tins of cocoa, one without its lid, sit side by side. A spoon lies on the countertop beside a tea caddy. The kettle is on the stove.

My father had been about to make a cup of tea. He was alone. Then *poof*. He vanished. What had happened?

Had Peter arrived one evening after dinner, announcing that he was returning to the States? Sweating, good-looking, maybe with straw still in his blond hair. His hands washed clean of the day's labours, but splashes of milk from the two cows still on his forearms. Fed by his aunt, probably a stew, followed by cups of tea and some soda bread.

Had the June evening still been bright, the sky not yet stained red by the imminent gloaming, shadows just beginning to lengthen, the day's work done? Had my father just put the kettle on to boil for his nightly cup of tea, then stood at the window, watching the fields, his fields, stretch to the horizon, layered in every shade of green? Maybe he thought of Andrew and me, wondered what we were up to now that the school year had ended. Did he plan a visit to us, or want our mother to put us on the train to come and stay with him? Then maybe Peter came in the kitchen door, as every visitor to the farm did, interrupting the reel of thought. Without my mother present, Peter didn't have to scrape his boots. The hens pecked at each other in the yard, their scratching noises puncturing the post-work hush.

Did Peter announce his departure? Say he could no longer suffer the claustrophobia of the two-cow farm and his unspeaking relatives? He was sure of who he was, what he was, even in those despair-edged days of repression and ignorance. He was leaving the following day, and my father could either go with him, begin again in a city that didn't care who or what he loved, or he could stay, chained to the land he owned through an accident of birth rather than any real belief in it. So my father phoned my mother to tell her he was leaving, moving to New York with the person who loved him. She, glacial, informed him that as far as her children were concerned he was dead. He was dead to her regardless, and it would be easier for everyone if he simply expired. So he did. An unremembered illness, an unfound grave, a vague story. It was the perfect plot: simple, unfussy, totally believable.

What did my father know of Andrew and me? Had my mother replied to any of those monthly envelopes, telling him of my brother's death, my disappearance into exile? Andrew's death he must have known about, because he left the land to me alone. Did he learn about my books, my awards? As much as my mother didn't want me, she desired even less that my father would have me. How difficult had it been for him to let us go, just to disappear into the dark with his suitcase of essentials and nothing tying him down? The house had been abandoned, the teacup unused, the spoon beside the caddy, the son and daughter grieving in their childish way for the father who chose death as his alibi.

Death is so easy, the cleanest of breaks. There's no arguing with it, no bargaining or beguiling. It simply removes. Did my father come to believe in his own death eventually? Did he drop all the layers of his life as a father, like discarded garments that no longer fit? Like foolish movie stars believing in their own hype, did Tom Perry pause in his Manhattan life, maybe while chopping vegetables for dinner, or while dodging cars crossing the road, to reflect that the story he told himself about himself was not entirely true? Possibly he'd been relieved to get away, anything to put space between him and the children he'd let down. Did we haunt him, his forgotten children? When he slept, did we visit him in dreams, remind him? He replaced us, found people, work, to occupy the empty spaces in his head, but he must have circled back in unguarded moments, found himself in the chair by the hearth, me on his lap, unhappiness weighing his heart down like a stone. Deception is an easy thing to discard at first, but it never fully goes away. Over time, it grows in size and importance, blanking out whatever gains were made by it in the first place. I don't like to think of my father pretending to be someone other than himself. We were out there, Andrew and I, his children, one of us wanting to forget and be happy, the other wanting to be dead. Andrew got his wish, but I kept on. I suppose I believed that things would turn out all right in the end, even if the end took a damn long time coming. If I hadn't believed it, who knows? Maybe I'd have joined my brother. The thing is, my father was who he was, but he ran from it. Running runs through my veins, just another part of my botched DNA. I find myself wishing again that he'd stayed. Even though it was Ireland, even though it was the horrible eighties and no one understood anything, we could have got through it. He was our father. He should have stayed. No use wishing that now, of course, and I'm not going to waste another minute regretting things that cannot be changed. But if he could have known how much we missed him, how much we needed him, maybe he would have changed his mind.

The cracked windowpane rattles in the rotten wooden frame. A mouse scratches behind a cupboard door. The whole place has a subterranean feel to it. Dark. Damp. Just being there makes me shaky and slightly sick. I want a drink.

In the living room, the ancient couch has sunk in on itself. Stuffing spills from gaps chewed through by mice, the fabric decayed and stinking. My father left without the old suitcase record player, but not without his records, his modest collection of jazz and big band. I lift the lid of the record player. It is perfect inside, protected from thirty-three years of damp and neglect by its case. I touch the three settings, the volume control, even the needle. This could fetch quite a bit of money on an internet auction. Everyone seeks out retro now, some bit of nostalgia to balance the rampant greed of modern life. The television can go too, the old black-and-white with its two channels and the dial that clicked when we turned it. The two-pronged antenna still squats on top. It was Andrew's job to manoeuvre them when bad reception ruined the cartoons on Saturday mornings. Two photographs, faded now, are propped behind my grandmother's clock on the mantelpiece. One is of my father's parents on their wedding day, my grandmother seated, wearing a hat, my grandfather frowning behind her, his hand stiffly on her shoulder, their sepia world better preserved than the one taken on what must have been my christening, my father holding me outside the church, my mother looking away, Andrew's eyes screwed up against the brightness. What photo did he pack of us?

Sadness gathers and collects in distant parts of me. No one forgets children, or replaces them. I must be kinder about my father. Regardless of what he did, what choices he made, leaving children is an impossible option. No one wins. I don't want to think of him, childless, and so far away, wondering if we thought of him, grieved for him, loved him. The sadness is heavy, and it pulls at me, draws me again to think of him as I have always thought of him. Sweet, gentle, kind. He was such a good man.

The stairs creak as I ascend. I step on the edges, mindful of the dilapidated wood. Upstairs is much the same. The taps in the single bathroom, which rattled and shook each morning as they suffered to bring us water, now run dry. Rusty water marks disfigure the once-white sink. The window has slipped from its frame, and cold April air courses in through the cracks. I call to mind how my mother had complained more about the bathroom than any other aspect of the house. Too young to comprehend her frustration, I hadn't understood, but now I can empathise. Vaguely I recollect her attempts at gentility, the fancy little towels, the perfumed soap, the embroidered cushions she'd put on the couch, the tiny watercolours she framed and hung along the stairs.

The house is a farmhouse, built at the turn of the century for a modest farmer with no knowledge of, or interest in, the world beyond his fields. It was suited to just such a person, his life revolving around crops and animals. Soap and matching wallpapers would remain forever outside his sphere of reference. My grandparents and their parents had been such people, uninfluenced by, and unaware of, city culture. Decades meant nothing to them. Trends didn't change. Worrying about what clothes to wear would have seemed trivial, insignificant preoccupations for a mind with nothing else to focus on.

I trace my fingers down the moist wall in the bedroom I shared with my brother. His Airfix models still hang suspended from fishing line, testament to the durability of the nylon line and the hooks our father screwed into the ceiling. Water drips from a leak in the roof, the sound hollow, echoing in the deserted landing.

An epiphany of sorts creeps over me, standing in that damp bedroom, with its mouldy bedclothes disintegrated into the rotting mattresses, the child-sized clothes in fragments in the wardrobe, the smell of fungus filling my senses. I feel my mother's frustration. How angry she must have been with her life, with the shitty deal she'd been apportioned. A house she couldn't keep clean or refined, regardless of her efforts. A daughter she never bonded with, who clearly preferred her father. A social life that revolved around two stations on the television that she insisted my father buy, and Mass on Sundays among people she considered peasants.

Instead of discarding it all when she left, instead of praising herself for the courage she summoned to escape, she allowed herself to sink into bitterness, holding on to her rage until it became the blueprint for her life. She hated me because I wasn't her. I was different, the unmouldable daughter. Her cast could not contain my form.

I cannot forgive her for flinging me aside, but standing in the cold little house, a city girl to my bones, I find a measure of understanding for my mother. It is only a miniscule amount, less, perhaps, than a teaspoon, but it is there, and I acknowledge it. The Pears soap, the cushions, the watercolours, the vases of wildflowers. She'd tried. The other things, all that came after we moved, I'll deal with eventually. I have no choice, not if I want to keep my sanity and refrain from following the prints her feet have so carefully outlined.

Poetry helped, and who knows, maybe it will again. I've learned not to rely too heavily on anything or anyone. In the end, all I have is myself. And for now, I am enough.

Bloodied light percolates through another hole in the roof. The sun has emerged and begun its descent. I untie my cashmere cardigan from around my waist and slip it on. Evening is falling, and the cooling air will chill me. The softness of the wool glides over my bare arms. This is the cardigan Isaac gifted me that terrible weekend in LA. I'd put it in a bag for donating, but retrieved it. Why bother? I still like beautiful things. Isaac doesn't have to haunt everything I own.

I consider opening drawers, sifting through the rest of the abandoned stuff, but it is mostly beyond recognition. My father had turned the key and left it all behind him. Other than his records and the clothes he wore, he'd brought little with him to his new life. How great his hurry must have been if he didn't even drink his tea. Peter had probably issued him with an ultimatum, *leave with me tonight or you'll never see me again*. My father, grasping at the straws of freedom, had turned off the kettle, put his records and a toothbrush in a bag, and shut the door firmly on the life he chose not to live.

I hope he was happy, that the shackles of his secrets had been blasted away by a world that cared little about whom he chose to love. What saddens me, though, is that he kept it from me. I wouldn't have cared. Just having him in my life would have sufficed.

By leaving me the farm, he knew I'd uncover what he'd buried. Secrets never stay unrevealed. They may hide their faces for years, but they eventually float to the surface, shocking us with their revelations. My father had known that, and he chose to disclose his from a place where I couldn't find him. Maybe bringing me back to the place of my birth was his way of telling me his truth.

Careful not to damage it, I drag the suitcase record player out to Adam's car. I relocate the drum of doughnut oil to the boot and wedge the case into the back seat.

Standing on the gravel, I turn on my heels, breathing in the fragrant oxygen, no hint on the air of the decaying heap that is the house.

The quiet is religious. It stretches infinitesimally around me. This is a safe place, holding the stillness like an ebony lake shelters its shimmering fish. It grips the scent of spring in its hands, new buds and fresh grass. Did my father miss it at all? In the midst of the insanity of New York City, did he ever pause to think of the flat land, or the way the heaped haystacks in summer must have looked like scenes from a Monet painting? Did he yearn for the hushed nights or their perfect darkness?

I imagine myself, pen in hand, dispelling poetry in this place, with nothing and no one to distract me. Would the ghosts of my family allow me the peace, or would they be forever knocking at my subconscious, demanding to be examined? Yet without my history, who am I? I can't wipe my slate clean, but I can begin again.

I start the car, giving it a minute to garner itself for the drive home. The day is fading fast. The house has taken on an ethereal aspect, its flaws dissolving as twilight purples the sky. The ancient Mercedes carries me back down the narrow lane to the road, the tall grass brushing off the windows. I wind down the window to throw the key out into the old well near the gate. It is useless to me. I examine it, just another brass key, nothing special. It doesn't open any doors I need to go through. Not any more.

But in the end, instead of discarding it, I drop it in my bag. Another souvenir of a life not lived.

CHAPTER 32

I resign my job in the boys' school after the Easter holidays, giving Jim Collins two weeks to replace me. It's a short term, only six weeks long. There won't be a problem. I must leave before my bump is noticeable, before Adam feels compelled to propose to me, to stand by his actions. It might be his, but it might not, and I would rather not know. That way it will be my child, and mine alone.

Aelita will move into this house. She and Seamus will occupy the rooms, bring new light into all the dusty corners. In return for keeping a close eye on Maude, they can stay as long as they wish. Forever, if that is their desire. Maybe Aelita will have more children, and the house will heave to their energy, their laughter. Old ghosts will be displaced, and new stories, new lives and histories set in motion. The house too deserves a fresh start.

Writing a letter to Adam explaining my departure is something I consider, but I decide not to. If I tell him, I'll never be free. He may feel obliged to stay with me out of duty, or some misguided sense of doing the right thing. I'd always be the abandoned girl he has to mind. I couldn't bear that level of deference. Like a disease, it would eventually consume us whole. Besides, Adam has his own life, his own child to take care of. I can't bring him his maybe-child, the possible cuckoo in the domestic nest.

In time I will work something out. When my child has grown somewhat, and paternity is clearer, I will reach out, make contact, tell the story. My mother's choices are being repeated by me, of that I am aware, but I won't withhold my child, will not deny it its father. Unlike my mother, I won't blame my baby for existing, for reminding me of this period in my life. It's been good, in all. I want to keep it that way. In time, things will be clearer, easier. I have come a long way. A short few years is little over the span of a life. In time. I will give it time.

That golden day in late April, the day my foot touches American soil in Kennedy Airport, all I'm aware of is the huge airiness within me and all around me. The sunlight bounces off the glass buildings ahead as the cab slides over the 59th Street Bridge. Below me, the East River shimmers in all its polluted glory. In front is the city I've called home for so long, this damaged, fractured, sooty city, harbourer of dreams, wishes, nightmares, brokenness. It stretches, a phosphorescent sprawl, as far as I can see, and farther still, and I love it. For now, this is all I need.

I book a room for a week in a boutique hotel in midtown. Next morning, I take the subway to the offices on Lexington that house my father's lawyers. My father has left me more money that I would earn in twenty years. The sum is unreal to me, a number with many zeroes, but it doesn't seem rooted in anything familiar. After the lawyers, in their Paul Smith suits and glass-filled offices, leave me alone for a few moments, I trace the numbers on the bank accounts with my fingers. Slants of light hit the pages. A phone trills outside. A copy machine clicks out sheets in a corner of the room. I rub my expanding bump, then return to the numbers again. So many of them. My father did this for me.

When they return, these two men, wearing suits that cost more than I earn in a month, I take the proffered pen, sign on the lines, shake hands with them. It is a pleasure doing business with you, they assure me. Ms Perry. A pleasure to have met you.

Outside, the city continues unabated. Yellow cabs clog the avenues, one-way traffic sitting at a standstill. Hot dog vendors hawk their wares, grease and onions smoking the air around them. A man selling pretzels in a Jets shirt sits in the shade of a crab apple tree. A garbage truck grinds past. Car horns splatter the late morning with their noise, invasive and unwelcome.

I sit at a pavement café, a mint tea cooling in a tall mug beside me. A book I started on the plane rests on the mosaic table, but I cannot read just now. Summer has arrived early in New York, and it cloaks the city in hot folds. Sweat beads my forehead and the sides of my nose. I dab my skin with a paper napkin. My eyes seek out the scenes I've missed for so long, the people, the purpose, the bustle of life.

Sitting at that table, I devour the city as it races by, fast-forwarding itself into a blur of frenzied activity. I watch a couple fighting over who will pay the bill, a child rummaging in her mother's handbag, a dog owner tying his charge to a lamp post. A girl in heels slips on the cobblestones. A homeless woman pushes her shopping trolley past. A waiter obliges me by erecting the large umbrella over my table. I've been in Ireland for eight months, and this heat is intense. Above me, the skyscrapers battle for height and space, reaching up and up, their glass windows winking in the saffron light. Down here, it always seems a shade darker, the buildings stealing so much of the glare. The city's sirens wail, and far beneath me the subway shudders the earth. A few blocks away is a dive bar I infrequently patronised with some colleagues from NYU. The worst kind of workingman's hovel, the floor sticky with spills, lifelong drunks slumped over their glasses at all times of day, but a place with friendly bartenders and cheap drinks. I have no urge to be there. I don't want to run into anyone, or feel the need to explain my expanding waistline. Mint tea is sufficient, and I'm proud of myself.

I check my watch. Peter should be here soon. This place was his suggestion, only two blocks from the attorneys' offices. Actually, I'm looking forward to seeing him, this man who occupied such a huge portion of my father's life. The connection is tenuous at best, but at least it's there. A good starting point.

The city air is blurred with heat. I adjust my dark glasses, rub my bump. A flash of blue linen, the scrape of a chair being pulled out. A kiss on my cheek.

'Eva. It's so good to see you.' His hand, firm on my arm.

I will stay here, in America. More than that I cannot say. Tiny steps, I remind myself. They're all that is needed. No need to hurry. The clock still ticks, the sand still seeps through the hourglass. No rushing required.

I don't know it now, but I will resign my post at NYU this summer and accept another job, in UCLA, where I did a semester's work before Isaac and I broke up. They will make me a professor of modern poetry by the end of my first year. A book I will write, on women and power in literature, will be published to acclaim, and will win me two awards.

I don't know that I will take evening walks along the ocean's edge each day, a short stroll from the pretty two-bedroomed house in Santa Monica that I will buy with part of my inheritance, or that settling into California life is something I'll achieve with ease. In that house near the edge of the ocean I will raise my son, my beautiful boy, and each night I will hold him till he sleeps as the Pacific crashes before us. From the moment this bundle of perfection is born, I'll wonder how it is possible that a baby could look so much like his father. One theory claims an evolutionary explanation, but whatever it is, this bewitching child has so much of his father in his face that it makes me cry. I don't know it now, but before this year has ended, at my desk in this house, by the enormous picture window with an unobstructed view of the ocean, I will sit down and I will pen a letter. *Dear Adam*, I will write. *I owe you an explanation.*

I may not know it now, sitting at this pavement café in New York with this lovely man who will be a huge part of my life, of my son's life, but I will be successful at shedding my past. Not denying it, but shrugging it off, stepping aside and moving on. No one has so far told me how easy it will be to do it, and it will be easy. After my gorgeous boy, it will be the easiest thing I'll have done. I will think of my brother, and he won't seal up the valves in my soul. I'll remember my mother, not with bitterness and rancour but with something approaching pity. And I'll thank my father for giving me this chance to move on with my life.

There will be days when a drink seems like the only thing that will get me through, but I'll manage. I'll manage very well. Adam will help, of course. How I'd imagined this journey without him is something I'll never quite understand.

When my son is still very small, I will rock with him on our porch each evening, the scent of lemons heavy as the twilight draws itself around us. And behind the dying light of day will be the hint of the one yet to come, and the one after that and after that again, and of all the tomorrows that will reveal themselves, one by one. Who knows, maybe occasionally I'll picture the other life, that buried life, and be grateful for what it has led me to.

The first of the stars will push through the pale purple sky, Jupiter maybe, or Saturn, the moon only a thumbnail, the tiniest curve of silver in the striped firmament. Not enough to see its cracked face or its vast arid oceans. The palm trees will rattle their fronds. Lizards will click their tongues. The Pacific, huge and dark at the magic hour, will glimmer all the way to the horizon, and my child and I will close our eyes and rock ourselves to sleep.

ACKNOWLEDGEMENTS

This book has been a long time in the making. Many people have helped me out in various ways, and I wish now to convey my sincere gratitude.

For reading (and printing!) early drafts and for cheering me on, Vanessa Doherty, Tracy Fung, Heather Dawson, Darren Lenton, Brid Brogan, Nessa Doyle, Liz Houchin.

For clearing the water and raising the Titanic, as well as for friendship, Janet Fitch.

For constant support, a place to stay and a lot of fun along the way, my brother, Alan Finn.

For answering my questions about academia and the world of the university, Bettina Knipschild and Jamal Ouhalla.

For taking a chance on an unknown, my agent, Caroline Montgomery.

Justin, Mariel, Edwin, Eoin and everyone at New Island for seeing potential in my book.

Mary Stanley, for her incredible editing skills and for all the laughter and coffee.

My parents, Ted and Yvonne Finn, without whom none of this would have been possible, for a lifetime of love, support, help and everything else in between.

My husband, Mark Schrier, for all his faith and help and for giving me the space to write.

My beautiful children, Emily and David, who make everything worthwhile.